Heating up the Holidays

A Hunky Holiday Collection

USA TODAY Bestselling Authors

JILL SHALVIS
JACQUIE D'ALESSANDRO
—∞∞∞—
JAMIE SOBRATO

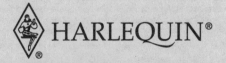

HARLEQUIN®

TORONTO • NEW YORK • LONDON
AMSTERDAM • PARIS • SYDNEY • HAMBURG
STOCKHOLM • ATHENS • TOKYO • MILAN • MADRID
PRAGUE • WARSAW • BUDAPEST • AUCKLAND

Recycling programs
for this product may
not exist in your area.

ISBN-13: 978-0-373-79439-3
ISBN-10: 0-373-79439-8

HEATING UP THE HOLIDAYS
Copyright © 2008 by Harlequin Enterprises Ltd.

The publisher acknowledges the copyright holders of the individual works as follows:

ALL HE WANTS FOR CHRISTMAS…
Copyright © 2008 by Jill Shalvis

MY GROWN-UP CHRISTMAS LIST
Copyright © 2008 by Jacquie D'Alessandro

UP ON THE HOUSETOP
Copyright © 2008 by Jamie Sobrato

www.eHarlequin.com

Printed in U.S.A.

ABOUT THE AUTHORS

USA TODAY bestselling author **Jill Shalvis** lives in Tahoe surrounded by her family, a few wild creatures and some of the sexiest firefighters on the planet. She is hard at work on her next romance novel. Visit her at www.jillshalvis.com/blog.

Jacquie D'Alessandro is an award-winning, *USA TODAY* bestselling author of more than thirty contemporary and historical romances. She grew up on Long Island, New York, where she fell in love with romance at an early age and dreamed of being swept away by a dashing rogue riding a spirited stallion. When her hero showed up, he was dressed in jeans and drove a Volkswagen, but she recognized him anyway. They now live out their happily-ever-afters in Atlanta, Georgia, along with their son, who is a dashing rogue in the making. Jacquie believes there's nothing like a hot firefighter to warm up those cold December nights, and she hopes Antonia and Brad's story adds some heat to your holidays. You can contact Jacquie through her Web site at www.JacquieD.com.

Jamie Sobrato lives inside her own head too much to be anything but a writer. When she's not writing, she can often be found hiking as she dreams up new story ideas. Jamie lives in Northern California, right across the street from the local fire station, where she does extensive visual research on firefighters.

CONTENTS

ALL HE WANTS
FOR CHRISTMAS...
Jill Shalvis

1

CRISTINA LEWIS walked into the florist's shop with a tiny bit of an attitude, which, at least according to those who knew her best, was nothing new. Whatever. She rarely wasted time thinking about her demeanor, or what people thought of it.

Probably not the best way to make friends, but she wasn't out to do so. Not in her world, where she was the lone female firefighter at station #34 in Santa Rey, California, a surfer-boy beach town. Her attitude was her shield, which she backed up by being good at what she did. The best, actually, and as a result, she was respected and trusted. And maybe a little feared, which worked, too.

Give her a burning building or a wrecked car threatening to explode any day of the week and she'd handle it. Unfortunately, today's task was picking out a Christmas bouquet for the new chief and his wife.

Cristina wasn't a Christmas person. Hell, she wasn't a people person, so the fact that she was the one in here while her crew waited outside on the rig was fairly ridiculous. "I know nothing about flowers," she warned the clerk who came around the front desk with a welcoming smile. "And even less about the whole ho-ho spirit, so we can skip the sales talk."

"Good. I hate the sales talk."

Okay, the woman was tough and had a sense of humor. Perfect. "Can you get me a Christmas bouquet and make it painless?"

"I'm an expert in painless." The clerk's professional smile never wavered. "For a boyfriend? Husband?"

Ha. Cristina didn't have a husband. She didn't have a boyfriend, either. The closest she'd come lately was her vibrator, but that had broken a few months back and she hadn't yet replaced it. As for a real live penis, that honor had all too briefly belonged to an extremely laid-back, easygoing, sexy-as-hell EMT named Dustin Mauer, whom she'd had to dump through no particular fault of his own—other than that he possessed the most baffling ability to make her want things. Things she didn't want to want. Things like a happily ever after, which she'd never believed in.

"It's for the new boss's wife." She slapped the seventy-five bucks the crew had all pooled together onto the counter. "In the name of sucking up to the powers that be, apparently."

"Well, you came to the right place."

"Great." Cristina just wanted to do this and get out, maybe fight a blaze or rescue someone. Anything but this. She knew damn well she was in here only because she had the lone vagina on the squad. Any one of those guys out there would have done a better job on this and they all knew it, but they were too busy cackling like little girls over making Cristina do it.

From some hidden speaker came a soft medley of Christmas tunes, and when she looked around, her senses were assaulted with a myriad of scents and colors. Flowers, plants, crafty stuff, it was everywhere, like a nightmare, all in green and red and silver and gold. Festive chaos.

It made her feel dizzy, and just a little like a bull in a china shop.

"Make sure it looks pretty," came Blake's voice over the radio at her hip. The radio issued by the fire department, the one supposedly to be used for emergencies only.

Cristina sighed. At the moment she didn't care that Blake had had an incredibly rough year and that she loved him like the brother she'd never had, she snatched the radio off her hip and snarled, "You sent me in here, you'll deal with what I pick."

"Scrooge."

So she wasn't a fan of Christmas, so what. She had no family to speak of other than the one she'd made at the station, and therefore didn't have a lot of happy yuletide memories. To her, Christmas was just another day at the firehouse, albeit with better goodies to steal out of the fridge.

"Make sure it has some red flowers on it," came Blake's voice again. "She loves red flowers, apparently."

Like she cared what some higher-up's wife liked. The last chief had been a serial arsonist. In her eyes, the new chief still had to prove himself. "You'll like what I pick," she informed him with plenty of her famed attitude. "Even if it smells like sh—"

"Wow, somebody *really* needs to get laid." There was laughter in his voice now.

Yeah, okay, so she *did* need that, desperately, but she'd done the stupid thing and dumped Dustin after one fantastic night of amazing sex, and now he refused to have additional amazing sex without "more," whatever the hell that meant.

Not that *that* was any of Blake's business.

The clerk cleared her throat and held up some sort of floral arrangement with what even Cristina had to admit was a gorgeous mix of red flowers and greenery, and a silver bow that managed not to look obnoxious. "Okay, you *are* good."

The clerk smiled. "Oh, I'm better than good. Do you want to take it with you or have it delivered?"

"Delivered, please." And while she pulled out the address she'd written down and waited for the woman to handle the paperwork, she eyed the store again. With her chore now completed, she could take a breath of relief and admit that maybe the place had a charm to it. It did smell damn good. She eyed the small tree on the counter, filled with tiny red envelopes. "What are those?"

"A present-in-an-envelope. Donate twenty-five bucks that will go to one of several local charities, and you get a surprise donated from a local business—a spa treatment or a dinner for two, things like that."

Cristina didn't know what came over her but she dug into her uniform pants and pulled out a twenty and a five. Scrooge, her ass.

"Pick an envelope, any one," the clerk told her cheerfully.

Cristina debated a moment, then grabbed one.

Feeling a little silly, she exited the shop. On the rig, Blake was on the radio with dispatch and waving to her to hurry up because they had a call.

As she hopped into the truck she read her card: Good for one night's stay at Santa Rey's most romantic getaway—the Sweet Pea B and B.

Terrific. There was only one man she'd want to spend the night there with, but Dustin wouldn't do it, not unless she gave him his damn "more." She stared at the card, rolled her eyes at the irony, then shoved it in her pocket and did as she did with everything that disturbed her. She brushed it aside and let it go.

DUSTIN MAUER drove his ambulance with easy purpose, as always. As an EMT, he knew the drill. Get to the scene as quickly as possible without risking anyone's life, assess the victims, get them the necessary medical care. He'd been doing just that for nearly ten years, since graduating from Cal Poly. It hadn't been his life goal to be an EMT, it'd been merely a means to an end, a decent paycheck with which to pay off his education debt while he and his brother Jason had gotten their renovation business up and running.

But then Jason had gone into the military and their business had become a sort of side deal, as in, they got to it when they got to it, and Dustin had gotten comfortable being an EMT. Plus he was excellent at it, and until a few months ago, had truly loved what he did every day.

Then he'd fallen for the stubborn, gorgeous Cristina Lewis and she'd dumped him, and he'd been restless ever since.

He pulled up to the multicar pileup on Hwy 1. James, his new partner, was talking to dispatch, but he could see what they faced—a big rig had hit the center divider, caught fire and then two other cars had impacted it, sliding beneath the trailer. It was a chaotic mess, and all units had been called to the scene.

The firefighters from his station were already there. Blake was working the flames, and Zach and Aidan were using the jaws of life to extract the people trapped in the first car, while Sam and Eddie rescued the woman in the second car.

And then there was the stubborn, gorgeous heartbreaker, Cristina. She stood right in the center of it all, surrounded by the blazing big rig and the smashed cars, feet firmly planted wide as she held a hose on the flames. She was in her fire gear from head to toe, including mask, so he couldn't see her face, but he didn't need to. Her expression would be calm, intense, determined as she concentrated on the job at hand.

Much as it had been when she'd dumped him after the best night of his life.

As he watched, a burning chunk of debris flew off the truck toward Cristina's head. Heart in his throat, he shouted her name even as he realized the futility of that—she couldn't hear him over the ruckus all around them. But she didn't need his help. She easily leapt out of the way with a casual agility, as graceful as a cat, never letting up on the flames she was drowning.

Sam and Eddie brought over the four victims from the first car, and Dustin tore his eyes off Cristina to do his job.

She'd be okay.

Hell, she always was. Like a cat, he reminded himself, always landing on her feet.

A talent he'd have to learn…

Unbelievably, he wrapped only a few minor scrapes and bruises, nothing serious, and then the woman from the second car was brought to them.

She didn't have any injuries at all. But as they sat there, her car exploded.

Dustin's head whipped back to the scene, his gaze anxiously searching for—

There. Cristina was there, still standing in one piece and he took a deep breath.

"My God," the woman said in shock ten minutes later when the flames were out. "I can't believe we're all still alive. It's a miracle."

"Actually, it's good firefighting."

They turned to the petite but toned firefighter who'd come up behind them. Except Dustin. He didn't have to look. He knew the sound of her voice, knew the sensation that hit him every time she was within a few feet.

"You okay?" Cristina asked the woman, pulling off her helmet.

"Yes, thanks to you. You got there just in time, I don't know how to thank you."

"It's my job. I'm glad to help."

Dustin knew she meant that utterly sincerely. Much as he'd like it to be otherwise, Cristina *was* the job. She lived and breathed for it, and little else.

As he'd learned the hard way.

She had a streak of dirt over one jaw, another across her forehead. She had her silky, long blond hair tied back as usual, hanging down inside the stiff collar of her protective jacket, though several strands were stuck to her damp, dirty forehead. She was a mess, and still drop-dead gorgeous.

Firefighter Barbie, her partner Blake had once dared joke.

Once.

Cristina had been so furious she'd tongue-lashed him for a week. Poor Blake—Eeyore to those who knew and loved him— had never made that mistake again.

To Dustin, Cristina was much more kick-ass warrior princess than Barbie, but he valued his life enough to keep that particular fantasy to himself.

"You really should take a ride to the hospital," he said to the woman they'd rescued. "Just to make sure."

"No, that's not necessary. I've called my fiancé, he's on his way." She whipped around as a man came running up to the rig, shouting her name hoarsely, in stark relief. The two of them hugged tightly. Dustin watched, trying to remain impartial, but he was a sorry sap, and these sorts of reunions got to him every single time.

"Are you okay?" the man demanded, pulling back to look the woman over for himself.

"I'm okay."

"Thank God." He hugged her tight. "You are my entire life, you know that, right? If something happened to you—"

"I'm okay. I'm right here." She hugged him as though she never intended to let go, her eyes closed as she breathed him in as if he were her very essence. "I love you so much."

Dustin had seen such scenes dozens of times. Hundreds. It still got him. He looked at Cristina, who'd already turned away.

Typical. She was uncomfortable with public displays of affection or love. "Cristina."

"Gotta go," she said.

He followed her off to the side, away from the victim and her fiancé. "Right. Because messy emotions disturb you."

She went still, then turned and looked at him. Things were

winding down behind them now. Several cops were taking statements and the tow-truck operators were working on hooking up all the disabled vehicles to pull them off the highway.

"Look," she said defensively. "It was just one night."

"And you had such a bad time that you can't bear to repeat it?"

She sighed. "Don't make me hurt your manly feelings, Dustin."

At that, he out-and-out laughed. There was nothing else he could do. "Are you going to tell me it wasn't good for you?"

Now she opened her mouth, then slowly shut it again. He arched a brow, waiting, knowing damn well she'd had a great night, too.

She rolled her eyes and took a step closer to him, so that their steel-toed boots were touching as she stabbed a finger into his chest. "Okay, so I came once or twice. Big deal, it'd been awhile and I was primed. It doesn't mean that I'd like to repeat the event. I can do that myself."

"Three times," he said much more tightly than he wanted to. He knew better than to take her bait and say anything, but when it came to her, The Most Irritating Woman on the Planet, he couldn't seem to help himself. "You came two times before, and then again when I was inside you. Can you give yourself that?"

He wasn't surprised when she spun on her heel and walked away.

A few minutes later, Blake clasped a hand on his shoulder, having come up behind him. "Not the smartest move, man, poking at the bear. You're going to get bitten."

Yeah. Been there, done that, bought the T-shirt.

2

THINGS didn't go any easier that night for Cristina, who, along with her crew, worked in twenty-four-hour shifts, three days on, two days off. They were going to need both days off to recover after the three fire calls in quick succession between midnight and dawn. It was still dark when Cristina finally made it back to the station, exhausted, filthy and starving.

None of those things were new. It seemed that she spent most of her shifts in some variance of exhausted, filthy and starving. It was a way of life. *Her* life.

Normally she yelled "Shotgun" for the shower before anyone even got off the rig, but today she let the guys go ahead of her because she felt…wiped.

The station was a comfortable, old, two-story brick building, decorated at the moment with Christmas ornaments made by various elementary schools in town, plus several small trees and what must have been an entire bush of mistletoe.

But she wasn't going to be kissing any firefighters, not this Christmas.

The station was on the main drag and directly across the street from the beach. The view was always gorgeous, no matter the weather. During the day she could stare at the waves and the surfers in it, and in the hours before dawn, she could watch the moonbeams bounce off the whitecaps as she did now.

As she slid off the rig into the cool December air, she glanced at her watch—4:30 a.m.

Dustin stuck his head out the front door, making the decorated wreath hanging there tinkle noisily. "Cristina."

Yes, that was her name. She really wished he wouldn't talk to her until she was completely over him, because he had one of those low, whisky-thick voices that made her quiver.

"Come on. Come in and get a hot shower."

"I'm not cold."

"Get in here anyway."

That was the thing about Dustin, the defining thing that grabbed her every single time—the way he could make an instant transformation from mild-mannered guy to tough, commanding alpha male. "In a few."

"You're filthy."

Yeah, she hated that voice's effect on her. Where were her knees? Suddenly she couldn't feel them. "Well, you're funny-looking. At least I can shower."

He just looked at her, not scared off like most, and she sighed. "I'll be inside in a few."

He gave her a long assessing look, then shut the door. She sank to the front steps and stared out at the water, too tired to move. If she had even an ounce of energy left in her, she'd kick off her boots and walk to the sand.

Twenty-nine years old and too damn tired to walk to the beach. That was so pathetic, she forced herself to bend over and untie her boots, nudging them off. She shoved her grimy socks into them and left them on the front step, crossing the street in her bare feet.

Even in California December could get downright chilly, and she shivered when the cool sand hit her toes. This year she had Christmas day off, and the two days after that, as well. A rarity. Maybe she should hop on a plane and go south. As in the South Pacific south. Yeah, that would work.

But she wouldn't, and she knew it. For all her bravado, she wouldn't enjoy such a thing by herself, and she had no one to take, a depressing thought.

She had been invited to Sam's house for a Christmas fiesta that he was making with his girlfriend, Sara. Or she could head with Eddie to his sister's house and be overrun with kids. Or Zach and Brooke had asked her to join them. So had Aidan and Kenzie.

She could do any of that, but she'd told them all she had plans, that she was having a thing. An alone thing, not that they knew that. Much as she loved her friends and even thought of them as family, when it came right down to it, they had their own.

The predawn air wasn't that bad, maybe fiftyish, but it was accompanied by a breeze that had the water just icy enough to make her gasp when the first wave washed over her feet.

"Are you crazy?"

She didn't turn to see who had spoken in that quiet, raspy tone. Her body didn't move at all, except on the inside, where something odd happened deep in her belly—a sort of quiver that she chose to identify as annoyance.

That her nipples tightened was sheer coincidence.

"I'm trying to enjoy a moment here." She shoved her hands into her pockets rather than face the urge she had to grab on to him, just haul him close by the ears and lay one on him. It was so ridiculous, this insane attraction she had for him. Seriously ridiculous. It wasn't as if he was going to give Brad Pitt a run for his money. In fact, he was the opposite of Brad Pitt, not *GQ* gorgeous at all.

Actually, he looked a lot like Harry Potter all grown up: dark, perpetually disheveled hair curling around his ears to just past his collar. Laser-blue eyes, magnified by the glasses he required to see a foot past his face. A crooked smile that was both self-deprecatory and contagious. He was tall, lean and lanky, and…hell. He *was* attractive, made all the more so by the fact that he had absolutely no idea how much.

Not that she was noticing.

Nope, that ship had sailed. She'd had him, curiosity over. Hunger sated.

Or so she told herself.

But did he take the hint and leave? No. Anyone else would have sensed something in her tone and backed away, but not Dustin. Somehow she didn't scare him off. Somehow she didn't *piss* him off.

It was really quite shocking.

And, she admitted to herself, just a teeny-tiny bit of a relief. People came and went in her life. That was just fact. Her father? Never knew him. Her mother? Traipsing through Europe with a backpack, or so she'd said the last time she'd touched base with her daughter, two years ago now. Any other people who had looked out for Cristina during her rough childhood, and acquaintances since that time, all had moved on and so had she. Apparently, she just wasn't the type of woman to inspire long-term relationships. In fact, her personal motto read something like a government health warning: Stay away from attachments, as they pose a serious threat to your brains, wallet and if you're stupid enough, your heart.

Somehow she'd become a firefighter instead of a statistic. Through time and sheer stubbornness on the guys' parts, she'd developed friendships. She adored Blake like a brother, adored Aidan and Zach, adored *all* of them—but she still had a limited amount of how much of anyone that she could take.

That didn't seem to be the case for Dustin, damn him. "I came out here alone. Which means I want to be alone. See how that works?"

"I hear what your mouth is saying, but everything else?" He shifted closer, standing next to her so that her shoulder brushed his arm. "Your body language, your body…"

Was it just her or did he sound all raspy and, *dammit,* sexy?

"Yeah, they're all saying something else entirely," he murmured near her ear, giving her a set of goose bumps.

So he'd seen the happy nipples. She crossed her arms over her chest. "For your information, I'm cold."

"Hey, whatever you have to tell yourself to sleep at night."

Now see, *that.* That was another thing that made him different. He called her on all her shit, every single time.

No one else did that.

She found herself staring into his glasses at those shockingly blue eyes. "Why aren't you afraid of me?"

"Maybe because I'm so badass myself."

She laughed.

"Okay," he muttered. "Not so badass. But I see the soft, marshmallow Cristina."

"I'm not soft. Anywhere."

"Well, we both know that's not true."

There he went with the sexiness again.

He shifted even closer, right into her personal bubble. "I see you, Cristina. I see the woman who feeds the stray cat her leftover sandwich."

"Only when the bread is stale."

"The one who always shoves all her spare change in the homeless guys' hands every time we go downtown."

"I hate having change in my pocket."

"The woman who looks at me and her eyes melt."

"Hell no, they don't."

He just looked at her, smiling knowingly.

Ah, crap. "Shut up."

He did, not because she asked, but because he liked to be quiet sometimes, as she did.

He got her the way no one else did.

All the others would get off their shift and go home to something, someone. She'd go to her apartment and bide her time until she could go back to work. Because, with no real family, work was her life.

Dustin had a great family: his mom, his sister, his brother… he'd lost his dad a few years back to cancer, and clearly missed him so much, but the rest of them were still very close. So close they constantly nosed around in his life and drove her crazy, and yet he loved them madly. Cheerfully.

He and Cristina were polar opposites. He knew this. She knew this. So why did he have to be the one to get her panties all twisted? Why him?

Ignoring her with an ease she'd never quite managed with him in return, he kicked off his own boots and socks and immediately hissed out a shocked breath as the waves splashed over his toes.

She laughed again.

At the sound, Dustin shoved his glasses further up on his nose and took a good, long look at her.

"What," she asked somewhat defensively. "You've never seen me laugh before?"

"Not since…"

"Since what?"

"Since we played strip poker and I lost."

Oh, boy, was that night imprinted on her brain. Her car had broken down. He'd taken her home, and then come in for a quick drink, and somehow he'd charmed her into playing a game of cards. Being a card master, she'd readily agreed, then scammed him, conning him right out of his clothes just out of curiosity.

Beneath his EMT uniform, he'd been hiding a sensual delight of long, lean muscle, and she'd gone from curious to aroused in zero point four.

They'd slept together that night. Even now her body tingled as it remembered, but she lifted her chin. "I laughed because you had SpongeBob SquarePants on your boxers."

He didn't look embarrassed but amused. That was the thing

about Dustin, he was comfortable in his own skin. "It was laundry day, and my mom bought me those boxers."

They'd made her hot. Another wave splashed over their toes and Dustin sucked in a harsh breath, backing up in surrender. "Okay, you win," he said. "You're the cool kid. *Now* can we go in?"

"I don't want to go in."

"What *do* you want?"

She let out a low laugh that inadvertently exposed her misery, and he shifted to face her, putting a hand on her arm. "Are you getting a migraine?"

Yeah, he knew her. *Really* knew her. And worse, he cared. Goddamm him. "No. Are you wearing SpongeBob Square-Pants now?"

The corner of his mouth quirked. "Not telling." He stroked a rogue strand of hair from her forehead, letting his finger trail over her temple, the rim of her ear.

She shivered and surrendered, as well, stepping into him. "Dustin…"

For a brief moment, his other hand came up, brushing down her back, settling low on her spine. He turned his face into hers, letting the tip of his nose run along her jaw, his mouth brush the underside of her throat lightly before he sighed and went to step back.

She grabbed him, fisted her hands in his shirt and held on tightly, so he couldn't go anywhere. "Please," she whispered, horrified to hear the neediness in her voice.

Thankfully, she didn't need to finish. He knew what she was asking. *Please let's get naked. Please make my body hum again. Please help me find oblivion tonight in your arms.*

For a blessed moment he held her close to his hard, warm body, and she felt a surge of triumph. But then with a low groan, he shook his head, setting her away from him. "No."

"Why? There's not someone else." Even the thought stopped her heart.

"You know damn well there isn't anyone else."

"Then—"

"Stop it." He met her gaze. "You know why."

"Suppose you tell me again."

"You run and run and run, never slowing down, always working, always keeping busy."

"So?"

"So then you're so exhausted that you can barely move. But when your body finally forces you to take a moment, you look around and realize you're alone. You hate alone. So you see who can fulfill you."

"And you fit the bill. Perfectly." She arched against him feeling the hard bulge beneath his zipper that assured her he felt the same way. "What's the problem here, Dustin? Suddenly you don't like sex?"

"I don't like *meaningless* sex. Not with you."

She managed another laugh. "That's ridiculous."

He didn't smile, and hers faded as she whirled away. But he pulled her back around. Their gazes met.

Locked.

Held.

She felt the jolt clear down to her toes, where it bounced and hit all her good spots. But now was not the time to melt. "So what now? You going to go find someone else?"

His fingers were tight on her arm. Not hurting her, never hurting her, but firm enough that she couldn't have pulled away without hurting him. His eyes were fierce, his brow furrowed, his glasses slipping down his nose. Beneath the hands she'd set to his chest she could feel the heavy beat of his heart. And it did something to her, made her feel something…basic.

His eyes widened slightly, signaling that she wasn't alone in this. Nope, the cool, laid-back, easygoing man was worked up, too.

Which was good, because she needed him. *Him.* No one else. No one else could make her sizzle like this—and she'd tried.

Fisting her fingers in his shirt, she tugged him close to kiss him, hard and deep. The rumble of his groan came up from his chest. The rasp of his five-o'clock shadow scraped her chin. The scent of him she couldn't get enough of, filling her nostrils as all her bones liquefied as his fingers tightened on her.

Dustin. Dustin was finally in her arms again, kissing her like he'd been dying without her.

His mouth was warm and delicious, soft yet firm, pure unadulterated pleasure. God, he was such a good kisser. She hadn't had time lately to dwell on that but she took the time now as his tongue stroked hers with the slow, sure precision of a master. He knew how to take *his* time, that was certain, and she fully appreciated his skill.

She couldn't have stopped, but that was okay because he dove into the kiss with her, making her feel marginally better about the whole thing. She wasn't alone in this. Not even close. He hauled her up against that chiseled, hard-earned body, his hands hot and rough, which matched the hot, rough, ragged groan torn from his throat.

Definitely not alone in this…

She strained against him as he rushed to touch as much of her as he could, making her body hum, and then…and then her nose bumped into his glasses and he pulled back so fast she staggered a step and nearly fell on her ass.

His glasses were fogged, and with a harsh, annoyed sound, he tugged them off and wiped them on his shirt before jamming them back on. "I told you. I'm not going to scratch your itch." His chest was still rising and falling from the kiss, but his voice sounded disturbingly weary. Bending, he grabbed his shoes. She expected him to walk away from her.

Most did. After all, she saw to that, didn't she?

But she should have known better. Dustin wasn't like most people. He wasn't like anyone she'd ever met. Straightening, mouth still wet from hers but grim, he offered her a hand.

She stared at it.

"Shower and bed," he said very quietly…in direct opposition to his breathing.

"Alone," he specified.

Damn. And yet a small part of her knew she'd be lucky to manage a shower before crashing.

She'd summoned the last of her energy to get here, to spar with him, to kiss him, but now she felt as if she'd hit the wall. Nothing left in the tank.

Empty.

God, she wanted her bunk almost more than she wanted her next breath, and yet it seemed like such a chore. But Dustin would get her where she needed to go.

Somehow, someway, he always did.

3

WHEN THEIR SHIFT ended at eight o'clock that morning, Dustin stepped outside and watched in disbelief as Cristina dragged her sexy but tired ass to the side of the building and unlocked her bike.

They'd just had a rough night, as rough as it gets, where they'd had maybe an hour of sleep broken into fifteen-minute increments, and she was going to ride her bike home.

Hard-core Cristina.

She was tough, so tough that people often forgot that she had a good reason to be so. She didn't talk about herself much, if ever. What information he had on her he'd pretty much pieced together from five years of knowing her. Her mother had had her when she was only sixteen, and while she'd done her best, her best had often meant hanging with men who weren't the greatest influence and ruled with a heavy fist. Cristina no longer kept in contact with her mother, and she'd never learned who her father was. She had no siblings, and as far as Dustin could tell, she didn't keep a lot of friends outside the station.

Inside the station, however, she loved them all fiercely, grumpily, and that love was returned, though not as grumpily. Any one of the guys would lay down his life for her, himself included, and she felt the same. Earlier in the year when her partner Blake had been wrongly accused of arson, she'd steadfastly and vocally objected, and had never wanted to believe the worst of him, even when all the evidence had been firmly stacked against him.

The people of station #34 were her family. *He* was her family. And she was afraid to mess with that. He got that, he really did, he just knew deep down inside that what they had could be so much deeper, if only she'd let it.

But, badass as she was, inside she was terrified. Terrified of letting go, terrified of allowing him too close, terrified of getting hurt.

What she didn't understand was that he felt those fears, too. But he'd always felt that life was worth living, fears and all, that if he didn't go for it, then why bother?

She fumbled with the bike lock and swore again.

Walk away, he told himself. He'd made the decision that she was bad for him. Bad for his self-esteem, bad for his ego, bad for everything.

Except…ah, hell, here came the excuses…except there was something about her. Something about the way her brain worked that was such a turn-on. And then there was the way she made him laugh. He came from a lively family. They were all opinionated and they all were thinkers, and they all made him laugh.

But Cristina slayed him.

God, that was sexy. She was sexy. That thought made him want to smile because at the moment she wore baggy sweat bottoms and a snug long-sleeved thermal top, with her long blond hair down and still wet from her shower. Not an ounce of makeup. He could see the exhaustion in every line of her trim body. She'd laugh her ass off if he told her he found her sexy, just as she was.

But she had a way of drawing him in no matter what she looked like. He came up behind her in time to hear, "Goddamn mother f—"

"Trouble?" he asked.

She spun the lock and rubbed her undoubtedly bleary eyes. "No." She attempted the lock again.

It was three miles to her apartment from here. Three miles in which she could run herself into a car or under a bus.

"Cristina."

She yawned, wide. "Yeah."

"Let me give you a ride."

Another yawn. "Nah, I'm good." But she rested her forehead on the lock and closed her eyes.

Setting his fingers over hers, he grabbed her hand and pulled her upright. She was so limp she actually let herself lean on him for a moment, which dammit, made his arms go around her and hold on tight.

Her wet hair stuck to the stubble on his jaw. It smelled good, like her, like warm, tired woman. God, he was such a sucker. "I'm driving you home." And a glutton for punishment, let's not forget that.

Surprising him, she allowed herself to be led to his truck, let him put her bike in the back for her. Once in the passenger seat, she leaned her head back and closed her eyes. "It's a good thing I'm so tired, or I'd have to kick your ass for bossing me around."

"Is that right?"

A hint of a smile crossed her lips. "No." She was so drowsy her words were slurred. "Actually, when you get all gruff and demanding like this, it turns me on."

"Stop it."

"It's true. When you go all rough and manly, it gives me the shivers."

She had a wicked grin on her face now, with her eyes still closed, and he had to smile and shake his head. She was teasing him. "And here I thought women wanted sensitivity and sweetness. I've been going about it all wrong."

"Seems like."

He pulled into her apartment complex, got out of his truck and came around for her just as she was getting her feet beneath her. "I've got it from here, sailor." She patted his cheek. "But thanks."

"Uh-huh." Instead of walking away, he took her arm and led her to her front door.

"This isn't necessary." She unlocked her door and blocked him from coming in. "See you in a few days."

Putting his hands on her arms, he gently but firmly pushed her inside, then followed her in, kicking the door shut behind him.

"Look, I just want another shower with hot water this time, and my bed," she said, sounding cranky now. "And I'd add sex to that list, but you've already shot me down on that score, so get the hell out."

He'd been inside her place a few times. A nice couch, a small TV, shelves with a few books here and there, and a plant that was either coming back to life or halfway dead. "Where's your Christmas tree?"

She didn't answer him.

"You said you were having a thing. You turned down all the invites you got because you were having a thing."

"I am having a thing."

An alone thing. He got that now. She'd lied, which he hated.

As if too burned out even to move, she sank to her couch and covered her eyes.

The soft, exhausted sigh did him in.

"Get up." He held out a hand. "Come on."

She opened her eyes and stared at his fingers. "For what?"

"Shower. Bed."

"Is that an invitation?"

Rolling his eyes, he pulled her up himself and took her down the hallway to her bathroom. In his experience, a woman's bathroom was her holy sanctuary, filled with all the mysteries of feminine beauty: bottles, creams, tubes, brushes, lingerie hung to dry.

Not Cristina's bathroom. As always, it was clean and *unlike* the woman herself, devoid of life. "I've always wondered. Where's all your stuff?"

"What stuff?"

"Your girl stuff."

She pulled open a drawer, revealing a brush, a tube of mascara and a bottle of body lotion. "Here."

"That's it?"

"No." She pulled open her other drawer, which held an un-opened box of tampons and an opened box of condoms.

He stared at the condoms and thought *down boy*. Telling

himself it didn't matter how many condoms were missing, he cranked on the hot water and turned to her.

She was looking at him curiously. "You're doing it again."

"What, breathing?"

"Being assertive."

"Yeah? How's this for assertive. *Strip.*"

She stopped in midyawn and raised a brow.

"Strip," he repeated. "Shower. And then if you're a good little girl, I'll tuck you in before I leave."

Now those eyes narrowed. "So you're being all sexy for what, just to tease me? Get out."

"Sure. As soon as I take care of you, since you're too stubborn to do it yourself."

"Seriously, what the hell is your problem this morning?"

The box of condoms was open, that was his problem. "Take your damn shower."

"Fine." She pulled off her shirt.

She wasn't wearing a bra. "*Jesus, Cristina.*"

"Hey, I'm just following directions." She shoved down her sweats, revealing a miniscule black thong. Then that was gone, too, and with a smug look on her face, she stepped into the shower and shut the curtain in his face.

He let out a slow, long breath. "Good. I'll just…" *stand here as hard as a rock* "…leave you to it."

"Oh, no. You promised to tuck me in." She stuck her head around the curtain and eyed him, her hair stuck to her head, framing her face, which was pale with dark circles beneath her eyes. Still, she batted them for all she was worth.

Spinning on his heels, he forced himself to leave the bathroom rather than strip down and join her. In the kitchen, he put water on to boil and searched the cupboards, which were pretty bare, but he found some tea bags.

He heard the shower go off while he was waiting for the tea to get good and dark, the way she liked. Then he drew a deep breath and headed back down the hall, reminding himself that he was only going to give her the tea, tuck her in and walk away.

No matter how freaking fantastic she looked naked, and no matter how much he wanted her.

No matter what.

CRISTINA STOOD beneath her shower and let the hot water pound at her sore muscles. She'd held up pretty well in front of Dustin, but she felt a telltale tightness in her chest, and the burning in her throat told her she was an inch from losing it.

If Dustin had stuck around for another minute he might have caught on, but this was a pity party for one only. Work had been tough over the past few days, but that wasn't what had gotten to her.

It was Christmas.

She hated the third-wheel feeling, hated how it made her feel like a stupid, unwanted kid all over again. She put her face right into the water and told herself that the prickle behind her eyes was simply from the spray, nothing else, but only when she ran out of hot water did she step out of the shower, grab a towel and go into her bedroom. She planned to pull on a big T-shirt and a pair of boxers and get into bed for at least eight straight hours.

But then Dustin walked into her bedroom, holding a mug of tea that smelled so good she nearly jumped him for it.

He handed over the mug but stayed in the doorway, carefully not looking at her bed, which meant he got a good look at her face, far too close a look for her own comfort.

"What's the matter?" he asked quietly.

Was there anything worse than someone asking that question when you were so close to losing it you could taste the tears? "Other than you won't do me? Nothing."

Stepping closer, he snagged her arm, reeling her in, staring into her eyes for a long moment.

"Let go of me."

He didn't. Of course he didn't. "Tell me what's wrong."

She felt her belly hitch for no stupid reason at all, except he wasn't being his usual laid-back, easygoing self today, but a new aggressive and assertive Dustin, and combined with the frustration simmering in his voice, it all equaled too much sexy for her. "I'm just tired."

His thumb glided over her jaw, his fingers slipping into the wet hair at the nape of her neck. "Cristina."

God, the way he said her name, as if she mattered a whole great big bunch. "Look," she managed in a bored voice. "If you're not going to get naked, then get the hell out. I said I'm tired."

He sighed, then lifted his hands with a quick shake of his head. "Fine." And then, just as she'd wanted, he turned away.

Good.

Perfect.

She could feel those unwanted tears stick in her throat so she ruthlessly held her breath. But he walked so damn slowly! By the time he got to the doorway, she had to suck in air or suffocate.

He whirled around. "What was that?"

She shook her head. "Nothing." *I'm fine. Look at me being fine...*

But then he took a good look at her face and said her name softly, and she shocked the hell out of both of them by covering her face.

"Ah, Cristina."

"Go," she managed in a perfectly even, perfectly pissed-off voice.

But his footsteps came closer instead of heading out the door. And the next thing she knew, he'd tugged her hands from her face and looked her right in the eyes. "You're not okay."

"Why the hell won't you just go?" she asked, baffled. "You want to, you know you do."

Grimly, he began to pull her in, though she resisted. The mild-mannered Dustin would have backed off, but he wasn't his usual mild-mannered self at all.

She could have fought him and won, but her fight had left her, gone south for the winter. Instead she sagged into him and pressed her face to his throat.

4

DUSTIN HAD no idea what was going through Cristina's mind as she stood there in his arms. He couldn't possibly guess, but he did know he wasn't going anywhere until he found out. He had a reputation for being quiet and easygoing, but being with this woman made him the opposite. Only she could do this to him, make him feel so revved up. "Talk to me."

She made a sound, a low, breathy sound that, if it had been any other woman, he'd have said was crying.

But this was Cristina. Kick-ass, rebel-queen Cristina, who never cried. She'd once proudly told him she hadn't cried since second grade, when one of her mother's boyfriend's dogs had eaten her one doll, and she'd only lost it because the dog had choked and died. "Cristina."

"Bite me."

He would, gladly. That was the problem. "Spill."

She muttered a long string of various four-letter words at that, and if she hadn't been so serious about it, he'd have smiled.

But then a soft sound escaped her, and he knew she wasn't anywhere close to smiling, and it tore a hole in his heart. "Baby, you're so tired."

"Just shut up a minute," she whispered. "Just shut up and stand here and hold me."

He could do that, for now. He had his arms around her, one hand in her hair, the other on the small of her back, fisted in the towel around her. He was hugging her. Comforting her.

That was it.

But suddenly in the huge, overhanging silence surrounding them, he became aware of the silky disarray of her wet hair, and how good it smelled. Of the imprint of her small body against his, covered only in that damp towel, which didn't matter because he could still see the picture of her in his mind dropping her clothes before getting into the shower.

Then her hand wriggled up between them, flat against his chest as she lifted her gaze to his.

In that very second, the embrace went from simple comfort to something else.

And he wasn't alone.

Slowly, she came up in tiptoe and touched her mouth to the corner of his. He went instantly hard.

Her mouth still touching his, she went still, preternaturally still, and then shivered.

And not from the cold.

He slid a hand down her side, reaching for her hand, entwining his fingers in hers, moving their now-joined hands to the small of her back because he couldn't bear her touching him and not having her.

But the motion arched her spine just enough to have her breasts pressing into his chest, belly to belly, thigh to thigh, and he groaned, unable to hold it in, the sound more a plea than anything else.

Her lips parted, answering that plea, and that was it for him. Ripping off his glasses, he opened his mouth on hers, kissing her, hard and long.

Not having her.

God, what a big, fat lie that was. He was going to have her, here and now, and he knew it.

They both knew it.

The kiss was everything, hot and giving, sweet and unbearably sexy, sending waves of desire and hunger through his body, pooling between his thighs in his groin.

He was lost, a goner, drowning in the sensations, the feel of her body against his, her sweet tongue in his mouth, the way they fitted against each other as if it'd been meant to be. Even when the kiss finally ended, he kept his mouth against hers, going still, just breathing her in.

Then she lifted her head, her eyes meeting his, filled with a question mark.

He moved his hand against the sleek strength of her back. She was small-boned, petite against him, almost fragile, but he knew that was deceptive. In reality, she was the strongest woman he knew.

Walk away now, he told himself. Run, or this time you're going to fall all the way, and she'll stomp all over your heart.

Again.

And yet he knew that with only the slightest encouragement from her, he'd pull her down to the couch and do something completely crazy and stupid and totally amazing, like yank off the towel and kiss every single square inch of that glorious body until she made those sexy little sounds in the back of her throat that she made, the ones that grew progressively more desperate right before she came, the ones that teased him into a sexual frenzy such as he'd never known.

"Dustin." She put her hands on his face. "How is it that you're always there when I need you?"

Yeah. He wasn't going to run or even walk. No way in hell. Not when she needed him.

"Dustin." She was still staring deeply into his eyes, which was the thing about Cristina. Everything about getting too close to him terrified her, and yet she didn't look away.

Nothing less than utterly direct at all times, she took his hand and turned, leading him back to her bedroom.

And he went willingly.

CRISTINA STOPPED at the foot of her bed and glanced at Dustin. God, the slightly befuddled, extremely turned-on expression he wore made her knees weak. Everything about him made her knees weak. Made all of her weak.

And wasn't that just the problem?

She didn't do weak, at least not knowingly. And yet…and yet this man. God, this man. When she was with him, she could give in, could be weak, because he was there for her.

Always.

She needed him, and she didn't understand why, when she'd never needed anyone in her entire life. Her vague anxiety about that wasn't going to stop her, not when she finally had him here again. Slowly she dropped her towel at their feet.

He squinted, focusing hard to see her, looking both adorable and sexy as hell. "Cristina—"

She put her fingers to his lips, not wanting to hear yet again why he wasn't going to do this with her. She knew all the reasons why they shouldn't do this again.

But she needed him, needed him like air, needed his mouth hot, his tongue wet. She needed— God. She needed so much that each touch stroked her from the inside out, and she stepped close and kissed him to get more.

Dustin lifted his mouth from hers.

"No," she gasped. "Don't stop."

With a low, ragged groan, he cupped her face and shook his head. "I'm not stopping. I'm not strong enough for that."

Actually, he was one of the strongest men she'd ever known, but she wasn't going to quibble, not when he was going to give her what she wanted.

Him.

Just him.

He pulled her in for another hot, wet, drugging kiss, her incredibly sexy EMT, a kiss that had her—no softie herself—quivering. He had a way of touching her, of *looking* at her, good Lord. She wanted this kiss to last until Christmas.

Of next year.

But then he stepped back.

"Dammit!"

"Shh…"

Oh, no he didn't.

But he only wanted to drag his shirt over his head, giving her a quick glance at sleek skin and hard sinew which made her melt, though not as much as his naked piercing gaze did as he yanked her back against him. "Where were we?"

"Right here." She slid her fingers into his hair, straining to reach his mouth, but he held her off, just looking at her, his eyes so dark and sexy her knees wobbled. "What?"

"You're beautiful."

"You're blind without your glasses."

"I have you memorized."

She sighed. God, she was a complete sap if that was working on her. "You're beautiful, too," she admitted. "And your eyes…"

"As blind as you said." He squinted with exaggeration and used his hands as if he couldn't see, copping a quick feel.

That made her laugh, but it backed up in her throat when he rubbed her up against him. Oh, yeah. Her soft, sweet, sensitive Dustin wasn't showing his usual side, and she loved it, both that and the slight rough edge to his hands as he kissed her again, his mouth binding her to him while he undid his jeans, letting go of her long enough to grab a condom from his wallet and shove the jeans off.

She sat on the bed, scooting back to make room for him as he crawled up her body and reached for her hands, holding them in his on either side of her face as he leaned over her. "Be sure," he murmured. "Be damn sure."

She looked up at him. He was so gorgeous, so much more than she'd let herself see, and so much more than she herself could ever be, and suddenly she faltered. For her this was a release, a great one, but nothing more. It wasn't the same for him, she knew that. What she didn't know was if she could do it to him—

"You've changed your mind, it's okay—"

"No." God, no. Her insides were trembling, making her fingers far too unsteady for her taste, and she uncharacteristically closed her eyes as she touched his jaw. "You don't understand. I—" *You're too good for me, for this…*

As if he understood, he touched his forehead to hers, his breathing rasping in and out roughly as he took in some air. "Cristina."

In a rare moment of cowardice, she squeezed her eyes tighter.

"Look at me."

Obeying that ragged command, she managed to open her eyes and meet his.

"It's just you and me. Just us. And we already know how good that can be. Let me show you how good this can be, as well." And he kissed her shoulder. Her collarbone. A breast, which he softly sucked into his mouth. When she gasped, he continued his little tour of her body, heading farther south, kissing a rib, her belly button, a hip…

Shifting, he ran his hand down her leg, gently nudging it open so that he could kiss first one inner thigh and then the next.

And then in between.

She stopped thinking then and stopped breathing, too, while he took her straight to implosion in five point four seconds.

When she came back to planet Earth, he was working his way up her body, looking quite hot and bothered. Once again, he laced his fingers with hers as he slowly eased her legs apart. "You do have the most beautiful eyes. Keep looking at me."

She could feel him hard and heavy between her legs, gliding against her throbbing and already very wet flesh. "I'm looking."

"You see me." He held her gaze as he slowly pushed into her, hard and thick, filling her so completely that she couldn't stop the small cry of pleasure from escaping her throat.

"I see you," she promised on a rough breath, arching up for more, for all of him, wrapping her legs around his waist.

"Keep seeing me." And he began to move inside her, making love to her with such beautiful fierce care that she found herself rocking into him, begging for her release long before he allowed it, showing her exactly how good he was for her, exactly how much she needed him and how much he could love her.

If only she'd let him.

And for that moment in time, she *did* let him, let herself. She completely gave in to it, letting herself soar, content to be in his arms for as long as he'd hold her.

Or at least as long as she could stand it before the doubts and fears overtook her again.

HOURS LATER, Dustin stirred and reached for Cristina, knowing when he felt the cold sheets that he was alone in her bed.

Rolling to his back, he sighed, not bothering to call himself a fool for believing that this time it would be different. He should know better by now.

It was never going to be different, nothing was ever going to change.

Except him.

He could change.

He could grow up and get over her and not give her the power to do this to him.

Not ever again.

5

WHEN CRISTINA came back from her punishingly long hard run, Dustin was gone. Which was perfect, she told herself. Excellent. She didn't need round two or an after-sex cuddle.

Nope, she was good.

Walking through the apartment she'd lived in for several years now, lived in and been content in, she found herself taking a good look around as Dustin had. When she'd first moved in, she hadn't been able to afford a west-facing apartment so she couldn't see the beach, but it was there, only two blocks away, and when she opened the windows, she could smell the salty ocean air.

She had minimal furniture but she didn't spend a lot of time here, so she hadn't found it necessary to fill the place up with stuff she would never use.

In fact, she hadn't filled much of it at all, and as she took the place in, saw the half-empty, clean rooms, she came to the uncomfortable realization that Dustin might be right.

She had nothing Christmasy out, no decorations, nothing personal at all.

She'd never cared before. It hadn't mattered, the holiday hadn't mattered. In fact, little did beside her work.

So when had that stopped being enough? When Blake had gone through such hell this year? When she'd thought he was dead and that she'd lost one of the few people she'd let herself care about?

Or when two others on her team, Aidan and Zach, had each found their respective soul mates in Brooke and Kenzie? Yeah, that had shocked her to the core, two staunch bachelors, both falling so hard.

With a sigh, she gathered her laundry, telling herself she didn't care that she didn't have a damn Christmas tree or some stupid decorations, and she sure as hell didn't care that she didn't have a soul mate, because if she had, then she might be doing laundry for *two* right now and that would suck.

Besides, she didn't even know if she believed in soul mates.

The idea of it, that there was one person in all the persons of the world, one, that was meant for her, seemed crazy. With those odds, it was no wonder that she'd decided not to look.

And yet…and yet a small part of her thought maybe it wouldn't be so bad to be doing two loads of laundry instead of one, if she had company while she was doing them. She dumped the first load into her washing machine, and, hearing the crinkle of paper, stuck her hands into her pockets. It was the red envelope, the one that had cost her twenty-five bucks on a whim.

For charity. There. See? She'd made a contribution to Christmas, and somehow, ridiculously, the thought cheered her slightly. Until she opened the envelope and remembered what her twenty-five bucks had gotten her.

That one-night romantic getaway. She and Dustin could have rocked that one night.

She should just throw the card away and chalk it up as a tax write-off. There was no reason even to keep it around….

But as she passed the trash can, she slipped the card back into her pocket instead.

DUSTIN WALKED IN the front door of his house and found his brother slouched on his couch, feet up, remote in hand, game on the television, as if he lived there.

Jason nodded a greeting, taking a few seconds to tear his gaze off the game, but once he did, he blinked at Dustin's disheveled appearance. "Either you got your ass kicked by the job, or you just got laid."

Dustin kicked off his shoes and dropped his keys and wallet, then sank to the couch next to his brother, whom he was damn happy to see. "You got off on leave a few days early."

"Yeah." Jason wasn't in his National Guard uniform, but wearing jeans and a vintage Van Halen T-shirt. "Thought I'd hang here, and we'd go up to Mom's for Christmas Eve together. Nice change of subject, by the way."

"I haven't seen you in six months, you don't want to talk about my job."

"Okay, let's talk about you getting laid."

Dustin rolled his eyes and leaned in to hug his brother, who met him halfway and pulled him in tight. "Missed your ugly mug a little."

"Same goes, bro. Same goes." Jason offered him a soda and the chips, both of which had come from Dustin's stash. "The house is coming along."

Dustin looked around him. They'd bought it together several years back, right before Jason had reenlisted in the National Guard. It was an investment over and above their usual renovation projects, and as a major fixer-upper, the investment part had been mostly faith.

But with Jason's down payment and Dustin's physical labor, the place really was coming along. They could sell, put the profits into another house and start over again. Their sister wanted them to do that and hire her part-time as a cash laborer, which would be both a blessing since she was a hard worker, and a damned headache because she was also a pain in the ass.

But it would be a nice transition out of his job, which Dustin had been restless at for far too long now.

"Shelly called me," Jason said, reading his mind about their baby sister. "She's seeing some guy named Chewy. I told her I was going to have to kick his ass for no reason other than he lets people call him Chewy."

Dustin laughed. "He's all right. And they're not serious."

"You checked him out?"

"Yeah. He's in college like she is, and a good kid, despite the unfortunate name."

"All right then." Jason stared at the game. Drank. Ate a few chips.

Dustin looked him over. Still the same dark hair, cut militarily short, and light gray eyes which could warm with a quick laugh or turn to steel. Jason had always been a big guy, nearly six foot four, and beefy, like the football player he'd once been, but over the past years in the military, he'd honed his body into a much rangier form, looking more like a lean boxer now than a high-school football star. Their mom had been worried about him ever since he'd gotten back from being in the South, working in and near New Orleans on clean-up and rebuilding, going out on search-and-rescue calls as his orders dictated. And indeed, as their mom had said, there was something different about Jason, something less easily accessible and definitely introspective.

"You could take a picture, it lasts longer."

Dustin didn't rise to the bait. "I'm just wondering if you're okay."

"Ah, and here I thought I looked so pretty today."

"Seriously, Jase."

"Seriously?" Jason set down his soda and hit Mute on the game, turning to face him. "Seriously, I was going to ask you the same thing. You look like shit. What's up?"

"I asked you first."

"Okay, what's wrong with me is that the big bad world out there sucks right now." Jason lifted a shoulder. "I work my ass off to do my part to fix it, but I can't, and if I think about it too much it seems stupid even to be trying, so I am not going to think about it. Not for at least the next two weeks before I have to head out again. Now you."

"Me what?"

"You might as well tell me before I knock it out of you."

Given Jason's new physical prowess, he could do it, too.

"Is it the job putting that look of misery on your face. Or a girl?"

Dustin let out a breath. "Both."

"So there is a girl."

"I don't think so, no."

Jason blinked. "A guy?"

"Jesus!"

"Well, use your words, dude."

Dustin rolled his eyes and ate some more chips.

"Come on, Dus. You're the middle child. You're the talker."

"Fine." Dustin pushed the chips aside. "I'm in a job that was supposed to be just a phase, a little fun before we got our renovation business going."

"Don't look now, but our renovation business is going. We've got good equity in this place."

"Sort of my point. We could be doing more and yet here I am, still driving an ambulance…."

"So quit and get a move on. I'm game. Let's sell the house. We can use my portion of the profit for a new down payment on another fixer-upper, and your labor. And I say we go big this time and do it right. Bigger house, bigger profit margin. If you're serious about being done as an EMT, you'd have the time to put in."

True.

"So…the girl," Jason said, leaning back to close his eyes. "Get to the girl."

Right. The girl. How to say that he was more than halfway in love with a woman who wasn't ever going to love him back? "She's a coworker, which is colossally stupid."

"Only if you intend to repeat."

"Last night *was* a repeat."

At this, Jason opened his eyes and turned his head to eyeball Dustin. "Is it that firefighter chick you've been hung up on since day one? The hot one who looks like…what do they call her? Kick-Ass Barbie. Cathleen?"

"Cristina."

"Ah, Christ," Jason said with a groan. "It is. Man, you're going straight down the path to Heartbreak City with that one. She's out of your league."

"Gee, thanks."

"Look, life's too short to get kicked in the balls or the heart, and with Cristina, you'll get both."

DUSTIN DIDN'T REALIZE exactly how true that statement was until his next shift. He got to the station, and found Cristina in the kitchen with everyone else. She was doing her usual dig through the refrigerator—she was the most notorious food thief in the entire station. "You stealing someone's lunch again?" he asked lightly, as if she hadn't dumped him.

Well, actually, you had to *have* a relationship with someone to be dumped. They didn't have a relationship, they had a thing. A sex thing. That was all.

At his question, Eddie and Sam, both at the table eating cereal, went still, swiveling wary gazes to Cristina. Blake, drinking coffee at the sink next to Aidan and Zach, raised a brow. It was unlike Dustin to start the bickering but what the hell. It was time for a new thing.

Cristina slowly turned to face him, her eyes unreadable. She hadn't changed into her uniform yet and wore army-green cargoes and a snug long-sleeved T-shirt that fitted her curves like a glove, curves he knew intimately. Curves he'd kissed every single inch of. "No, smart-ass," she responded. "I made cookies."

"Made them? Or bought them?"

It was a long-standing joke that the only girl in the station couldn't cook, but still, the entire room held their breath and swiveled their gazes to Cristina as if watching a tennis match.

"I baked them myself," Cristina said. Stiffly. "I'm actually leaving them in people's lunches to make up for all the stuff I've…borrowed."

"Wow." Dustin leaned back against the wall, crossing his arms so that he couldn't reach for her, which is what he suddenly wanted to do, even surrounded by everyone else. She looked good, he thought, rested, with color in her cheeks. She had gloss on her lips, her only makeup. Her hair was loose, which made him remember how it'd felt brushing his chest.

He wanted both to touch her and to strangle her. "I'm impressed."

"That's because whatever we women do, we have to do it twice as good as a guy to be thought of as half as good. Luckily, that's not difficult." She shut the refrigerator, and avoiding looking at him, headed across the kitchen.

"She's escaping, man," Blake said to Dustin out of the side of his mouth.

"They must have slept together again," Sam whispered to Eddie as if Dustin was deaf. "She's looking relaxed and he's not."

"You doing it wrong?" Eddie asked Dustin.

Dustin sighed. "Cristina." He watched her stop and go a little stiff in the shoulders. "Are we going to talk about it at all?"

"What, the orgasms?" She didn't turn to face him. "That's a little too risqué a topic for the workplace, don't you think?"

Eddie snickered, only to be silenced by Sam's elbow in his gut.

Dustin took a step toward Cristina. "Maybe we could discuss this in—"

The alarm bell interrupted him, then dispatch, calling for Dustin and James's unit. No firefighters required.

"—private," Dustin finished on a sigh, grinding his back teeth together in frustration as he was forced to head out. He brushed past her, making sure to touch her as he did, getting some satisfaction when her breath caught at the contact.

Which didn't change the fact that they were back at square one—her holding him at bay with her sarcasm and sharp wit, and him nursing an aching heart.

6

THE MOMENT Dustin was out of sight, Cristina sagged to a kitchen chair. "I'm such an idiot."

"Yeah," Eddie said, patting her knee. "You are."

Sam nodded.

Blake lifted a shoulder in silent agreement.

Cristina looked at Aidan and Zach, two of the most logical men she knew, hoping…but they also nodded.

It was unanimous. She was an idiot.

"I know you don't like to clutter your plate with relationships," Blake said tactfully. "Because you have to be free for… What is it exactly that you have to be free for?"

"Well…" Everyone waited for her sage, intelligent response. "I have to be free for…" Jeez. She suddenly had no idea. It'd started out because she'd spent so many years watching her mother *never* be free, always trapped in a bad relationship with one man or another, over and over again.

Trapping Cristina, as well, so she'd learned to gather her mistrust close to her like a cape. Once she'd gotten out on her own, she'd gone the opposite route, always staying on her own. She was, after all, nothing if not a creature of her own habits. But that all seemed short-sighted and a bit pathetic now. "I don't know," she admitted, and thunked her head to the table. "I guess I don't know how to do things differently."

"You can fix this," Blake said so calmly, she raised her head.

He nodded.

The others nodded, too.

"All you have to do is stop running scared," he said gently, rubbing her back.

"Whoa. I'm *not* scared."

Five patient but amused faces just looked at her.

Okay, so she was scared. Oh, damn. "But what if I mess it up?"

"Well, you probably will," Zach said.

"Gee, thanks."

"No, everyone does once or twice, at *least*."

"You can still turn this around," Blake promised. "If you want it bad enough."

She looked at the door through which Dustin, her mild-mannered best friend by day—big, bad, confident, sexy lover by night—had vanished. There'd been something different in his eyes just now.

Distance.

Her fault. He thought he'd been ditched. She knew that now. She'd pretended to want distance, but that wasn't really what she wanted at all. She knew that now. "I want it bad enough," she whispered. "What do I do?"

"You could tell him you love him," Blake said.

"What?" She nearly choked. "I'm not— I can't— I can't say that— I mean, it's not…*that*." She grabbed Blake by the lapels. "There has to be something else."

"Well, for one thing, you relax," Aidan said as Blake pried her hands off him. "Ask him out. Show him you're in this. Plan something fun. Take him jet-skiing, or something he wouldn't do for himself. You know, show him you know what he likes."

"Feed him," Zach suggested, patting his belly. "Food always works."

"You don't have to cook it," Aidan said quickly. "In fact, you shouldn't cook it. Go out to a restaurant, or make a picnic."

"But if you do the picnic," Eddie interjected. "Make sure it's not silly little finger food. Bring *real* food."

"And try smiling," Zach said. "You have a great smile, on the rare occasions you use it. He'll be so stunned, you'll have time to spit out the fact that yes, you're an idiot, but you're working on it."

"It would help if you took off all your clothes first," Eddie said.

"Guys like that," Sam agreed.

"You could practice here," Eddie suggested, nearly falling over when Sam shoved him.

Blake was shaking his head. "Just tell him you love him."

No. No, she liked the other ideas much better. She'd just ask him out, that's what she'd do. Plan that picnic. Smile. Bring food. Maybe wear some sexy outfit and let things take their course. She'd show him how much he meant to her.

Yeah. She was going to turn this around. Time was on her side.

DUSTIN'S UNIT was run ragged for the rest of the day, one call after another. So it was inevitable that one of his calls would bump up against one of Cristina's. He'd been brooding all damn day, and braced for the awkwardness of seeing her, given that she kept sleeping with him and then breaking his heart. But if she felt weird, she didn't let on. In fact, she smiled at him.

Dazzled the brood right out of him.

She was working a small fire caused by a toaster while Dustin treated the young woman who'd attempted to put it out by herself only to fall on her butt, knocking the air out of her.

"I can't be in a cast for Christmas," she wailed, holding her bottom in both hands. "Not this year."

"I don't think they cast your ass," Cristina said helpfully from where she stood near the toaster. She winked at Dustin.

Winked.

"I can't have any bandages, either, my boyfriend's coming to town." The woman tried to get up and gasped in pain. "Ouch, ouch, ouch… Do you think it's broken?" As she asked this question, she turned and yanked down her pants, revealing a quite perfect tightly toned ass. "Anything?"

Dustin stared at it, then lifted his gaze to find Cristina looking at him, eyes amused, brows raised. Oddly enough, given that he'd been pouting all morning, the air crackled between them. "I don't think it's broken." He cleared his throat. "You look…fine."

"Fine," Cristina mouthed, and rolled her eyes.

Afterward, outside, she sidled up to him. "Hey."

"Hey," he said, and to keep that crackle at bay, he went light. "Need me to look and see if your ass is broken?"

She flashed a smile and almost blinded him. "You just want to see my ass."

True enough. After all, it was world-class.

"Little tip, ace." She patted his chest, voluntarily touching him outside of sex. "Next time a woman pulls her pants down for you, find a better description than *fine*."

"I'll work on my adjectives," he said, hoping despite himself that it was *her* ass he saw next.

"Um, Dustin? You want to have a picnic sometime?"

He stared at her. "Huh?"

"You have a hearing problem? I asked if you wanted to have a picnic."

"Like a *date* picnic?"

"Yeah. A date picnic."

"A date," he repeated. He wouldn't have been more shocked if she'd asked him to marry her.

"Well, if it's that stupid—" She started to turn away but he grabbed her hand and pulled her back around.

"I'm sorry. You surprised me, that's all. I've asked you out before and been shut down."

"You know what? Forget it. Forget I said anything about anything."

"Cristina…" He shook his head. "You drive me crazy."

"I realize I tend to have that effect on people." Again she tried to pull away and again he held her.

She looked at his hand and then up into his eyes. Something was happening between them, the same odd phenomenon that always happened between them, and it was heat, pure heat.

"Mostly it's in a good way," he said a little thickly. "The driving-me-crazy part."

"Mostly?" Her voice was husky, too.

"Yeah. Well, you do have your moments."

She stared at him for a long beat. "You say the nicest things." A small smile flashed. "And you're funny."

"I'm a keeper."

She paused, suddenly looking as though she'd been struck, then touched his chest. "I know."

The air felt changed, his heart too full. "Cristina—"

"But I'm not," she whispered. "A keeper."

And with that, she turned away.

"Cristina."

She kept walking.

"So…no picnic I'm guessing?"

Still walking…

Okay. Shit. Once again he'd gotten his hopes up but no more. He couldn't do it again. This had to be it, he had to be done bashing his head into a wall. He wanted her, more than he'd ever wanted anything, but it wasn't healthy. Shaking his head, he pulled out his cell and called Jason. "Okay."

"Okay what?"

He let out a shaky breath. "Let's sell. Go big."

"You're outta there then? You'll give the new project the time it'll need?"

He leaned back against the wall and nodded, until he realized that his brother couldn't see him. "Yes and yes."

"Hot damn. I have a real estate agent on hold right this minute who says she can sell the house, and already has a list of properties for us to look at."

"Good. I'll meet you after work." Dustin shut the phone and turned, nearly running into Cristina.

She slapped his clipboard against his chest. "You left this inside. What are you selling?"

"My house."

"Why?"

"Because the time's right."

"You mean, the market?"

"That, too." And then, for the first time ever, he walked away from her.

THEIR PATHS crossed again later, at a duplex fire in an older part of town. The building had been undergoing renovation; now flames were taking care of the reno, and at least fifteen construction workers were unaccounted for.

Cristina and Blake were on scene, as well as Aidan and Zach and the others, putting their own lives on the line.

That was their job.

Dustin knew it as he stared at the inferno, his gut pinched, but he never got used to it, never, so he concentrated on the victims as they were pulled out, rather than wonder exactly where Cristina was and if she was safe.

He had to believe she was safe.

Eddie and Sam came barreling out of the fire, a big guy between them, hunched over. Dustin ran toward them, meeting them just beyond the porch and barely out of the smoke from the fire. The guy slumped to the ground just as above them they heard screaming.

"I've got him," Dustin told them. "Go!" He dropped to his knees next to the victim, who was over six foot four and close to three hundred pounds.

And out cold.

The heat was overwhelming. Only a moment ago Dustin hadn't been able to see the flames from here, but now the entire front wall of the duplex had started to burn, and just to his right, one of the windows exploded.

He dropped over the victim, protecting him. Above him, flames leapt out of the huge gaping hole where the glass had just been, enraged by the new burst of oxygen. As he watched, horrified, the flames coalesced in a ball, heading right for him, and he thought, *ah hell, I'm done. Toast, burnt toast—*

But he didn't die, so he opened his eyes and realized the

flames had been abruptly held back by a long line of water, coming from a hose—

In Cristina's hands. "Get back!" she yelled.

In the movies, their gazes would have met and in hers Dustin would have seen love and fear for him, but she didn't take her gaze off the fire. Dustin got behind his unconscious victim, sliding his hands beneath the guy's arms, and tugged, hard, not looking back.

He didn't have to. He didn't need the movie stare to know Cristina had his back, she always would. He could trust that.

But in spite of their chemistry, he couldn't trust her with his heart. That had finally settled in his head. It was why he was getting out, cutting his losses. For self-preservation, he had no choice.

He and James left the scene with two of the victims in their rig, heading to the hospital. By the time they got back to the station, the shift had ended and Cristina was gone.

He showered and changed before heading out to look at houses with Jason. Afterward, he drove to Cristina's place…to say goodbye.

She opened the door and looked at him in surprised relief, and also anticipation.

That hummed through him, so instead of saying goodbye, he decided to show her how he felt. He stepped over the threshold, pushing his way in past her.

"What—"

That was all she got out before he got his hands on her, spun her around, and pinned her to the door.

"Dustin—"

"I can't do this anymore."

"Can't do what?"

"This." And he kissed them both stupid.

7

CRISTINA PULLED BACK to stare into Dustin's unbearably familiar face because she had to see him. She'd been standing in her living room, worked up at how he'd put his life on the line today.

If she hadn't been right there with her hose—

But she had been and he was okay, she told herself. But her? Not so okay. She'd been wondering what the hell was wrong with her that she couldn't just go for what she wanted, when the one thing she wanted had knocked at her door.

And then he'd said he couldn't do this anymore. They should discuss that, but this was not her mild-mannered EMT geek. This was a pissed-off, frustrated, on-the-edge Dustin, tough and implacable in his resolve.

He'd stepped all over her personal space and was kissing every single brain cell out of her head. "If you'd gotten hurt today," she murmured, "I'd have killed you."

"You really are the most annoying woman on the planet."

"I think it's time that we start annoying other people."

"Later."

"I mean it, Dustin."

"I believe you." His eyes darkened. "It's why I'm here. Saying goodbye."

Her heart caught. "Oh. I…see."

"I've got to, Cristina. You're killing me."

Right. She knew that. He was killing her, too. As was her own inability to figure out what to do about that. "I don't want to kill you. I like you alive."

"You just don't like me close." He was still holding her against the door, her hands held in his on either side of her face. Eyes narrowed, mouth grim and tight, he stared down into her face with an expression that said *I'm pissed, frustrated and worked up. And I want to take you right now, right this very minute.*

God, the man made her forget she had knees. "I'm sorry," she whispered.

"Me, too." He let out another breath. "But I want you to know how much it meant to me that you were there for me today."

She stared at him, the words *I always will be* stuck in her throat, because she could feel that goodbye to the very corners of her soul, and knew he meant it. "Forget the thanks. Get back to the goodbye, which I was so enjoying."

She needed to keep this light.

Very light.

Or she'd fall apart, and she didn't allow herself to do that, ever. So she lifted her mouth to his and he met her halfway, going back to ravishing her mouth as if he were a man starving after a two-week fast and she was a twelve-course meal.

She felt the same. She needed to fill herself up with him. Straining against his leanly muscled form, she ran her mouth along his jaw, impatient at not being able to reach any of the good stuff. "My hands, I need my hands to touch you."

"You touch me with your eyes. You touch me with your voice. You touch me with your damn heart, you just can't admit it."

Stung by what was undeniably the truth, she went still, but he tilted her face up to his, stared into her eyes, swore roughly and kissed her again. "You touch me every time I look at you," he managed gruffly when they both came up for breath. "Or when I think of you. Hell, I dream about you. It pisses me off, Cristina."

"Then you shouldn't have come. You shouldn't have come."

"Damn right, but I did. I came to say goodbye."

"What does that mean exactly? Where are you going?"

"I'm leaving the station and going back to what I wanted to do in the first place. It might take me a little time to get it all in gear, I still have to sell the house, but I wanted you to know."

Her heart had stopped at the words *I'm leaving the station.* She tried to turn her head away to blast him with some more words, words that would scare him off, make him get the hell out, but he wouldn't allow it. He took her mouth with his, nipping at her resistance with hot, hungry bites until, with a moan of surrender she arched closer, clutching at him, giving in to everything, anything, he wanted of her.

It was insane, this surging swell of need and hunger she felt.

It flooded her, nearly blinding her, and before she knew what she was doing, she'd torn her hands from his and yanked at his pants, desperate to get them open, even more desperate to get him inside her. While she fought his zipper, he had her jeans down completely and a condom out of his pocket. "Wrap your legs around my waist," he commanded in his low, rough whisper, the one that had her shivering and rushing to do what he asked.

"Yeah, like that," he ground out. "God, just like that." Lifting her up against the door, he pushed inside her.

As she cried out in sheer, unadulterated pleasure, her head thunked back against the wall and she gripped his shoulders for all she was worth. She had no idea how she could want him like this, but she did. "Dustin—"

"I know." Sliding a hand up her back to cradle her head, protect it from the door, he began to move. "I know." Leaning into the door, he pressed her between the hard wood and his equally hard body, thrusting into her over and over again, until her toes curled, until she was panting out his name like a mantra in mindless plea as he kissed her, using his tongue in a matching rhythm to his body.

Within moments, she burst, and he was only seconds behind her, and for long ragged breaths they were both gone. Then his knees wobbled, and with an oath, he slapped a hand back on the door to hold them upright, his muscles still trembling. But instead of letting her go, he turned his face into the curve of her neck and nuzzled there, softly kissing her damp flesh.

"I can't feel my legs," she gasped.

"I've got you."

And wasn't that just the thing. The terribly confusing thing. "I…need to feel my legs."

Lifting his head, he looked into her eyes as he let her legs slide down his body. When her toes touched the floor, her legs nearly buckled, but he caught her, his jaw against hers, his breathing—still uneven—disturbing the hair at her temple.

"I'm good." Proving it, she stepped back, coming up against the door, but holding her hands up to show him that she was fine.

Dustin just stared at her. "What the hell was that?"

"Some damn amazing goodbye sex."

"Yeah." He turned in a slow circle, shoving his hands through his hair as he came back around. "I really don't want to do this, to say goodbye."

"Well then, don't. Don't say it."

Stepping back, he shook his head. "I want more."

She closed her eyes.

"And you still don't," he said quietly.

"Dustin—"

"Goodbye, Cristina."

She was standing there, mouth open when he walked right out the door.

ON DUSTIN'S next shift, his unit was called out just as he set foot in the door of the station.

Just as well. He needed to keep busy, because after this shift he was giving his typed resignation to the chief, and he didn't want to think about it.

At midday they met up with Cristina and Blake's rig outside a small grocery store on the corner of Main and Third. Inside there'd been a brawl in the liquor aisle over the last of the peppermint schnapps, leaving the manager with a black eye and a customer headed for a night behind bars.

"I guess that guy really needed that peppermint schnapps," Cristina said.

"Maybe he should have gone for a beer instead."

She gave him a tough-girl stare. "Sometimes, you just have to have what you have to have."

"Yeah?" Knowing he was stepping into the frying pan, he shifted close. "And what is it that you have to have?"

She paused, then sagged a little, losing the attitude. "That's the problem. I always figured it was one thing and now I'm thinking it's another entirely."

Just then Blake called her away. Dustin had to restrain himself from yelling, "What the hell does that mean?" after her.

They met up again several hours later, outside a small house. "People are so stupid around the holidays," she said.

He happened to agree. People *were* stupid around the holidays, as evidenced by the fact he was loading a guy into the ambulance minus his fingers, which he'd cut off with his new turkey carver, right into his kitchen sink. Earlier he'd had a guy who'd fallen off his roof putting up the Christmas lights, and a woman who'd accidentally electrocuted herself when she had stuck too many strings of lights into one socket and then touched it with wet fingers.

Yeah. People were stupid around the holidays. Including himself.

And then came the defining moment of stupidity. He and James were called *back* to the grocery store from earlier that day for another unknown injury.

"The call came from the deli," one of the clerks in the front told them as they came through. "Someone's down."

"I'll go get the stretcher," James said.

Blake and Cristina entered, as well. "They said they might need a fire unit," Blake told them. "What's up?"

"Don't know yet." Blake radioed dispatch for more information while Dustin headed in, extremely aware of Cristina at his side. At the back of the store, a wide-eyed clerk peeking out from a swinging door behind the deli counter waved them over. "You're just EMTs, right?" she whispered frantically. "No police?"

"What's happening?" Cristina asked her.

"No questions!" The clerk grabbed Dustin's arm. "He said no questions! Oh, God, you have to hurry, or it'll be too late!"

Dustin went with her, with Cristina right on his tail. They both looked at each other, nonplussed, when the clerk locked the door behind them. "He said just two EMTs."

Dustin opened his mouth to correct her that Cristina was a firefighter, but Cristina stepped on his foot. "It's just us two," she said quietly.

"Okay, good." The clerk gulped in air. "Because if I let anyone else in, he'll kill all of us. Hurry!"

Kill?

The back area was empty, except for two people—the manager they'd met earlier, down on the ground, still sporting his black eye, but now holding on to his shoulder, as well, which was bleeding all over the floor.

And the customer from earlier, who stood over him.

With a gun.

"Well, it's about time," he said, tightening his grip on the gun. "This idiot made me shoot him."

"You're crazy!" the "idiot" yelled, writhing in pain, bleeding out on the floor as Dustin watched. "And so is the courthouse for letting you out on bail! They should have put you in a seventy-two-hour hold! And for the record, all I said was that you're more stupid than you look if you think I'm going to apologize to you!"

"And you're not only as stupid as you look, you're also going to be dead." He aimed the gun between the manager's eyes. "Now say it. Say you're sorry."

The wounded man was bleeding fast and furious, and going very pale. "No."

"Say you're sorry!"

"No!"

"You have another shoulder, you know. And I'll shoot you in it— Hey!" The shooter turned his head toward Dustin, who'd shifted closer to the victim. "Stay right where you are until I tell you to move!"

Ignoring him, Dustin went down on his knees to look at the wound. The bullet couldn't have hit any major arteries or the manager would probably already have bled out completely—one thing in the guy's favor.

Dustin lifted the torn and bloody material away from the entry wound.

The manager hissed out a pained breath. "I'm going to die, aren't I? How long before I die?"

Cristina went to move closer to help but crazy-gun-guy protested. *"Stay where you are!"*

Her hands fisted but she stayed. "He needs helps."

"Let me repeat. Move and I'll shoot."

"Okay, let's all just try to relax," Dustin said quickly, still crouched by the injured man. "You let us in here, right? So I know you don't want anyone to die." He went to open his bag, until the gun ended up in his face.

"No funny business!"

"No funny business." Slowly, Dustin pulled out gauze and pressed it to the wound. "He needs a hospital."

"Not until I get my apology."

"For what?"

"He said I was a worthless loser."

"You hit him," Dustin pointed out. "And then you shot him. I think you're even."

"Mom said he has to apologize, that I shouldn't give in until he apologizes."

"Mom?" Dustin divided a look between the two guys as sirens sounded in the distance. "You're brothers?"

"Only temporarily," the brother holding the gun said. "Because I'm going to shoot him dead if he doesn't apologize, and then I'll be an only child."

The manager groaned and lay back. "Jesus. You're crazy."

"Say you're sorry!"

"Just say it," Dustin grated out, trying to stop the bleeding and having little luck.

"No way in hell!"

The armed brother waved his weapon, looking quite pissed off at the world. When it ended up in the vicinity of the terrified clerk, she let out a low cry and started to back away.

"Don't move!" The manager, gray from blood loss and pain, yelled from his position on the concrete floor. "God, Tess, don't get shot for me!"

The gun was in her face now. "Yes, Tess," the manager's brother said. "Don't get shot for him."

"Okay, let's just all stay very calm," Dustin slowly rose, holding up his hands. "You don't need the clerk anymore, right? You can let her go. Let both women go."

"They can identify me."

That didn't sound promising. For any of them. The police were probably outside by now, maybe even making their way in somehow, or so he hoped, so he figured stalling was key. "Look,

why don't you tell me what it is you want, and I'll try to negoti-
ate it for you."

"I want an apology, or he dies." Emphasizing this, he pointed
the gun at his brother.

Tess screamed and scrambled backward, turning to race reck-
lessly toward the door.

"Stop!"

Knowing it was all going to go bad, Dustin grabbed Cristina
and shoved her behind him, dropping them both down as the guy
waved his gun around like a mad man over their heads.

Well, shit, he thought. He should have quit *yesterday.*

8

FROM BEHIND Dustin, where he'd shoved her, Cristina couldn't
see, but what she heard stopped her heart.

"Stop!" crazy-gun-dude yelled. "Stop or I'll shoot you!"

"Don't shoot her!" his brother cried.

Cristina lifted her head.

Tess wasn't stopping. Heart in her throat, Cristina tried to get
free from Dustin's grip but then he was surging forward, throwing
himself at the gunman.

In Cristina's life, she'd been afraid many times, but never like
this, never such a gut-wrenching horror. *"Dustin!"* She reached
for him, grabbing, but catching only his belt, and the holster for
his scissors.

Dustin landed on the gunman and they rolled around on the
floor, each grappling to be on top.

Cristina held the scissors like a weapon, planning on stabbing
gun guy, but the two men kept moving, rolling, bizarrely in tune
to the clerk screaming her head off. Then the man with the gun
shoved free of Dustin, whose face was bleeding. He'd lost his

glasses and squinted, as crazy-gun-guy leapt to his feet and aimed at the clerk's back.

"No!" all of them yelled. Dustin lunged to his feet, the sudden motion causing the gunman to whirl on him just as the manager, still on the floor, yanked on his brother's leg hard, causing him to lose his balance.

The gun went off.

Time stopped and so did Cristina's heart as she watched Dustin jerk. She dove for him as the deranged brother fell, and they all hit the floor in unison.

"Shit, shit, shit," she gasped, grabbing Dustin as he doubled over and grabbed his leg, his face a mask of agony.

The room was suddenly filled with police and everything was a blur.

Except Dustin, still in her arms, eyes closed, his precious blood pumping out of a hole in his thigh. *"Dustin."*

James was suddenly there, as were two paramedics from station #33, all getting in her way, pulling Dustin out of her arms.

"He's going to be fine," she told them, stepping back out of the way so they could get him on a gurney.

Blake was there. He hugged her hard, and into his chest she said it again. "He's going to be fine."

"I'll take you to the hospital," he said, far too solemnly.

Which was odd because Dustin was going to be fine. *Fine.*

BLAKE GOT Cristina to the hospital right behind the ambulance. As they rushed into the E.R. alongside Dustin, Cristina never took her eyes off his pale, pale face. A nurse cut away his pants while a doctor barked orders over his head.

Cristina tried to get a good look but another nurse eased her back out of the way. But she stayed in the room. "Look at that, Dustin. I'm getting you out of your pants without even trying."

Dustin's mouth quirked, but his eyes stayed closed. "Be gentle."

There was a lump in her throat the size of a football. "Hey, I'm always gentle with the lightweights, ace."

"I'll have you know I'm no lightweight. I know what I'm doing…"

Cristina choked out a laugh. He did. He did know what he was doing, always. "Dustin—"

"Yeah…" His voice was fading away, which terrorized her. But it was just the drugs, she told herself.

He was *fine*.

Out of the speakers came some soft, elevator Christmas music, reminding her that tomorrow was Christmas Eve. Someone had the small TV at the nurses' station on CNN, muted, and ticker after ticker spelled doom and gloom for their economy. "You know, it's really not a good time to be selling a house," she whispered.

Blake reached for her hand and squeezed it. "Cristina—"

"Seriously. He should just forget about selling his damn house."

"I think I can get this bullet out without sending him to surgery," one of the doctors said.

"Do it." Dustin sounded as if he was breathing through gritted teeth.

"Give him more pain meds," Christina demanded. Why weren't they giving him more? "Blake—"

Blake held her back, whispering in her ear. "They know what they're doing. You know they know what they're doing."

"Do you feel this?" the doctor asked, poking at Dustin's bare foot.

"Feel what?"

Oh, God. "He's going to be fine…" She stared at Dustin's too-pale face. "You hear me, Dustin Mauer?"

The doctor gave Blake a look that had the firefighter holding on to Christina very tightly, but she was very aware that no one was making any promises. "He's going to be fine," she repeated for herself.

"Yes," Blake said, sounding a little tense. "He is."

The alternative was far too painful to contemplate. A world without Dustin? Without those eyes, that smile, that gentle, giving, sweet nature that he could turn just a little rough and edgy when he had to? No way. She couldn't imagine not having him in her life. "Goddammit, we have a picnic to go to."

Dustin didn't respond to that and she tried to move closer to the gurney, but Blake caught her. "We have to stay back or they'll make us leave."

"He practically jumped in front of that gunman!" she cried. "To protect that girl. To protect me!" *She* did the saving, dammit. No one needed to save her.

Blake kept a good hold of her, probably afraid she was going to jump the line of nurses and start yelling at Dustin again. She gripped the front of Blake's shirt, giving him a shake when it was herself that needed one. "I'm not done with that man!"

Very gently, Blake pulled her in for a hug. "I know."

"I have things to tell him." She wasn't exactly sure what they were yet, but she'd figure that part out. She tried to look at Dustin through the throng of people now working on him. "Do you hear me, Dustin Mauer? I have things to tell you!"

"Cristina, come on now," Blake begged her. "The drugs have just knocked him out. Stay back. You'll get your second chance. Everyone gets a second chance."

If anyone should know, it was Blake, who'd come back from the dead, literally.

But suddenly everyone in scrubs was on the move, with Dustin between them, far too still and quiet on the gurney.

"Going into X-ray," the doctor called back. "Checking bullet and bone placement. Is his family here?"

"Not yet," she managed, her gut tight.

"We'll be back."

It didn't escape her that he moved off without having ever given anything away.

In the movies that never boded well. As Dustin's gurney moved past her, she reached out and touched his foot. It was all she could reach. "You're going to be fine," she whispered after he was long gone behind the double swinging white doors. *"You are."*

9

DUSTIN LAY in the hospital bed, wriggling his toes. He was never going to get tired of wriggling his toes, not ever again. That was the good news.

The bad news? He hadn't quit his job soon enough.

"You feeling sorry for yourself?"

Dustin craned his neck and eyed Jason, sitting by his bed. "Hey. What are you doing here?"

"Waiting for your pansy ass to wake up. So…does getting shot hurt as bad as everyone says?"

"Nah." He sat up and grimaced at the pain. "Piece of cake."

Jason's smile faded. "You scared the shit out of us. Don't ever do that again."

"Believe me, I don't intend to. They got the bullet out."

"Yes."

"And I'm okay."

"Yes."

"And the other guy who got shot?"

"Also okay."

"So do you have the getaway car?"

"You're not clear to go yet. And Cristina and Blake had to go to the police station to give statements, but they were going to come back to see you."

"I need out of here."

"But—"

Dustin struggled to toss off the covers. He was wearing a hospital gown. Great. "Either drive me or call me a damn cab. And where are some damn pants?"

"Jeez, those drugs you're on are supposed to make you happy."

"I'll be happy. Out of here."

BY THE TIME Cristina got back to the hospital, she was seriously losing it.

Dustin was recovering.

She knew this because she'd called every ten minutes. "I need to see him," she said to Blake, who was sitting in the passenger seat.

"He's probably sleeping."

"Okay, but I still need to see him. I think I might…have feelings for him. Real feelings, you know?"

Blake laughed softly. "Yeah, I know."

"Well, I didn't!"

"That's because you're a little slow on the uptake. But we love you anyway."

She stared at him for a beat. "You do?"

"All of us, Cristina. Every last one."

She struggled with this concept, wanting to believe that could actually even be possible, but not sure, even now, if she could. "Why?" she asked suspiciously.

"Maybe it's your sweet, sensitive nature."

"No, really. Why?"

He took in her tense features, and softened. "We love you because you're the best of the best, Cristina, and because you're fierce and intense and amazing. You'd lay your life down for any single one of us. Hell, you'd do it for a stranger. Now you have a guy, also one of the best of the best, who feels the same way about you, and you're sitting at a green light looking at me."

"Oh!" She hit the gas and didn't let up until she'd pulled back into the hospital. She rushed past the E.R. cubicle where only a few hours before Dustin had lain bleeding, not able to feel his toes, to the information desk, where she was directed to Dustin's room.

And found an empty bed.

An aide was cleaning up the sheets. "Where is he?" she demanded hoarsely.

"Who?"

"Dustin Mauer. The patient who was here. *Where is he?*"

"He's gone."

FOR THE FIRST TIME in her entire life, Cristina left the job in the middle of a shift. Abandoning Blake at the hospital, she drove to Dustin's house and banged on his door, opening it herself when she couldn't wait. "Dustin— Oh."

A Dustin look-alike was on the other side of the door. He was tall, leanly muscled, and so much like Dustin she had to blink.

"Hello," he said.

"I'm sorry, I—" She looked behind her, back outside, to make sure she'd driven up to the right house.

"Oh, you're at the right place," he told her. "You're the heartbreaker, right? Cristina."

"Jason." Dustin said this from his perch on the couch, his voice low and raspy and so familiar it nearly brought her to her knees. "Let her in."

"She's already in." But Jason stood back and gave her room.

"My brother, Jason, the watchdog," Dustin said. "Jason, this is Cristina."

Cristina managed a small smile and then moved past Jason to stand in front of Dustin, so relieved to see him she could scarcely breathe. He looked like shit, like death warmed over really, but he was breathing, so that was good. Still, she wanted to wrap him up in her arms and never let go. "You scared the hell out of me."

"So we're even."

"*I* scared *you?* What the hell are you talking about?"

"Why are you here?" he asked instead of answering her.

She shoved her hands into her pockets. Probably she should have figured out exactly what to say to him. "Isn't it customary to visit someone who's been shot? Even idiots who check themselves out of hospital against doctors' advice?"

His eyes gave nothing away behind his glasses. "So this is a friendly visit then? A how-are-you-doing visit? Well, I'm pissed off and in pain. There. Now you know. Thanks for coming."

As if on cue, Jason opened the door in a not-so-subtle invitation for her to walk back out again.

"Wait." She let out a breath and shoved her fingers in her hair. "Just wait a damn minute."

Dustin waited with a patience that stretched hers thin for no reason that she could put her finger on. "I just wanted to see you. Is that so weird? We—we're—"

Completely unhelpful, he lifted a brow.

"I mean, I thought we—"

He still just looked at her.

Goddammit.

"Okay, let me help you," he said.

Well, finally!

"We've been friends," he murmured. "Close friends."

She'd never been good with the word *close*, but it was hard to dispute the truth. "Yes."

"We've been sleeping together."

She shot a quick glance at his brother. "Well, not regularly or anything. At least until this week," she muttered.

Jason pursed his lips. "Sounds like you kids have some talking to do. I'll be eavesdropping from the kitchen."

He left, and a heavy silence filled the room.

"Here's the thing," Dustin said.

Good. The thing. She was so glad he was about to define the thing.

"I'm tired."

"Well, of course you're tired. You were shot!"

"No, I mean, I'm tired of this. I'm tired of the yo-yo. I'm tired of making all the moves."

A burning panic began to rumble low in her belly. "What are you talking about?"

"If I don't push you, then we stand still. But I'm tired of pressuring you into each and every single tiny step forward we take. It's why I came to your place the other night to say goodbye. Which didn't stick, obviously. So if you want to make the first move today, then make it already. If not, I'd like to be alone."

Hurt, stunned and more hurt, she just stood there.

"Yeah, that's what I thought." Sounding extremely tired, he lay back and closed his eyes. "Lock the door behind you."

Well, wasn't that subtle? She'd just lock the door then. Asshole. She let herself out and not only locked the damn door, but slammed it first.

And drove herself home to think.

And think some more.

And in the thinking, found her mad. How dare he go along with whatever the hell it was they'd been doing all this time, and then suddenly decide that wasn't working for him?

It wasn't like it was working for her, either. Not even close.

She spent a very long night stewing, and when she woke up, she stormed back to his house.

Only to find it empty.

It was her day off, but she drove to the station and sought out Zach, who was doing pull-ups on a bar in the hallway, shirtless. Once upon a time she'd harbored a secret crush on Zach. They were friends, and twice they'd been friends with benefits, but it had been a long time ago, and, while he was one of the most gorgeous men she'd ever met, he was a better friend than most.

Plus he'd found true love with Brooke, and been taken off the market.

But even before that, she'd fallen for Dustin. She hadn't known back then the why or how of it, but Dustin had taken her off the market, too.

It was time he damn well knew it. "Where's Dustin?"

"Gone."

The same queasy panic she'd experienced yesterday flooded her again. "What do you mean, gone? Where does a guy who's been shot go?"

Zach released the pole and hopped down. Letting out a long breath, he looked her in the eyes. "He's at his mom's house in San Luis Obispo."

Which was an hour north of Santa Rey. "Why?"

"For Christmas."

There was something funny to his tone. "He's coming back though," she said. "Right?"

"He didn't tell you?"

Oh, God. She wasn't going to like this. "Tell me what, Zach?"

"He gave his notice. He's going full-time into the renovating business with his brother."

Cristina chewed on that for a moment while a very bad feeling sank in her gut. "Okay, I'm going to need his mom's address."

Five minutes later she was on the highway heading toward San Luis Obispo. She didn't want to think about why she was in such a hurry, or why the panic had grown and spread from her gut to every part of her body.

Dustin had quit.

He'd walked away.

And she'd let him.

10

CRISTINA GOT STUCK in holiday traffic, which only upped her blood pressure, but finally, she got there. Dustin's mother lived in the middle of suburbia, complete with a white picket fence and a well-kept yard decorated for Christmas with lights strung in the trees and boughs of holly along the patio decking.

It was Christmas Eve.

It was Christmas Eve and she stood on the porch, hand raised to knock, about to completely impose on a family she'd never even met.

Because she had to see Dustin. She had to tell him—

Oh, God. She still didn't have the exact words but she had the gist now. She was going to get it right this time.

Jason opened the door to her knock. Perfect.

In an exact imitation of his brother, he arched a brow and waited patiently.

"Um," she said brilliantly.

"Still working on your greeting, huh? Need a moment?"

"No." *Yes.* She stepped into the living room, filled with comfy, worn furniture and a huge Christmas tree, around which were so many presents they came halfway out into the room. "Wow."

"Yeah," Jason said, amused. "We don't get to see each other too much during the year so we tend to go a little overboard at Christmas."

She had no understanding of this. Christmases in her world were a whole different ball game. "Oh. Uh, I don't want to intrude."

"You're not. Everyone's out doing their last-minute shopping. Probably be gone for hours. I was just leaving, too. Dustin's upstairs."

And with that, he walked out the front door. She stared at the tree, gulped and headed toward the stairs. "Dustin?"

He didn't answer, and she began to make her way up, her

heart in her throat. Upstairs in the hallway, all the doors were shut. "Dustin?"

She heard a soft oath, some rustling, and then one of the doors opened and Dustin stood there in a thick, dark blue robe, braced on a crutch, looking pale and tense.

And at just the sight of him, her heart warmed. "Hey."

"Hey."

He was hurting like hell, she could tell, and without a word, she went to him, slipped her arms around him, and took him back to his bed.

Lying back on the mattress, he gritted his teeth and pulled himself into a better position. "If you're here to have your way with me, I'm going to disappoint you."

"You could never disappoint me."

"Yeah? Try me."

As usual, he told it like it was, holding nothing back. What was it like to wear your emotions on your sleeve, she wondered, not to have a deep, dark secret festering inside?

Her deep, dark secret was killing her. "You win," she told him. "Your evil plan worked."

"Huh?"

It was so clear to her now, and, needing it to be clear to him, she stripped out of her clothes while he sputtered, and then she climbed into bed with him.

Two warm, hard arms came around her. "Cristina."

She kissed his jaw, and then his chest, and he groaned, the sound bringing her such raw relief she felt the sting of tears at the base of her throat. "You're not mad at me," she let out before she could stop herself.

"Frustrated. Irritated. Hurt." He shook his head and sighed. "But not mad."

"I'm so sorry, Dustin," she whispered, slipping her hands into his robe, warming at the discovery that he was naked beneath. She tugged the robe off his shoulders so they could both be naked together. "This day really sucked golf balls."

"Tell me about it."

"Don't ever get shot again."

"Amen to that."

"Dustin, I—"

But his hands were busy skimming over every inch of her, wrenching a heartfelt and appreciative deep groan from his chest. It tugged at her, from loins to the tips of her hair, and she kissed him. She meant it to be a sweet kiss, a prelude to the I-love-you speech she'd prepared, but his hands swept down her back and cupped her bottom, nudging her closer until he let out a hiss and went still.

"Careful," she gasped. "I don't want to hurt you—"

"You're killing me." But he wouldn't let her pull away. Rolling to his back, he urged her over on top of him until she straddled his waist.

She understood. It was her move. If she wanted him, wanted them, then this one was on her. No problem there. Her fingers curled around him. He was ready. She reached for the condom she'd brought.

"You came prepared."

"In many ways—" She broke off to put it on him, leaving them both gasping by the time she was done. "Are you okay?"

"I will be. When you— Oh, yeah," he managed on a rough breath when she sank down on him. Their twin moans mingled in the night, and she dropped her forehead to his, swamped with emotion. "Dustin."

"Much as I want to be the macho guy here and show you a good time, I can't move. My leg—"

"I've got you." And for once, she did. She cupped his face and breathed his air and repeated it softly. "I've got you, Dustin." Heart and soul…

When she began to move, it seemed as though her entire world moved along in sync. For the first time she felt completely transformed, transfixed, beyond herself. He gripped her hips in his hands and let her ride him, and just when she began to go over, he stroked her where they were joined, making her his…except she already was.

His.

She let herself fall, and one stroke later, he fell with her.

It took her a long time to recover. Still breathless, she rolled off him, shocked at the depths of what they'd just shared. "How was that for a first move?"

He reached for her hand, bringing it to his mouth. "Nice."

"I have more. First moves, that is."

"You're going to have to give me a minute."

"No," she said, and laughed. Rolling over, she lay on his chest, looking through the dark to find his eyes glittering with interest. "I meant a different first move." Her smile faded, replaced by nerves. "I've been an idiot, Dustin. A stubborn, closed-minded idiot."

His lips quirked in silent agreement, but he didn't respond. His hands though, they moved, up and down her naked body, producing a set of anticipatory shivers. He had the most amazing touch.

"And also—" She paused. "Okay, this is the hard part because I've never said this before—I was wrong." God, those hands. And now his mouth got into the fray, too, nibbling at her shoulder, over her collarbone… "About me being able to be in a relationship. About us. About so many things—" His fingers were driving her crazy. "Are you listening?"

"Mmm-hmm."

He sounded laid-back and sleepy-eyed and sexy as hell, and she breathed him in. "I don't know why I'm so anxious. It's just words. Three words." She drew a breath. "I love you."

His hands went still and he stared at her. "What?"

"I'm sorry it took me so long to tell you, but as you know, I have a few issues."

His eyes were bright, warm and filled with love for her even as his lips quirked. "I love you and your issues."

"I know. And that's my own miracle, believe me." She shot him a shaky smile. "I want you, Dustin. EMT or whatever it is you want to do—I don't care. I just can't imagine you not being in my life." She held her breath for his reaction, but he merely smiled, too, a slow beautiful smile that stopped her heart.

"About time," he murmured, and pulled her close.

* * * * *

MY GROWN-UP CHRISTMAS LIST

Jacquie D'Alessandro

This book is dedicated to all the brave and heroic firefighters who put their lives on the line every day to save and protect us. Thank you for all you do. Also, to Jill Shalvis and Jamie Sobrato for making this such an enjoyable project; to Brenda Chin, editor extraordinaire, for bringing us all together; and Jenni Grizzle, for her unfailing loyalty and friendship. And, as always, to my fantastic husband, Joe, who, even though he isn't a firefighter, has always been my hero; and to our wonderful son, Chris, aka Hero Junior.

1

BRADLEY GRIFFIN closed his locker at the firehouse and breathed a sigh of relief that his stress-filled twenty-four-hour shift was finally over. After picking up his duffel bag, he waved goodbye to the guys polishing the pristine red ladder truck. He hoped their shift would be quieter than his had been, but he doubted it—the Christmas season always proved busy for firefighters.

Fires and emergencies were always difficult, but they just seemed much more so to him at this time of year, when good cheer was supposed to prevail. In his mind's eye he could still see the soot-and-tear-streaked faces of the family whose house had burned last night. The parents and two young children had made it out alive, thank God, but their home and all their belongings, including the Christmas presents stacked under their tree, were lost, leaving them with nothing except each other. How many times over the last seven years had he seen that same heart-wrenching combination of terror and desolation in people's eyes? Too many to count. Yet, he still wouldn't trade jobs with anyone. Wouldn't trade those moments when a life was saved, a loved one brought back from the brink. That family last night…they'd clung to each other and the fact that they were alive to rebuild. Unfortunately not everyone was so lucky.

He walked toward the open bay doors, the sight of the bright California sunshine a welcome relief after the smoke-blackened dawn sky he'd stood beneath only hours earlier. He pulled in a deep breath, loving the smell of the firehouse—the lemony cleaning fluid the guys used to keep the place spotless, combined with a hint of what he called automotive potpourri, mixed with a whiff of the salty breeze blowing off the ocean. Through the doors he caught sight of the sparkling blue Pacific running onto the sandy beach. Lots of skaters, walkers and joggers already out and about this morning, he noticed. A beautiful sunny day like this always brought the crowds to Ocean Harbor Beach, the laid-back surfing town where he'd lived his entire life. And now that he had forty-eight off, he couldn't wait to join them. Two days to regroup. To put the pressures of the job behind him. To concentrate on happier things, like Christmas. Which was only a week away. Which meant it was about time he started Christmas shopping.

"Yo, Brad."

Brad turned at the familiar greeting. His best friend and fellow firefighter Jim Ballard exited the station's kitchen and loped toward him. Jim had come on duty an hour ago and clearly it was his turn to cook; he carried a spatula and wore an apron that advised in bold print: Firefighters Do It With Heat. Brad sent up a silent prayer of thanks he was off duty. He loved Jim like a brother, but he was the station's worst cook.

He gave Jim's black-and-red-stain-splattered apron a skeptical glance. "Soot and…ketchup?" he guessed, hoping it wasn't blood. "Doesn't bode well for the morning meal."

Jim looked down at the apron then shrugged. "Had a little mishap with the huevos rancheros. Nothing a few handfuls of jalapeños won't fix."

Brad's stomach clenched in sympathy for those poor bastards polishing the truck. "What's up?"

"Been looking for you. Found out something you might find interesting." Jim lowered his voice. "About Antonia Rizzo."

Brad's entire body quickened at the mention of her name, which totally annoyed and confused him—as it had from the first moment he'd seen her three months ago, when her florist shop, Blooming Pails, had opened in Santa Rey, the town just south of Ocean Harbor Beach, famous for its seaside boardwalk. He'd stopped by on opening day, not so much to buy flowers—really he didn't need any flowers—but more because he was walking right by the store and figured he'd be neighborly. Not to mention score one of the free cannoli set on a huge ceramic tray just inside the door. He'd taken one bite of the delicious, chocolate-chip-and-cream-filled Italian pastry and his eyes had glazed with sheer bliss. In the next instant he'd taken one look at Antonia—or as everyone called her, Toni—Rizzo and forgotten how to swallow.

Damn near forgotten how to breathe. Sure as hell forgot how to speak English.

Holy smokin' cannoli.

His stupefied gaze had tracked over a mass of shiny, dark brown, spiral mess-with-me curls that loosely danced around her shoulders. Her chocolate-brown eyes sparkled as she wrapped a colorful bouquet in green paper and chatted with the customer purchasing the flowers. Her smile…damn, her smile was gorgeous and sexy all at once, her full lips glossy with something dewy-pink and flanked by a pair of shallow dimples. She laughed, a deep, throaty sound, followed by a slightly husky voice that brought to mind hot, sultry nights and tangled sheets.

His gaze had skimmed lower and he knew that as delicious as that cannoli was, it didn't hold a candle to Antonia Rizzo's feminine form. Damn. Even her curves had curves. She was striking and vivid and sexy as hell, and everything male in him went on red alert. In the space of a nanosecond he fell totally, irreparably in lust. Which admittedly had happened to him before, but never to this extent. Never to the point where he actually forgot where he was. What he was doing. And what his damn name was.

Once he recalled he was Brad—or Bill—or at least something that started with a *B,* he approached her. Smiled. Complimented her on her fabulous cannoli. Flirted. She was polite, but didn't return any of the flirtatious lobs he tossed. He bought a bouquet of flowers, which he immediately gave to her, along with an invitation to dinner. She'd thanked him, handed him back the flowers and broken his heart by saying she was already involved.

Whoever he was, the guy was damn lucky. Brad had departed the shop deflated, unable to shake the feeling that he'd lost out on something really great. He'd never experienced such a strong reaction to a woman, and she was unavailable. What kind of crap was that?

He told himself he was better off, that he wasn't looking for a girlfriend. Reminded himself of the wringer his last two girlfriends had put him through. Sandy hadn't been able to deal with the dangerous aspects of his job; what had started out as concern for his safety, which he'd appreciated, had eventually deteriorated into constant nagging to quit the fire department, which he hadn't appreciated. And then Janna had been Sandy's complete opposite—she loved everything about the fire department. Unfortunately she loved firefighters a little too much, as Brad learned when he caught her riding a guy from a neighboring town's hook-and-ladder company like he was the winning horse in the Kentucky Derby. A guy Brad had considered a friend.

Ever since that unappetizing scene four months ago, he'd flown under the radar. He supposed he should have jumped right back into the dating whirlpool, but his heart just hadn't been in it. He wanted another girlfriend like he wanted a gaping hole in his head. But for reasons he couldn't figure, even picking up one of the endless smorgasbord of bikini-clad babes who frequented the beach and local bars and engaging in a few hours of mindless, no-strings-attached sex didn't hold the allure it once had. After Janna he'd indulged a couple of times, but both occasions had left him feeling empty and filled with an unsettling loneliness.

Yet even before his last two breakups, he'd felt the stirrings of this weird discontent, one he finally traced back to last July, when he'd served as best man at Greg and Tanya's wedding. He'd never seen his older brother so happy. As they'd watched Tanya walk down the aisle, he'd said to Greg, "She's beautiful." Greg had nodded. "Best thing that's ever happened to me." And Brad had thought it was too bad Tanya didn't have a sister. Two months later, he'd seen Toni Rizzo and it was as if he'd been hooked up to a nuclear reactor.

Even though she wasn't available, he couldn't stop thinking about her. He kept comparing his reaction to other women to his reaction to her. And every other woman came up short. It had quickly turned into something of a quest—find a woman who turned him on and attracted him the way she had. He hadn't succeeded, and because he hadn't, he'd spent a lot of nights alone in his bed, tossing and turning, frustrated, lonely and wishing like hell he could forget her.

Unable to keep from doing so, he found himself frequently stopping by her shop in the hope that she'd respond to one of his opening conversational gambits, and maybe he'd find her no longer "involved." No such luck. Toni was unfailingly polite, but her "I'm not interested" vibe never wavered. And after three months of buying flowers and plants he didn't need, his small ranch house looked downright girly and his mother had received so many bouquets from him, she was convinced he was up to something. Or that she'd contracted some dread disease and he wasn't telling her.

"What about Toni?" Brad asked, keeping his tone casual.

"Good news and bad news." Jim grinned. "And you're gonna owe me."

"Fine. Good news first."

"She doesn't have a boyfriend."

Whoa. That wasn't good news—that was freakin' excellent news.

"Not only that," Jim continued, "but apparently she hasn't had one for a while. Like six months."

Brad's eyes narrowed. "She told me she was involved."

"Right. Obviously to blow you off. Which leads to the bad news."

"Which is…?"

"She doesn't like firefighters."

Brad frowned. "What do you mean?"

"She. Doesn't. Like. Firefighters. What part don't you get?"

Great. Was she another woman who couldn't handle the danger his job entailed? As soon as the question entered his mind, something told him the answer was no. Whereas Sandy had turned out to be a needy, clingy sort of woman, Toni struck him as very confident. And far too independent and smart to be unreasonable about a man's job involving some danger. There had to be another reason. "Why doesn't she like firefighters?"

"Don't know." Jim shrugged. "If I had to guess, I'd say she probably got her heart broken by one, but who knows? Who can figure out women?"

"How do you know all this?"

Jim rolled his eyes. "Because I'm thirty years old and in spite of knowing a lot of them, women are impossible to understand."

This time Brad rolled his eyes. "I mean, how do you know she doesn't have a boyfriend or like firefighters?"

"Oh. Bobby T told me," Jim said, referring to the bartender at Breezes, one of Santa Rey's most popular beachfront bars. Since Bobby's last name contained about seventeen letters and was completely unpronounceable, especially after a couple of beers, he was simply Bobby T. "Toni and that gal who works with her went to the bar last night and had one of those long, boring, involved chick chats. Since business was slow, Bobby couldn't help but overhear bits and pieces. They even drew him into the convo a few times. I saw him this morning before I came on duty and he told me. And now I'm telling you. Figured you'd want to know, especially if you plan to make a move. Once word of this gets out, guys'll be all over Toni like wet on water."

A sensation that felt exactly like jealousy rippled through Brad. "Right. Except, in case it's escaped your notice, I'm a firefighter."

"Uh-huh." Jim pointed his spatula at the ladder truck. "Yeah, the big shiny red truck kinda gave it away. But I doubt that's gonna stop you. You've been panting after this woman for three months. Keeping your distance because you thought she was involved. Now you know she's not."

"I haven't been panting," Brad felt compelled to object. "Breathing heavy, maybe."

"Panting," Jim insisted. "Dude, I've known you since tenth grade and I've never seen you so… I don't even know the word to describe it, about a woman. Discombobulated. Stupefied. Like a deer in the headlights." Jim shook his head. "Maybe I shouldn't have told you. I'm thinkin' this could only lead to trouble."

Brad knew what Jim meant by trouble—a serious entanglement. But who said anything had to be serious? He grinned. "*Trouble* is my middle name."

"Like hell." Jim's smile turned downright evil. "It's Theodore."

Damn. There were definitely disadvantages to having friends for years. Brad shot Jim a glare meant to deep-fry him on the spot. "Those will be interesting last words, should you make the mistake of repeating them." His nickname at the station was already embarrassing enough. He didn't need a derivative of Teddy Bear or some such cutesy crap to live down. "Don't you have eggs and toast to burn?"

Jim lifted his hands in an exaggerated backing-off gesture. "Yup. You wanna stay for breakfast?"

"Tempting as that sounds, I'm gonna blast outta here." He nodded toward the guys polishing the truck. "Don't poison those poor boys."

"Are you kidding? They'd eat tire treads if I poured melted cheese on them."

"Do you know how to melt cheese?"

"Sure. That's what blowtorches are for."

Brad wasn't sure Jim was kidding. "Good thing we're fully equipped with fire extinguishers." He clapped his hand on Jim's shoulder. "Hope your shift's quieter than mine was."

"Enjoy your days off. Got any plans?"

"Since Christmas is next week, figured I'd better start shopping."

Jim laughed. "Bet I know where you're going first."

Brad chuckled. "Oh, yeah. Got me some flowers to buy. Wish me luck."

"I wish you luck, dude. I have a feeling you're going to need it."

Maybe he would. But he was determined. He didn't fear going after what he wanted—no one had ever given him anything so he'd been doing that his entire life. And he wanted Toni Rizzo—in a way he hadn't wanted any woman in a long time. Yeah, he wanted her. Naked. In his bed. Under him. Over him. Putting out the damn fire she'd lit in him the moment he'd seen her.

Yet he wanted something more. Wanted to get to know her. He didn't have any doubt they'd get along in bed, but he also wanted to know if they'd get along outside the bedroom, something he hadn't been interested in finding out about a woman for a very long time. He couldn't explain it, it didn't make sense, but there it was. So in-his-face he couldn't deny it. She was at the top of his Christmas list. At the bottom, too. And everywhere in between. And now that he knew she wasn't taken, there was nothing to stop him.

Well, except her crazy aversion to firefighters. But he had every intention of changing her mind.

After all, how difficult could that be?

2

TONI RIZZO stood behind the long granite counter at Blooming Pails and deftly worked sprigs of mistletoe, poinsettia, red and white roses and fragrant pine into the two dozen centerpieces she was putting together for this evening's Wilson/Mayberry wedding. Nothing like December nuptials to boost business, which was precisely what she needed. Only three months remained until the bank's first six-month evaluation, and she had to make damn sure her revenues showed growth. The loan she'd taken out to open the shop included a clause that she was subject to a twice-yearly review for the first two years. If sales were maintained or grew each quarter, she kept her low interest rate. If she failed to maintain or increase sales, her interest rate would go up. Which would put a financial strain on her fledgling business she simply couldn't afford—one that could result in her losing Blooming Pails and everything she'd worked so hard for.

So far, sales had been decent for the holiday season, but it was an active time of year for any business and she needed her sales to be much better than merely decent. This month was do-or-die time to generate enough revenues to keep that interest rate down. She had to cultivate customers to keep the sales up after the holidays were over. Because if her business failed, she'd find herself right back where she'd been three years ago—out of work, her career in tatters, and being smothered by her well-meaning but overwhelming family who were relentless in their quest to drag her ass back home and into the family business. That alone was incentive enough to make sure Blooming Pails succeeded. The fifty-mile buffer she'd put between herself and the fam when she moved to Santa Rey had saved her sanity. She had every intention of keeping her ass right here, and working that ass off in her shop.

She shot a quick downward look over her shoulder and grimaced. Yeah—if only it were possible to actually work her ass off. Of course, even if she ever managed to—and in her twenty-eight years she hadn't managed—her mother would whip up a few trays of antipasto and lasagna to put some meat on her bones. And if her mother failed, Nana Rose would take up the banner. Her grandmother would fix her eyeballs on Toni with what she called the Stare of Death and command, "Eat, Antonia. *Mangia.* Men do not like women who look like pencils."

Thanks to the Rizzo boobs and butt, which had been passed down through generations of Rizzo women, along with the wildly curly hair from which her surname was derived, she'd never know if Nana Rose's statement was true.

Not that she currently gave a rat's ass about what men liked. Hell, no. Men were, in a word, pains in the ass. Okay, so that was four words, but still. After freeing herself from her last disastrous romantic entanglement, she'd sworn off the male species. Someday, after she'd gotten Blooming Pails off the ground and the shop didn't require all her attention, then she'd consider dipping her toe back into the shark-infested dating waters. But even then only if she met someone worthy of her attention. Someone who accepted her as she was—flaws and all. Who didn't cheat. Who had some integrity. Who made her laugh. Whom she wanted to share her life with.

"Good luck with that," she muttered.

But for now, she had zero time for a man. Blooming Pails required all her focus and tender loving care. Unfortunately Blooming Pails didn't keep her warm at night, and after six dateless, sexless months she was feeling definite twinges of loneliness. Not to mention sexual frustration. Sexual frustration that became more acute with each passing day.

She glanced out the window and caught sight of a young couple across the street walking a puppy on a leash. The small dog yipped and ran in circles, chasing its tail, then rolled over for a belly rub. When the laughing couple crouched down, the puppy jumped into the woman's arms and covered her chin with exuberant kisses.

"If only that adorable, loving, amusing dog came in a man," Toni said with sigh.

Yup, she should just forget about men and get herself a dog.

Just then her attention was caught by a familiar figure striding past her window. A tall familiar figure with broad shoulders, sun-streaked golden-brown hair and a killer smile. And just as it always did when Brad Griffin came by, her pulse skipped a beat. Which was really annoying since a skipping pulse was the last thing she wanted around him. Yeah, he was good-looking—okay, great-looking—but it didn't matter. Even if she had time for a man—which she didn't—he was a firefighter and she absolutely wasn't having any of that. Bitterness welled in her throat and she pressed her lips together. Never again.

The first time she'd seen him, on Blooming Pails's opening day, she'd nearly swallowed her tongue. Standing in a shaft of dazzling sunlight, biting into one of the homemade cannoli she'd put out to tempt customers, was the personification of her every sexual fantasy. Yowza. Big, strong and utterly gorgeous, he looked like a cross between a sun god and one of those beautifully rugged guys who populated men's cologne ads. Everything female in her had snapped to attention and in a heartbeat she fell in lust. She might not have time for a relationship, but she could carve out a few minutes to relieve her sexual drought with *this* guy.

But then she'd noticed the emblem on the T-shirt which stretched across his broad chest. The T-shirt bearing the words *Ocean Harbor Beach Fire Department*. And she'd deflated like a popped balloon. How freakin' unfair was it that the first guy in months to give her a jolt—and a freakin' lightning-bolt jolt it had been—was a firefighter? Just to be sure, she'd casually asked him while she wrapped up the bouquet he ordered, hoping he'd tell her the shirt belonged to a friend or he'd bought it secondhand and he was an accountant. A waiter. A mechanic. Anything but a firefighter.

But he'd confirmed his occupation. And sealed his fate, at least as far as she was concerned. Even though her hormones screamed in protest, there was no way she'd act on that spark of attraction. When he'd given her the bouquet she'd just wrapped and asked her to dinner—and okay, it was a romantic gesture that from anyone else would have worked—she'd claimed she was involved. Which wasn't a lie. Exactly. She was involved. With her new business. Settling into this new town. Keeping her busybody family at arm's length.

She'd hoped her claim, along with her cool demeanor, would deter him, but he came in every week. And each time her pulse annoyingly jumped through hoops. He was always friendly and talkative and amusing and subtly flirtatious and way too tempting and she wished like hell he'd go away. On each visit he purchased something, either flowers or a plant, although it was clear he barely knew the difference between a daisy and a rose. Obviously he either had one woman in his life who really liked flowers or a bunch of different women. Given his good looks and the number of beach babes populating the boardwalk, she'd bet on a bunch of different women.

And now here he was again. Walking by her window. She hoped he was just taking a stroll, enjoying the lovely day. Maybe he wouldn't come in—

The door opened, announcing his presence with a tinkling of the Christmas bells she'd attached to the top of the jamb along with mistletoe. Damn. And she couldn't fob him off on Jayne as her assistant was running an errand. Maybe she'd return soon and Toni could perform the Brad pass-off. For now, however, she'd have to deal with him.

Their gazes met and her stupid pulse performed a somersault. Crap. Why did he have to be so attractive?

He's not merely attractive, her suddenly alert hormones informed her. *He is steaming* hot.

Okay, fine. Steaming hot. Lots of men were steaming hot. Didn't they litter those men's cologne ads? Yes, they did. So what was it about this one that got under her skin? Maybe she was allergic to him. She instantly brightened. That's all this was—a pesky allergy. One antihistamine and she'd be cured.

It'll take more than an allergy pill to purge this guy from your system, her talkative hormones whispered. *And he hasn't even touched you. Or kissed you.*

Touched her…kissed her…

An image popped into her mind, of him walking toward her. Not stopping or slowing down, just wrapping those strong arms around her, picking her up and still walking, until her back hit the wall. Settling his beautiful mouth on hers. His tongue slipping past her lips. His hard, muscular body pressing against her—

"'Morning, gorgeous."

The deep masculine voice yanked Toni from her sensual reverie and she blinked. And realized he'd walked to the counter. And that now only the three-foot-wide slab of granite—and a dozen centerpieces—separated them. Three feet and a bunch of flowers she could easily reach across. Or jump over.

Heat rushed into her face and she inwardly winced. Great. Now she'd look blotchy. Annoyance—at herself for her runaway thoughts and at him for looking so damn tempting—skittered through her. A good dose of irritation followed, thanks to the way her heart sped up because he'd called her gorgeous. He undoubtedly called every woman that. It irked her no end that she wasn't as immune to such meaningless flattery as she'd thought.

"Good morning," she said, looking down, partly to keep from staring at him, partly to hide the flame scorching her cheeks. She stabbed pine into the centerpiece in front of her with far more force than necessary.

"You okay?" he asked, tilting his head to the side. "You look sorta…flushed."

Her head jerked up at that. Their gazes collided and she found herself staring into his beautiful, ocean-colored eyes, the sort you could drown in while trying to figure out if they were more green or blue.

"I'm fine," she said, her voice laced with a hint of challenge, daring him to disagree.

Instead he nodded. Then grinned. "You sure are."

That damn grin crinkled the corners of those beautiful eyes and annoyingly seemed to peel away several layers of muscle from her legs.

"It's just the reflection of all these red leaves and decorations and lights," she said, waving her hand to encompass the store.

His gaze followed her hand, pausing on the Christmas tree set in the window. "Pretty tree," he said. "Is that a new addition?"

"It's been there for the past two weeks."

He returned his attention to her and smiled. Whoa. The grin

was pretty damn great, but the full smile was potent with a capital *P*. Warm, flirty and intimate all at the same time. Another few layers of strength fled her knees without a backward glance. She stabbed in another piece of pine and pretended she didn't feel it.

"Guess I was too busy looking at you to notice," he said. "What are all those little red envelopes hanging on it?"

For an answer she handed him a flyer from the pile on the end of the counter. "The Twelve Steamy Nights of Christmas," he read. His gaze flicked back up to hers. "Sounds promising."

"It's for charity," she said quickly, groaning inwardly as the words poured from her like a flood—a curse that occurred whenever she was nervous. And dammit, he made her nervous. "Each envelope contains a gift for a…sensual night out." Crap. Her tongue had tripped on the word *sensual*. "Local restaurants have donated meal cards, shops in the area gave gift cards, that sort of thing. For a twenty-five-dollar donation, you can pick any envelope you want. All the proceeds go to local charities."

He nodded. "Very nice. Your idea?"

"Yes. It seemed a good way to introduce myself and Blooming Pails to the community and do some good at the same time." Which was absolutely true—although the full truth was that after six months with zero sex, the idea was also inspired by her own deep desire for a steamy, sensual Christmas gift. But since nothing remotely resembling sexy, steamy, sensual—all those lovely *S* words—hovered in her immediate future, she'd just live vicariously through her customers.

"Great idea. Lots of folks need help, especially this time of year. A fire last night in Ocean Harbor Beach left a family homeless."

Toni's stomach clenched. "I'm sorry to hear that. Anyone hurt?"

"No, but they lost everything."

"If they're still alive, they didn't lose anything that really matters."

"True," he agreed. "But it's still a tough situation. The guys at all the stations in the county participate in a toy drive every Christmas. It's really hard to think of kids not having a present from Santa to open."

Toni nodded. She recalled the faces of such children, such families, who'd lost everything. Even now, three years later, with that life behind her, the images still haunted her. To this day she still jumped at the sound of a fire alarm, and adrenaline pumped at the sight of a fire truck. She blinked away the heart-wrenching memories and said, "The toy drive's a great idea. Even as we speak, my assistant is dropping off our donation at the Santa Rey station." An errand Toni had thought she was so smart sending Jayne off on so she wouldn't have to visit the firehouse. Little had she known Brad would show up here while Jayne was gone.

"On behalf of all of us, I thank you." He glanced back down at the flyer. "It says if you bring your little red envelope here the day you're using the contents, Blooming Pails will provide a free rose for the date." He looked at her and zoom went her pulse. "Pretty romantic."

Was he laughing at her? It was impossible to tell, just something else annoying about him. She could usually read people very well, but Bradley Griffin and his unwanted sex appeal kept clogging up her receptors. "You have something against romance? Or roses?"

"Heck no. And to prove it, I'll buy one of the red envelopes." He reached into the back pocket of his jeans and she absolutely didn't notice the fascinating play of muscles beneath his snug black T-shirt. Or the way his jeans clung to his lean hips and long muscular legs. Nope. Didn't notice a thing. Besides, what was the big deal? She knew damn well what great shape firefighters had to be in. Just because his shape looked better than most didn't mean she had to stare.

He pulled out his wallet and handed her twenty-five dollars. Their fingers brushed as the money exchanged hands, shooting a tingle straight up her arm. "Which envelope should I pick?"

Any one. Then take your tempting, sexy self out of here and don't come back. She shrugged. "Your choice."

He leaned a bit closer and she pulled in a quick breath, one that filled her head with his scent. God, he smelled good. Clean. Like sunshine and freshly showered man. She had to lock her knees and grip the edge of the counter to keep from giving in to the temptation to bury her nose against his neck and simply breathe him in.

"What if I said *you* were my choice?" he asked softly.

She forced her gaze to remain steady on his—his gaze that was filled with unmistakable interest. And heat. Enough heat to make her feel as if someone had just set a match to her skin. "I'd say you were trying to pick something off the wrong tree."

For an answer he just smiled—which was bad enough on her already weakened knees, but then he winked.

Oh, God. *Why* did he have to wink? A man that good-looking shouldn't be *allowed* to wink. Especially at her—a woman who harbored a freakish weakness for winking. And what this man could do with one wink…good lord, she needed to ring up his purchase and send him on his way.

She turned and headed toward the cash register. From the corner of her eye, she watched him peruse the tree, as if choosing a card was a monumental decision. Finally, he plucked one from an upper branch then walked toward her waggling the envelope between his long, strong fingers. "Wanna see what I got?"

God, do I ever. I wanna see everything *you've got.* She firmly told her inner voice to shut the hell up then picked up several roses and resumed her work. "If you want to show me."

The heat that flared in his eyes stilled her hands. And damn near stopped her heart. Okay, wrong thing to say. Why, oh, why didn't life have a rewind button? Or a judge to rule on such things. *Your honor, I'd like my last statement stricken from the record.*

"Oh, I definitely want to show you."

Her mouth went dry. It simply wasn't right how this man turned her on just *standing there*. Why couldn't he be an accountant? Anything but a firefighter? She briefly wondered if Nana Rose had put some sort of Sicilian curse on her love life.

With his gaze on hers, he opened the credit-card-sized envelope and slipped out its contents. Then he looked down. And smiled. Then looked up at her. With a heated expression that threatened to melt the soles of her sneakers.

"This must be my lucky day," he murmured. He pulled out his wallet and handed her another twenty-five bucks. "I'll take another."

Before she could recover from her surprise, he headed back toward the tree. Her gaze zeroed in on his ass. And what a fine ass it was. The man definitely had a great walkaway. When he crouched down to mull over the envelopes near the bottom of the tree, her head tilted to admire the view, while in her mind's eye his jeans—along with the rest of his clothes—miraculously disappeared. When he returned a moment later holding another envelope, she realized she was still standing precisely where he'd left her, holding the twenty-five bucks, her head still tilted to one side, and the fantasy-induced image of his bare backside fried into her brain.

"Wanna see what I've got now?"

I just saw it. And it was fiiiine. She blinked away the image of a naked Brad and shrugged. "You can show me what's *in the envelope*—since I have a feeling you will no matter what I say."

"C'mon, you're as curious as I am."

True, unfortunately. Insatiably curious about what his skin would feel like beneath her fingertips. What his kiss would taste like. How his large hands would feel skimming down her body. How quickly they could bring each other to orgasm. How long they could make it last before coming together.

All things she desperately wished she wasn't curious about.

He opened the envelope and perused its contents. "Perfect. This really is my lucky day." He set the gift card from the first envelope he'd opened on the counter and slid it toward her.

Toni looked at it and her eyebrows shot up. "Perfect? Really? A red-and-white peppermint-striped lace Christmas thong from Mimi's Intimate Apparel on Third Street?" She pushed the card back toward him. "Congratulations, although really, I would have pegged you for a boxer man myself."

He pushed the card back toward her. "Glad to know you've been thinking about what's under my clothes."

"I've done no such thing," she lied, ignoring the fact that she sounded like a prudish schoolmarm. A *lying* prudish schoolmarm. She pushed the card back toward him. "Have fun with that."

"That's my fondest hope." With a single fingertip he once again pushed the card back toward her. "For you."

Again, her brows shot upward. "Me?"

"You. Doesn't take much of a leap of imagination to figure that that peppermint-striped thong would look a hell of a lot better on you than me."

She slid the card back at him. "Thanks, but no thanks."

He slid it right back to her. "C'mon. Help a guy out." He flashed a devilish grin. "The boys at the station would razz me no end if I showed up in something from Mimi's Intimate Apparel. You have no idea how brutal those guys can be."

Actually she did. All too well. *Never again.* She pushed the card back to him, this time with a bit more force. "As much as I appreciate the thought, I have to decline. I'm sure you won't have any trouble finding someone else to give those panties to."

"Seems I already am having trouble." Once again he pushed the card toward her, this time setting the red envelope next to it. "Since you don't want it, why don't you just put the card back on the tree? And instead, I'll offer you this one." He set the second card on the counter and nudged it toward her.

She looked down at the gift card for dinner for two at Sea Shells, Santa Rey's most popular beachside restaurant.

"Have dinner with me," he said softly.

Her insides threatened to melt into goo and she gritted her teeth against the appalling affect he had on her. She turned the card around so it faced him then pushed both it and the other one back toward him. And stiffened her rapidly weakening spine. "Thanks, but we already had this conversation. I told you I was involved."

"I know. But I heard that you aren't."

"You heard wrong."

"You have a boyfriend?"

She hesitated, cursing the fact that she wasn't a better liar. That brief hesitation clanged out like a choir of church bells that she didn't have a boyfriend. A triumphant gleam entered his eyes. "You don't."

"That doesn't mean I'm looking for one," she said.

"So I won't be your boyfriend. I'll just be the guy you go out to dinner with. What's the harm in one little date?"

"I'm trying to get my business off the ground. I'm too busy right now to date."

"Then what's the harm in one little dinner? Or are you going to tell me you're too busy to eat?"

Toni tucked a wayward curl behind her ear and drew a deep breath. "Look, I might as well tell you, Brad…you're just not my type."

"Because I'm a firefighter."

It wasn't a question. So clearly he'd heard something from someone. Well, good. It saved her from making explanations she wasn't inclined to give. "That's right."

"Care to tell me what you have against my occupation?"

"No. And I can't see how it matters. Listen, you seem like a nice guy—"

"I am. Ask my mom. She'll tell you." He leaned closer and lowered his voice, as if imparting a great secret. "Don't ask my older brother, though. He'll tell you I'm a pain in the ass."

She had to force herself not to grin. "I appreciate you buying the gift cards, but I won't go out to dinner with you."

"Because I'm a firefighter."

"Yes."

"So, if I were say, an accountant, you'd go to dinner with me?"

"You're not an accountant."

"But if I were?" he insisted.

She desperately wanted to tell him no, but knew she'd never make it sound convincing given that every hormone in her body was shouting *yes!* "Fine. Yes, if you were an accountant, or a cowboy, or even a circus clown, I'd go to dinner with you. But you're not, so I won't." She nodded toward the dozen centerpieces. "And now, unless there's something else you'd like to purchase, I really need to get back to work."

He studied her for several long seconds and she forced herself to hold his gaze so he could see she meant it and wasn't being coy. Finally he gave a tight nod. "Can't blame a guy for trying." He scooped up the two gift cards and slipped them in his back pocket. "See ya, Toni," he said softly, then turned and walked toward the door. The bell tinkled as he departed and Toni stared at the now-empty doorway. He was gone. Good. And undoubtedly wouldn't be back. Even better. She'd probably never see him again. Excellent. She was glad. Really, really glad.

She returned her attention to her centerpieces. And ignored her little inner voice that told her she was a big fat liar.

3

LESS THAN a minute after Brad departed the shop, the door opened again. Toni's heart jumped, thinking he had returned, but instead Jayne hurried in, her cheeks flushed, eyes bright, toting a shopping bag. Toni told herself that the odd feeling rushing through her was relief. Of course it was. It certainly wasn't disappointment.

"Sorry I took so long," Jayne said. "I got tied up at the firehouse. Not literally, of course," she added with a laugh. "but when I arrived bearing toys, I was an instant hit with the firefighters."

"Uh-huh. And I'm sure the fact that you're blond and cute had nothing to do with it."

"Uh-huh. And I'm also very happily married, and in case you've forgotten…" she turned to the side and struck a pose, one that emphasized the gentle swell of her belly "…five months pregnant, which is why I drank nothing but seltzer at Breezes last night. Speaking of firefighters, wasn't that Brad Griffin I just saw leaving the shop?"

Toni nodded. "He bought two gift cards from our tree." *Have dinner with me.*

"That was nice of him."

I'm a nice guy. Ask my mom. "The Twelve Steamy Nights of Christmas is a big hit. Every card makes a great gift."

"And speaking of gifts…I have not one, but two for you. And both of them have to do with Brad Griffin."

Toni's gaze shifted to the shopping bag Jayne set on the counter. "There's a voodoo doll of him in that bag that I can stick pins in to make him go away?"

"Nope. Even better." Jayne reached for her bright green Blooming Pails apron. "I got scoop on him."

Toni shook her head. "Forget it. I know everything I need to know. Not interested."

Jayne joined her behind the counter and set to trimming roses for the centerpieces. "Not even in his nickname at the Ocean Harbor Beach firehouse? It's very…interesting."

Toni pursed her lips. What the hell. Might as well make conversation. "Fine. You can tell me, but only because you're clearly dying to. What is it, and how did you find out?"

"The guys were only too pleased to tell me when they gave me those." She nodded her chin toward the shopping bag she'd placed on the counter.

"Those?"

Jayne set down her clippers and reached into the bag. "One for each of us."

She handed Toni a calendar. The front showed a muscular firefighter sporting six-pack abs, leaning against a fire truck. Bright crimson letters proclaimed that Firefighters Like It Hot.

"Very nice," Toni said, setting the calendar aside. "But I hope you didn't pay too much for it. This calendar is from two years ago."

"It was free. The calendar was made to raise funds for fire safety and awareness after those tens of thousands of acres burned a few years back. The station had some copies left over and the guys are giving them to folks who donate toys."

"But who needs a calendar that's two years old?"

"Eye candy never goes out of date. For instance—check out Mr. December."

Suppressing a sigh, Toni picked up the glossy calendar and turned to December. And found herself staring at Brad. Brad whose skin gleamed wet from the water trickling out of the fire hose nozzle draped around his broad, muscular shoulders. Brad who wore only a sexy smile and his yellow bunker pants, which hung dangerously low on his lean hips, held up by a single red suspender. Brad, whose gorgeous blue-green eyes seemed to bore into hers, inviting her to join him in a little water fun.

Her gaze skimmed over his defined pecs and ridged abdomen and she barely resisted the urge to fan herself. A small Cross of Saint Florian tattoo, the badge of firefighters, adorned his chest, right above the place where she'd feel his heart beat if she were to touch him.

"Nice hose, huh?"

Jayne's voice yanked Toni from the stupor into which she'd fallen. To her dismay she was tracing her fingertip over his tattoo.

She snatched her hand away as if the paper had burned her. "I didn't know he'd posed for a calendar."

"I think there's a lot you don't know about him—something he'd clearly like to change since he's in here every week. And if you think it's because he likes flowers, you're nuts."

Toni somehow managed to pull her gaze away from the photograph. "He asked me out again when he was here this morning."

"Please tell me you said yes."

"I said no."

Jayne shook her head and pointed to the picture. "Are you crazy?"

"No, I'm *busy*. And not looking for any distractions. Especially with a—"

"Firefighter. I know. But who says you have to marry the guy? Just use him for sex."

"What would Tim think if he heard you talking like this?" she asked, referring to Jayne's studly husband, who owned Santa Rey's largest surf shop.

"As long as *I'm* not using Brad for sex, he wouldn't care." She looked over Toni's shoulder at the photo and heaved a gushy sigh. "That is one fine-looking man. Too bad about the nickname this picture spawned."

Bad? There was nothing bad about it. Mystified, she asked, "What's his nickname?"

"Would you believe…Elf?"

"Elf?" Toni shook her head. "How'd they get Elf from this picture? He's gotta be six-four, and nothing on him looks small." Nope, not a thing.

"The hat."

Toni's gaze shifted to his head. And for the first time she noticed that a green hat, the sort Christmas elves in malls wore, was perched on his head at a rakish angle. "Oh."

"Definitely not what one notices first about this picture," Jayne said.

Toni hadn't noticed it at all. "Uh…no." She could think of a few nicknames the photo would inspire, and none of them were

Elf. Steamy, for instance. Or Red-Hot. She doubted he cared for
Elf, and she couldn't blame him.

"He certainly has a nice body," Jayne said, picking up her
shears once again.

An understatement if Toni ever heard one. "Uh-huh."

"And really nice eyes."

"I guess."

"And a great smile."

"I suppose." If you liked slightly crooked, devilish and devastatingly sexy smiles. She forced herself to snap the calendar
closed then slipped it back in the shopping bag. After setting the
bag beneath the counter, she once again returned her attention to
the centerpieces.

"And lovely lips," Jayne said.

Toni heaved an inward sigh. Really lovely lips. The kind that
looked soft yet firm at the same time. The kind that undoubtedly
knew how to kiss extremely well.

"After we finish these centerpieces, we need to start on the
floral arrangement for the Chamber of Commerce," Toni said.

"You're changing the subject."

"Yes, I am. Because there's nothing left to discuss."

"Has anyone ever told you you're extremely stubborn?"

"Yes. My mother. And my nana. And my three brothers. And
my sister."

"Not your father?"

"I'm sure he would have if he'd been able to squeeze in a word
around Mom, Nana and the siblings. Now, about the Chamber of
Commerce arrangement…"

For the next hour, Toni kept the conversation strictly business.
A steady stream of customers trickled in and she took several
phone orders. She and Jayne had just finished the wedding arrangements when the door opened. Toni looked up from the box
where she was packing the fragrant centerpieces. And stared. At
Brad. At least she thought it was Brad. It looked like Brad, but
his golden brown hair was flattened down and parted on the side.
And what the hell was he wearing?

Her gaze skimmed over black-rimmed glasses whose hinges

appeared held together by tape. A white dress shirt with half a dozen pens sticking out of the pocket. Black dress pants that were hiked up way too high on his waist which showed off the dreaded white socks/black shoes combo.

He walked toward her and she realized it was indeed Brad. He stopped in front of the counter and smiled. "Hi, Toni. Hi, Jayne."

"Is that you, Brad?" Jayne asked, squinting at him.

"Sure is. How do you like my new look?"

"It's, um, interesting," Jayne said, clearly trying to be diplomatic.

"What do you think?" he asked Toni.

"You look kinda…nerdy."

Instead of appearing insulted, he smiled. "Perfect. That's how accountants are supposed to look, right?"

"So this is for a costume party?" Jayne asked with a laugh.

Brad shook his head. "No. It's for a date." He reached in his back pocket and pulled out a gift card. Toni instantly recognized it as the one he'd bought just an hour ago—dinner for two at Sea Shells. He set the card on the counter and pushed it slowly toward her. "You wanted an accountant—you got one. Have dinner with me."

Warmth rushed through Toni at the gesture. It was funny and annoying and romantic and ridiculous, and to her horror she felt the word *yes* rush into her throat. She forced it back and fixed him with a stern stare. "I've heard of makeovers, but this is definitely a make*under*."

Looking confused, he pushed up his taped glasses. "Isn't this what accountants look like?"

"Yeah—in comic strips and cartoons. You look like you got attacked by a copy of *The Nerd's Complete Guide to Bad Fashion*."

"Is that so? Well, at the last accountant convention I attended, this is what I wore and I was the height of fashion. Really. I mean that."

"Uh-huh."

He held up his hands in a gesture of surrender. "Hey, you're the one who wanted an accountant. I'm just trying to be accommodating."

"I was actually thinking more along the lines of an accountant who might wear an Armani suit."

"According to *The Nerd's Complete Guide to Bad Fashion,* accountants don't wear Armani. They wear high-water pants and pocket protectors." He pointed to the array of writing implements in his shirt pocket. "And always carry bandages in case their pens stab them in the boob."

A giggle escaped her and she coughed to cover it. "You're not an accountant."

"Oh, yeah?" He leaned closer and flashed her a naughty grin. "Wanna see my assets?"

More than I'll ever let you know. "Keep talking like that and I'll report you to the IRS." She pushed the gift card back toward him.

"So even though you said you wanted an accountant and I've turned into an accountant, the answer is still no?"

"Correct." Although she had to give him props for ingenuity. Not that she had any intention of telling him that, of course.

He leaned back and stared at her through those ridiculous glasses and she had to press her lips together to keep from laughing. "What would you say if I told you you're a hard woman to please?"

"I'd say you were right."

He muttered something under his breath about women being fickle-hearted creatures then retrieved his gift card and slipped it back in his pants pocket. "No argument here. Well, I guess I'd better go. I have um, accounting-type things to do."

"You mean like tax returns?" Toni asked.

"Yeah. Stuff like that. See ya."

How unfair was it that even dressed in high-water pants, the man looked utterly delicious? As soon as the door closed behind him, Jayne planted her hands on her hips and shot Toni The Look.

"I guess you're wondering what that was all about," Toni said, ignoring The Look and reaching for another centerpiece.

"Actually, I was able to connect the dots pretty well. What I want to know is how you could possibly turn him down! Did you not see how *sweet* that was? How romantic? Obviously the guy is totally into you. When's the last time a man made such an effort?"

Since she couldn't remember if any man had ever made such an effort, she merely shrugged.

"If I weren't so in love and so knocked up, *I'd* have dinner with him. What *are* you, made of steel?"

"Titanium," Toni corrected, although, given how tempted she'd been to accept his invitation, she had to wonder if it was true.

"Well, just remember that even titanium can melt if exposed to hot enough temperatures."

"Noted. Why don't you start on the Chamber of Commerce piece while I finish boxing these centerpieces?"

"Fine," Jayne grumbled, her lower lip sticking out in a pout. "I'll do that while you box centerpieces and regret letting that beautiful man get away."

"No regrets," Toni said with a smile, but even as the words left her mouth she wondered if they were true.

Forty-five minutes later, Toni was just adding a bright red satin bow to a poinsettia for her latest customer when the bell above the door jingled. She glanced that way, noting the tall man dressed in jeans, a denim shirt and a ten-gallon hat whose brim shadowed his features. Smiling, she handed the woman the plant then turned toward the man. And froze as recognition hit her.

"Howdy, ma'am," Brad said in a slow drawl, his lips curving upward in a smile. He then touched the brim of his hat and nodded a greeting to Jayne.

Jayne shot him a grin. "Don't tell me—she said she'd rather date a cowboy than a firefighter."

"That's the truth," Brad replied in his exaggerated drawl. He stepped up to the counter and slapped down the dinner gift card in front of Toni. With his eyes gleaming at her, he said, "Thought I'd mosey on over here and see if I couldn't convince you to share some vittles with me." He pushed back his hat and gave her a sexy smile that she suspected could actually melt titanium. "Whattaya say, little lady? Have dinner with me. If you do, I'll dazzle you with some of my cowboy wisdom."

Dammit, she was having a hard time resisting this. God knows if he really were a cowboy, she'd take him up on his offer in a snap. But he wasn't. So she crossed her arms over her chest and shot him a skeptical look. "Cowboy wisdom?"

"That's right. Such as, don't squat with your spurs on."

Toni considered, then nodded. "Makes sense."

"Always drink upstream from the herd. If you're riding ahead of the herd, look back once in a while to make sure it's still there. Never slap a man who's chewing tobacco." He gave a solemn nod. "Yes, ma'am, words to live by." He pushed the gift card closer to her and lowered his voice. "Have dinner with me."

The heat in his eyes, the intimacy in his tone, touched something deep inside Toni. Something she didn't want touched. Especially not by him. For three years she'd never once wavered from her resolve to avoid firefighters. Had never been even remotely tempted to do so. The fact that she was now so sorely tempted confused and irritated her. And actually scared her. And on top of that, the timing was all wrong. She simply didn't have time for this. For him. For anyone.

She pushed the gift card back. "Look, I appreciate the effort you've put in here, but—"

"So have dinner with me."

She had to force herself to shake her head. Force herself to say, "No. Thank you, but no. And I recall the rest of our earlier conversation. Please don't show up here dressed as a circus clown. This is very flattering, but the answer is still no."

He heaved a sigh and slipped the gift card back in his pocket. "Well, as they say on the ranch, if you find yourself in a hole, the first thing to do is stop digging." He tipped his hat, then without another word, turned and loped out of the store.

"Okay, that does it," Jayne said, reaching for the phone. "I'm calling the men in the white coats. You're totally certifiable. You must have a lump of granite where your heart belongs. Not to mention rocks in your head to turn him down."

"I'm sure you mean that in the nicest way," Toni said, unable to keep the traces of hurt and annoyance from her voice.

"Actually, I don't. Look, I understand your aversion to firefighters—"

"Thank you. Because it doesn't seem as if you do."

Jayne reached out and clasped Toni's hand. "I really do, sweetie. And I agree with you. What happened to you was awful and wrong and very, very hurtful. You have every right to feel the way you do. But in this particular case, I think you're making a mistake to pile Brad into the same category as those idiots you worked with. They're the ones who hurt you—not Brad. He seems really sweet and sincere, and God knows, he's sexy as hell. And obviously he has a sense of humor. How many times have I heard you say you'd love to meet a man with a sense of humor?"

"And I would. *Someday.* Not now. And never, if he's a firefighter."

"It's only dinner. A simple meal."

A humorless sound escaped Toni. "A simple meal. The problem is I somehow don't think it would remain simple. And that…scares me." There. She'd said it out loud.

"Of course it could be simple—if that's what you want."

"You really think I should have said yes?"

"Yes. I really think you should have. Maybe he's a really great guy whose only fault is saving people's lives for a living. That beast."

"Maybe he's a real jerk."

"Maybe. Don't you want to know? I know I would."

Toni pulled in a long breath. Dammit, she did want to know. She didn't want to want to know, but she did. Which was really annoying. And frightening.

"What if I discover he isn't a jerk?"

"Would that really be so terrible?" Jayne asked, her big blue eyes filled with compassion.

"Yes. No." Toni raked her hands through her curls. "I don't know. I have so much on my plate right now, with the shop and upcoming bank review— I need a man like I need a bad rash."

"I disagree. After six months with no sex, I think a man is exactly what you need. A few man-induced orgasms would be a perfect Christmas gift to give yourself."

Toni refused to consider how perfect a few man-induced orgasms would be. "If he isn't a jerk…I'm afraid…I don't want to end up liking a guy whose occupation would remind me every day of something I've worked very hard to put behind me and forget."

"Well, as I said before, it isn't necessary that you marry the guy. Again—you haven't had sex in *six months.*"

"Way to rub it in."

"I'm just stating a fact." Jayne grabbed the calendar from the bag beneath the counter and flashed Mr. December's picture. "If that's not enough to make you want to end your sexless streak, you don't have a pulse."

Toni grabbed the calendar and shoved it back beneath the counter. "Fine. He's hot. Fine. I'm horny. Doesn't matter since he's gone and won't be back. It's for the best." Right. Completely for the best.

"But if he came back?"

"He won't. I was very clear."

"But if he did?" Jayne persisted.

"If he did, then I'd—"

The door opened and the jingling bell cut off her words. She turned and her pulse stuttered as Brad, dressed, she guessed, as himself, in jeans and a green polo shirt, entered. With his gaze steady on hers, he approached the counter. God help her, he looked good enough to eat. An image instantly popped into her mind. Of her running her tongue down his torso. Licking her way beneath his waistband—

"It occurred to me," he said when he stood in front of her, "that you never mentioned a teacher."

Toni had to swallow to find her voice. "Teacher?"

He nodded. "In addition to being a firefighter, I'm also a teacher. At the Ocean Harbor Beach Community College."

"What do you teach?"

"An Emergency Medical Technician training course. I worked as an EMT before joining the fire department. I teach on my off days."

"I see…Professor."

He flashed a grin then pulled out the now-very-familiar gift card from his back pocket and set it on the counter. "Another cowboy bit of wisdom is—when you get to the end of your rope, tie a knot and hang on. So that's what I'm doing." He nudged the card toward her. "Have dinner with me. C'mon, Toni. Just one little dinner."

Dammit. Her resolve was melting like chocolate left in the sun. "How do you know so much about cowboy wisdom?"

"I spent three summers during high school working on my uncle's ranch in Wyoming. I'd be happy to tell you all about it over dinner."

"Are you always this persistent?"

All traces of amusement faded from his eyes, which now looked more green than blue thanks to his shirt. "No."

That single softly spoken word rendered a direct hit to her rapidly weakening resolve.

"And just so you know," he continued, "I can keep this up for a while. I have the next two days off."

"What about your class?"

"The semester ended last week. School doesn't start again until after the new year." He nudged the card closer to her. "So…are you free tonight? Please say yes. I *really* don't want to come back here dressed as a circus clown."

Her lips twitched. "Would you?"

His gaze dipped to her mouth and heat flared in his eyes. Heat that sizzled over to her like an electric current and whooshed straight to her core. He raised his eyes to hers. "Yes, I would."

Somehow resisting the urge to wave her hand in front of her flushed face, she fixed him with a hard stare. "Just one dinner." After all, what could be the harm in one little dinner? A girl had to eat—right?

Relief flickered in his eyes. "One dinner," he agreed. "Tonight?"

Might as well make it tonight and get it over with, she decided. Surely this one ill-advised meal that she annoyingly couldn't seem to resist would drive home the fact that getting involved in any way with a firefighter was a bad idea. Meanwhile, she'd just pretend he was nothing more than a teacher. A really hot teacher. A really hot teacher she already knew looked incredible all wet.

"Tonight," she agreed. She'd give him one evening, then put

him from her mind. And put her focus back where it belonged—
on her business.

A huge grin split his handsome face. "I'll pick you up—"

"I'll meet you at Sea Shells," she said firmly. "Eight o'clock."

"Eight o'clock," he agreed. After saying goodbye to Jayne, he
left the store. The instant the door closed behind him, Jayne said,
"Thank God you said yes. If you hadn't, I would have told Santa
to let a reindeer kick you. *I* would have kicked you."

"It's just dinner," Toni said, trying to ignore the fissure of jit-
tery anticipation running through her.

"Of course it is," Jayne agreed in a calm voice. "Still, be sure
to bring some condoms. Just in case you decide you want dessert."

4

BRAD SAT in a corner booth at the bustling Sea Shells restaurant
and forced himself not to look at his watch; he knew less than a
minute had passed since he'd last peeked at the time. Which
meant it was five minutes to eight. Five minutes that he suspected
were going to pass ve-e-ery slowly.

Dammit, he was nervous. He tried to recall the last time he'd
felt so jumpy about a date and realized it was probably in high
school. Great. Thirty years old and struck down by teengeritis.
It was just a date. Just one little dinner.

*Yeah. With a woman you've wanted for three months. With
a woman you clearly have one shot with. Screw this up and
you're finished.*

No pressure.

Yet in spite of his nervousness, he felt more alive than he had
in months. Because of the number of women who made themselves available to the guys at the station, it had been a long time
since he'd actually had to do any pursuing. In fact, he didn't know
one firefighter who was single who had trouble finding a woman.

When was the last time he'd had to put any effort into getting a date or a one-night stand? Damned if he could remember. But then, when was the last time he'd experienced the sort of wild attraction he felt toward Toni?

Never. He never had.

In an effort to relax and not glance at his watch again, he looked out the window at the foamy waves rushing onto the sand. The star-studded sky resembled diamonds tossed on inky velvet, and the full moon cast the beach with a bright silvery glow that reflected off the water. A few people walked along the sand: teenagers jostling each other, a family with two small children who chased the seabirds darting near the waves' edge, couples holding hands. He studied one couple in particular, their arms wrapped around each other. They were chatting and laughing, smiling, completely absorbed in each other. Even though they didn't look anything like Greg and Tanya, the love and happiness that radiated from them reminded him of his brother and his bride, and a pang of unmistakable envy hit Brad right in the chest.

"It's a beautiful night. Can't remember when I've seen so many stars."

His head jerked around at the slightly husky feminine voice, and he found himself staring up at Toni. Toni, whose shiny dark curls spilled over her bare shoulders. Toni, whose big brown eyes were locked on his. Toni, whose full lips gleamed with a touch of gloss that looked good enough to lick. Toni, whose killer curves were highlighted by a strapless Christmasy-red dress that immediately set him on fire.

Talk about a hit right in the chest.

He stood and tried not to stare, but failed. "Hi," he managed, feeling like a tongue-tied teen standing before his fantasy girl. "You look… Wow."

His gaze swept over her, noting the smooth, creamy skin that showed just a hint of cleavage, the way the dress hugged her feminine form to her hips then flared to flirt around her knees, the sexy peep-toe silver heels, the red-polished toes that matched her dress. Damn, even her feet were beautiful. And those heels made her legs look endless. He raised his gaze back to hers, and noted her looking him over. He hoped his dark gray dress pants and white dress shirt met with her approval because he sure as hell met with his.

He wanted to add that she looked amazing. Gorgeous. Classy. Incredible. Instead he could only repeat, "Wow."

Color rushed into her cheeks. "Thanks." Her gaze wandered over him again and her lips twitched. "What happened to your high-water pants?"

"I retired them. Apparently I need to look for something by Armani."

He stepped behind her to hold her chair, and found himself less than a foot away from her bare shoulders. The expanse of smooth, satiny skin beckoned his fingers like a siren's call and he had to grasp the back of the chair to keep from touching her. The subtle scent of flowers wafted toward him and he couldn't keep from leaning a bit closer to catch the elusive fragrance. She smelled incredible. Like a garden in the sunshine.

She shot him a half smile over her shoulder, murmured, "Thank you," then gracefully sat. After pushing in her chair, he resettled himself in the seat opposite her. And wondered how he was going to make it through the meal without giving in to the overwhelming urge to touch her. The craving to kiss her. How the hell was he even going to make conversation with her when all he could do was stare? She'd done something to her eyes... applied some sort of smoky makeup that reeled him in like a fish on a hook. Made it impossible to look away from her.

"For you," she said. He managed to drag his gaze from hers and saw that she held out a single red rose. "As the Twelve Steamy Nights of Christmas flyer promised, if you come into Blooming Pails the day you use your gift card, you receive a rose. Since you came in—several times—I thought it only fair that you get yours."

He reached for the bloom, taking the opportunity to brush his fingers against hers. An electric tingle rushed up his arm. One that kept on going and settled in his groin. She stilled at the contact and he wondered if she felt this same...whatever the hell it was...that he did.

"No woman has ever given me a flower before."

"How many flower-shop owners have you taken to dinner?"

"You're the first."

She flashed a smile. "That could be why."

"I have something for you, too," he said, reaching down for the small silver-and-green gift bag he'd set by his feet.

She frowned when he placed the bag on the table in front of her. "That's a…gift."

"Well, 'tis the season. You gave *me* one."

She shook her head. "No, I didn't. I brought you the flower you were entitled to."

"Then don't consider this a gift. Consider it a favor."

Still frowning, she peeked in the bag. Then looked at him over its bright foil edge. "The gift card for the thong at Mimi's Intimate Apparel?"

He nodded. "Seriously, you'd be doing me a huge favor by taking it off my hands. It's not like I can wear it."

"There must be fifty other women you could give it to."

"Actually, no. And even if there were, I want you to have it. Since it came off the tree in your store, it's only fitting it be yours."

She said nothing for several seconds and he could almost see her internal debate as to whether she should accept the present. Finally she said, "Thank you."

"You're welcome." He shot her a wink. "I hope you'll think of me when you wear it."

Another crimson blush suffused her cheeks and he nearly groaned. He tried to remember the last time he'd seen a female over the age of fourteen blush, and came up blank. Silence swelled between them and he frantically searched his mind for something to say. Something other than *I want to kiss you so badly I can hardly think straight.* He was saved when the waiter appeared with their menus and the wine list.

"Do you prefer red or white?" Brad asked her. "Or maybe champagne?"

"Chardonnay, please."

He consulted the list and ordered a bottle. After the waiter departed, Brad opened his menu, but couldn't concentrate on it since he was so busy looking at her. After a quick perusal of her menu, she closed it and set it aside. He gave up and did the same. Before he could think up anything brilliant to say, the waiter reappeared with their wine. After he'd poured them each a glass, he turned to Toni to take her order. Brad's gaze zeroed in on her glossy lips, watching her form each word, imagining that gorgeous mouth pressed against his.

"And for you, sir?" the waiter asked, turning toward him.

"The same for me," Brad said, unable to look away from Toni. He had no idea what she'd ordered, but since he pretty much liked everything except broccoli, it didn't really matter. Hell, he'd even eat broccoli if that's what she'd ordered. As far as he was concerned, this meal definitely fell into the category of "it doesn't matter what you're eating, it's who you're eating with."

After the waiter left, he picked up his wineglass and held it aloft. "To…" He hesitated, unwilling to say what he really wanted to for fear of scaring her off. *Us. Beginnings. An incredible night.*

"An enjoyable evening," he finished.

She inclined her head and touched the rim of her glass to his. After taking a sip, he set down his drink and said, "So, tell me why you don't like firefighters."

She raised her brows. "Boy, you don't waste any time."

"If this is the only date I'm going to get, I don't have any time to waste."

"This isn't a date," she reminded him. "It's just—to use your words—one little dinner."

Not if I can help it. If he had his way, this one little dinner was going to turn into one hot night followed by one hot morning. Then repeat same. Until neither of them could move and this fire she had lit in him was put out.

Obviously a plan best not put on the table right now.

"Okay," he agreed. "So since this is the one little dinner I'm going to get, tell me why you don't like firefighters." He studied her for several seconds then guessed, "Bad breakup?"

"I suppose you could describe it like that, but not in the way you're suggesting. It's nothing to do with a boyfriend." She drew a deep breath, then with her gaze steady on his, said, "I used to be a firefighter."

Brad couldn't hide his surprise. "Used to be? What happened? Were you injured?"

"Not physically, although it came close. You sure you want to hear this?"

"Absolutely."

"All right. During college I dated a firefighter—nothing serious, but it whetted my interest, and even after the guy was gone, the interest in a firefighting career remained. I enrolled in fire school and became certified as a paramedic. Four years ago, I was hired by a station in Woodton, a small city about one hundred miles east of Santa Barbara, which is where I'm from. It was my first experience living away from home, and I thought everything was going to be perfect."

She paused to take a sip of wine and he sat back, waiting for her to continue. "But I take it everything wasn't perfect," he said.

"Everything was a disaster. I was the first woman to be hired at that station. I think the only reason I was is because the chief felt pressured to break that gender barrier. Unfortunately, almost without exception, the men I worked with resented having a woman there. I was the interloper in the all-boys' club and they let me know from day one that they weren't going to make it easy on me."

Brad nodded. As much as he disagreed with that mentality, he knew it existed. "They made your life difficult."

She made a humorless sound. "*Difficult* would have been a blessing. It was hell. I have three brothers so God knows I can take teasing, practical jokes and potty humor. But this was…mean. Even vicious. The guys who weren't actively harassing me just turned a blind eye to what was going on. In spite of passing every physical and written test with flying colors, none of them believed that a woman who 'looked like me'—" she made air quotes around the words "—could do the job. The stress was incredible, but I was determined not to quit. The abuse got so bad I finally filed a sexual-harassment suit, figuring things couldn't get much worse. I was wrong."

She looked away from him and ran her finger around the base of her wineglass. Sympathy for her plight, the unfairness of it, filled him, and unable to keep from doing so, he reached out and touched her hand. Her skin was warm and silky and a tingle sizzled up his arm. "What happened?"

"It got to the point where I actually feared for my life because I didn't trust any of them to have my back." Her eyes bored into his. "You know that your life depends on your partners. I didn't have any. It was a small station and we all needed each other, but I couldn't depend on them. Not one of them. I knew that with every fire, every rescue, my life was endangered. I accepted that risk. But I wasn't willing to accept that I could be injured or even die because my coworkers wouldn't have my back. So I quit."

Outrage on her behalf joined sympathy and he squeezed her hand. "I'm sorry, Toni. How long did you tough it out?"

She slipped her fingers from his and again picked up her wineglass. Her hand shook slightly. Obviously the memories still distressed her. "A year and a half."

He nodded, impressed. "I give you a lot of credit for hanging in that long."

She looked at him over the rim of her glass. "You don't think I'm a quitter?"

"Hell, no. Given the impossible circumstances, I think you did the right thing. What became of your sexual-harassment suit?"

"I dropped it. Once I quit, I didn't want anything to do with any of it. I packed up my things and moved back home to Santa Barbara."

"And that's why you don't like firefighters," he murmured. "Now I get it. But, Toni, you know we're not all like that. If I'd been at that station, I would have had your back."

She shot him a clearly skeptical look. "You wouldn't have gone along with the crowd?"

Her question hit him like a slap. "No. Not my style. Never has been." He leaned forward and fixed his gaze on hers. "As much as I'm sympathetic to what happened to you—and believe me, I think it sucks—you're making assumptions about me based on the bad behavior of people I don't even know. I've been a firefighter for seven years and during that time I've worked with some great people and some real jerks. Here's a news flash—there are great people and real jerks in every profession." He cocked a single brow. "Probably even in the flower business."

She blinked. Then narrowed her eyes and studied him for a long moment. He strongly sensed he was about to pass or fail some test he hadn't studied for, so he remained silent under her regard and wished he knew what she was thinking. Finally, a sheepish expression crossed her face. "You're right, of course. I don't know you. You might be a prince among men—"

"My mother will tell you I am," he broke in.

"No doubt. But it's her job to think so. My mother would say the same about my three brothers and all of them are pains in the butt."

"And as their sister, it's your job to think so."

"Touché," she said with a quick laugh, then sobered. "I…I didn't mean to insult you. I'm afraid that given my experiences, I cast a dubious eye on everyone in your profession."

"Understandable—I'd feel the same way. But I'm not one of those guys. So I'm asking you not to feel that way about me. At least until you get to know me better. Then if you think I'm an asshole, well, okay." He smiled and held out his hand. "Deal?"

Her gaze shifted down to his hand then back to his face. He could almost see the wheels turning in her mind. Could tell that she was fighting her desire to stay away from anything that had to do with firefighters, and what he hoped was desire for him. Or at least a desire to give him a chance.

Finally she extended her hand. "Deal."

His fingers wrapped around hers and a combination of relief and anticipation raced through him. Instead of shaking her hand, he brought it to his mouth and pressed his lips against the back of her fingers. Her breath caught slightly at the gesture—definitely a good sign.

"I'll have you know it took some effort for me to put aside my prejudices and make that deal," he said. "I've had some very difficult dealings with florists. Most recently today."

She nodded. "I don't doubt it. Florists can be notoriously hard to deal with."

"Lucky for me I like a challenge."

Encouraged by the fact that she didn't pull her hand away, he lightly brushed his fingers against hers, exploring their softness. Her hands were small but capable-looking, which they'd have to be for her to have passed the grueling firefighter tests. Clearly, on top of having an incredible shape, she was in good physical condition.

"So, continue your story," he urged, scooting closer. He snagged her other hand and slowly played with her fingers. "How did you get from returning home to Santa Barbara to owning a flower shop fifty miles away in Santa Rey?"

"My family owns the largest nursery in Santa Barbara, so I grew up learning the business."

Damn, she had the softest hands he'd ever touched. He slowly traced the length of each of her fingers with his fingertips. "You didn't want to work at your family's place?"

"I did. But after a few years I wanted to be my own boss. Create something that was *mine*. Plus, I needed to put some distance between myself and my loving but smothering family." She looked down at their touching hands then back at him. "That's, um, really distracting."

He brushed the pad of his thumb over the velvety skin of her inner wrist. "Distracting in a good way?"

"Distracting in an I-can't-remember-what-we-were-talking-about way."

"That's a good way. You were telling me how much you like me."

Amusement glittered in her eyes. "Was I?"

"Yup. And you were about to tell me how it's possible that a gorgeous, intelligent woman like you isn't taken."

"What makes you think I'm intelligent?"

"I'm a very good judge of character." He smiled. "Besides, the fact that you accepted my invitation proves it."

She rolled her eyes, but then smiled. "You know I didn't want to."

He turned one of her hands over and lightly traced the lines on her palm. "Yeah, I got that. I'm hoping you're not sorry."

"Not yet. But the night's still young." Her eyes seemed to darken. "That feels really…hmm…nice."

The smoky tone of her voice had him shifting in his chair.

Damn. Just her voice turned him on. What would happen if she touched him? Stupid question. He knew damn well what would happen. He'd go up in flames.

She slowly spread her fingers wider, a gesture that shouldn't have struck him as sexy as it did. But then, he found everything about her sexy and had since minute one.

"So, why aren't you taken?" he asked, continuing to caress her fingers.

"Actually, I am—by my business. It requires all my time and attention. Now, and for the foreseeable future."

Obviously a not-very-subtle warning that she didn't have time for him. A warning he was determined to ignore, and convince her to ignore, as well. "Okay, I'll rephrase. How is it possible that an intelligent woman who looks like you, who smells as good as you do, whose skin is as soft as yours, doesn't have a boyfriend?"

"After I discovered my last boyfriend required a dictionary, I gave him the heave-ho and haven't felt inclined to replace him."

"Dictionary?"

"Yes. He didn't know the definition of some pretty basic words. Like *honesty*. And *integrity*." She leaned a bit closer and lowered her voice as if imparting a great secret. "He thought monogamy was a type of wood."

Brad could only shake his head. "What kind of idiot would cheat on you?"

She flashed him a smile, one which raised his temperature several degrees. "Compliment noted—thank you."

"Compliment sincerely given—you're welcome. How long ago since you heaved him?"

"Six months. What about you? How is it possible that an intelligent man who looks like you doesn't have a girlfriend?"

"Sadly, my last girlfriend couldn't even spell *monogamy,* let alone mistake it for a type of wood. Like you, I gave her the heave-ho and haven't felt inclined to replace her."

"Not to repeat your words verbatim, but what kind of idiot would cheat on you?"

"Not to repeat *your* words verbatim, but compliment noted— thank you. I'm lucky I came out of it as unscathed as I did. I wasn't heartbroken. Just royally pissed off. I'd considered the guy a friend."

She winced. "Ouch. At least my dirtbag ex didn't cheat with anyone I knew…" Her words trailed off and her gaze dipped to the table where he was lightly massaging her fingers, one at a time.

"That feels…ahhhh…incredible, especially after putting together dozens of arrangements today." When she looked at him again, her eyes were half-closed. She made a low, sexy sound of approval that had him shifting against the swelling going on behind his pants' zipper.

"So why haven't you replaced your girlfriend?" she asked. "Obviously you don't lack opportunity. Firefighters attract women like bees to honey, and this town and Ocean Harbor Beach are both littered with young, gorgeous women, who wear bikinis most of the time. You can't walk two feet without bumping into a dozen of them."

"Exactly. And after a while, they became…interchangeable. They can't seem to talk about anything other than clothes, their drama-filled lives, their girlfriends and former boyfriends and celebrities. I think the operative word you used is *young.* When I was in my twenties, that was fine, but since hitting thirty…my tastes have changed. So I guess it's actually more accurate to say that I hadn't met anyone in a long time who really interested me." He lifted her hand and with his gaze steady on hers, pressed a kiss against the warm palm he'd been caressing. "Until three months ago. When I walked into Blooming Pails."

5

TONI WATCHED heat flare in Brad's eyes as he pressed another kiss against her palm, liquefying her insides. Whoa. His mouth felt *reeeally* good against her skin. And looked *reeeally* good there, too. And…oh, God, had he just touched her palm with his tongue?

Oooh, yes. He had. *Mama mia.* Good thing she was sitting down, because that single tongue flick left her legs feeling like melted wax. It left her spine feeling that way, too. So much so that she'd like to lie down. With Brad. Right now.

He brushed his lips against her inner wrist and she actually felt her eyes glaze over. When the hell had that little bit of skin become so sensitive? And who had run the electric circuit from her wrist straight to her nipples—which were now hard and aching? Clearly her six-months-long sexless state had screwed up her internal wiring.

His gaze dipped and he stilled at what she assumed was the sight of her erect nipples pressing against the velvet of her dress. When he raised his gaze back to hers, his eyes all but breathed smoke. "Toni," he said softly.

Just the way he said her name rippled a heated shiver down her spine. Good grief, *how* had she resisted this man for three months? She was either insane or deserved a medal of fortitude. How could she hope to resist him tonight?

You can't, her inner voice flatly informed her.

Her inner voice was right.

Sure, she could try to lie to herself, but what was the point? She might as well face it. The guy was hot, sexy, gorgeous, funny, romantic, smart and totally into her. He oozed sex appeal and sex sounded so incredibly…appealing. In a word, he was irresistible.

Exactly, agreed her triumphant inner voice. *So stop trying to resist!*

Sex on a first date wasn't normally her style, but hey—they'd agreed this wasn't a date. It was just one little dinner. One little dinner that would lead to one little bout of sex. One little dinner during which it was now time to turn the tables and make *him* suffer for a while. Heh, heh, heh.

He appeared about to say something else, but just then the waiter appeared bearing their salads. After pressing another quick kiss to her palm, Brad released her hand and Toni curled her fingers inward to keep the warmth of his mouth against her skin. After topping off their wineglasses, the waiter faded away. She reached for her fork and speared a bit of radicchio, watching him do the same. She waited until Brad had taken a bite then slipped her foot from her shoe.

"Tell me about your family," she said. Under the cover of the long tablecloth, she slid her bare foot against his calf.

He stopped in midchew. Went perfectly still while she slowly rubbed her instep along his shin. For several seconds his hot gaze bored into hers. Then he chewed twice and swallowed. "Huh?"

"Your family. Any more at home like you…Elf?"

She had to fight to hide her smile when his face colored slightly. He groaned and shook his head. "Who told you?"

"Word gets around. I saw your picture, Mr. December. Very nice."

"You mean, embarrassing. I'll never live that down."

"Believe me, you have nothing to be embarrassed about." Her foot snaked up to his knee.

He set his fork down so quickly it clanged against his salad plate. He shifted slightly, and she felt him stretch out his leg. "Thanks. Glad you approve."

Her gaze flicked to his chest. "I liked your tat. Did it hurt when you got it?"

"Not a bit, thanks to an overindulgence of…" He sucked in a quick breath as her toes brushed against his hard thigh.

Several long seconds of silence passed during which he looked at her as if she were a glittering diamond and he was a jewel thief. Finally she prompted, "You were saying?"

"Saying?"

"About your tattoo."

"Oh. Right." He shook his head and gave a short laugh. "Sweetheart, if you want to make conversation *and* touch me, you'll need to expect some lulls."

She popped a bit of cucumber into her mouth. "Turnabout is fair play."

"Believe me, I wasn't complaining." He picked up his fork and stabbed a bite of tomato. "Tequila," he said to finish his sentence. "A well-documented tattoo-painkiller."

"You mentioned a brother—is it just the two of you?"

He nodded, somewhat jerkily as she continued to stroke his

leg with her foot. "Greg's two years older and got married this past summer. Never seen a guy so happy."

Toni sighed. "I wish *my* brothers would get married. Then maybe they'd concentrate on their own love lives rather than mine. I love them and they're good guys, but ridiculously over-protective. They can't seem to grasp that I'm not twelve years old any longer."

"Is that why you put some miles between you?"

"Yes. I love my family, but we clash. I guess I'm something of a rebel and the black sheep. My mother literally took to her bed when I said I wanted to be a firefighter. You'd have thought I'd announced a plan to blow up a major city. I'm the first one not to work in the family business."

"But you did for a while."

She took a sip of wine, then said, "Yes. But I found it impossible to live my own life. Mom and my sister—who's married— were always trying to fix me up, and Mom constantly poured on the guilt that I wasn't married and giving her grandbabies. Yet she hated every guy I dated. And believe me, dating wasn't easy with three overprotective brothers scowling at anything with a penis that came within ten feet of me.

"Then, last year, my Nana Rose moved in with Mom and Dad. She's exactly the same as my mom, only feistier. I like peace. Quiet. But there's practically this glowing ring of nitpicking tumult surrounding all of them. And when they form groups…". She shook her head. "Run for the hills. I truly do love them and I know they mean well, but I can only handle them in small doses. Sometimes I think even fifty miles isn't enough distance between us. Five hundred might have been smarter."

"What about your dad?"

"The calm eye in the storm. He just smiles and goes to work and enjoys his hobbies and lets all the chaos roll off him like water off a duck's back. I think he's the only one not hoping I'll fail."

"Fail at what?"

"My business. Even though they haven't said so out loud, I strongly suspect the rest of the family secretly hopes Blooming Pails will go belly-up, thus making it necessary—in their minds—for me to move back home and work again at the family nursery."

"Any chance that'll happen?"

"The business going belly-up or me moving back home?"

"Both."

"Absolutely not to moving back home. I've fought too hard for my independence. As for Blooming Pails not making it…a lot depends on what happens in the next three months." She gave him a brief overview of her loan situation and the bank evaluation coming up at the end of the next quarter. "If my interest rate goes up, I'm afraid that will be the beginning of the end, so this is really make-it-or-break-it time for me. Which is why I'm devoting all my time and attention to work. Which is why I don't date." She didn't bother to add *especially not firefighters.*

"No problem, since we've agreed this isn't a date—it's just one little dinner."

"Right." She skimmed her foot beneath his pant leg, brushing her toes over his sock until she encountered warm, firm skin. "Now that you know all about my crazy family, what about yours?"

The way his eyes smoldered made her feel as if she'd stepped into a furnace. "My folks are great. Very little nitpicking and tumult. Like you, I like peace. My job is stressful enough—I'm lucky I don't have any extra because of my family."

"Very lucky. Is your dad a firefighter?"

"Nope. Schoolteacher. So are my mom and brother. Right in Ocean Harbor Beach, where I was born and raised. I might have followed that path except the summer I was fourteen I worked on my uncle's ranch in Wyoming."

"Where you learned your cowboy wisdom."

"Right. There was a drought that year and a brush fire broke out on some back acres. It quickly spread, and if not for the fast work of the firefighters, my uncle might have lost everything. Watching those guys work…the die was cast right then and there. Made me the rebel who broke with the tradition in my family."

"Well, not completely—you're still a teacher."

"True. I guess it's in the blood. Still…" He raised his wine-glass. "Here's to rebellion."

She touched her glass to his. Then slipped her toes from beneath his pant leg to shimmy her foot along the top of his thigh. "Right. To doing things we probably shouldn't."

He briefly closed his eyes. When he opened them, the fire in their depths scorched her. There was no doubt he wanted her. And God help her, she wanted him. More than she'd expected to. Certainly more than she wanted to. But no way she was willing to stop now. She shifted her foot to slowly caress his inner thigh, stopping just short of touching him where she was most tempted to touch.

"You're driving me crazy," he said in a strained voice.

"Just like you did to me. Want me to stop?"

"Hell, no."

"Good." She enjoyed another taste of her salad, chewing slowly, still stroking him, watching him watch her. After she swallowed, she asked, "So what do you like to do when you're not fighting fires or teaching classes?"

"Take beautiful florists to dinner."

"Thank you. Besides that."

"Surf. Swim. Hike. Kayak. Fish. Kick back and watch TV. Take beautiful florists to dinner."

She shifted her foot a hair higher on his leg. "You said that last one already."

"Did I? I'm afraid I'm…distracted. But at any rate, it bears repeating." He cleared his throat and took another bite of his salad. "So, what else do you like to do besides arrange flowers and play a wicked game of footsie?"

She smiled. "Swim. Run. Hike. Read. Cook. Play tennis. Fix up old cars."

"Fix up old cars? Seriously?"

She nodded. "Something I inherited from my dad who's an automotive genius. I drive a '64 Mustang convertible that I rebuilt. Took me six years to do it, but I love that car."

He leaned forward. "That's my dream car."

She glided her foot a bit higher, until it just brushed his groin. He sucked in a sharp breath. "Maybe you'd like me to take you for a ride."

With his eyes burning into hers, he set down his fork, reached beneath the table, and lightly clasped her foot. Then he shifted a little lower in his chair and pressed her instep against his erection. "There's no maybe about it."

Oh, my. Whoever had nicknamed this man Elf didn't know what the hell they were talking about.

"The question is," he said in a low, husky voice, "are we still talking about cars?"

"What if I said we weren't?"

He rolled his hips slightly forward, a gesture that set up an insistent throb between her legs and made her yearn to touch that lovely hard, male flesh with more than her foot. "I'd say you'd been peeking at my Christmas list." Then he did something exquisite with his hands on her arch that brought a gasp of pleasure to her lips.

"Ohhh…that feels…hmmmmm. If you don't stop that in about three or four hours, I'm going to get really angry."

"Did you just give me permission to touch you for the next three or four hours? It sounds like you've been peeking at my Christmas list again."

"I thought only children made Christmas lists."

"Clearly not, as I have one. And you're all over it. And there's nothing childish about it."

Good God, Toni was ready to slither to the floor. She *loved* having her feet rubbed and he had *very* talented hands. Hands that she wanted on more than her feet. As quickly as possible. Summoning the remnants of her wilted strength, she slid her foot from his grasp and slipped it back into her shoe.

"You didn't like?" he asked.

She pushed back her hair from her overheated face. "Oh, I liked. But if you kept doing whatever glorious thing you were doing to my foot, I was going to have an orgasm."

His eyes darkened. He pushed aside his forgotten salad and reached for her hand. "I wouldn't have minded that one bit. Seems to me that when you reach boil…well, that's a bad time to turn down the heat."

A breathless laugh escaped her as his fingers entwined with hers. "I think Santa needs to know that you're naughty."

He gave her a slow smile that melted what was left of her spine. "And that you're nice. And that I really like you."

The unsettling realization hit her that she liked him, too. Which she hadn't counted on. And wasn't particularly happy about. In an effort to lighten up a moment that suddenly felt way too serious, she said, "You don't know me."

"Aside from the obvious fact that you're gorgeous, I've managed to pick up quite a bit over the last three months during my visits to your shop. I know you're creative, talented, independent, smart, hardworking and have the most beautiful smile I've ever seen. And now I know a lot more than I did an hour ago. And I like everything I've seen. And heard." He drew her hand to his mouth and touched his tongue to the center of her palm. "And touched."

"You want to go to bed with me."

"True. But that's a statement you could safely make to any breathing guy on the planet." He reached out his other hand and traced his fingers gently over her cheek. "*But*—I also want to get to know you."

It took all her willpower not to lean into his hand and purr like a kitten. Her mind was warning her to slow down, reminding her that as charming as he was, he was a firefighter and she wanted no part of that ever again. That, except for tonight, she had no time to devote to getting to know him. But her heart and her body were screaming at her that for the purposes of sex, his occupation didn't matter, and to move full steam ahead. And those screams quickly drowned out everything else.

"What if I said I'm only interested in sex?" she asked.

She expected him to agree instantly, but instead he studied her through very serious eyes. Finally he replied, "I sure as hell wouldn't turn you down, but I think we'd both be missing out. I know we'll be great together in bed—I think maybe we could be great together out of it, as well. For the purposes of full disclosure—I'd like to find out."

Given his honesty, she couldn't give him less than the truth in return. "For the purposes of full disclosure—as much as I appreciate that, I'm not looking for a boyfriend. I'm not looking for anything past tonight."

His gaze searched hers. "I'll take tonight." He traced the outline of her lips with a single fingertip. "But be warned—I'm going to do my damnedest to change your mind."

A sensation that felt alarmingly like eager anticipation rippled through her. "I won't change my mind." And she meant it. She'd take this night to douse the fire he'd lit in her, but that was it. No point in prolonging something that couldn't lead anywhere.

"Well, in that case, I don't want to waste any time. What would you say if I suggested we get our meal to go?"

Toni captured his hand and gently bit the end of his finger. "I'd say how fast can you get the waiter over here?"

6

THE SIX MINUTES and forty-two seconds—not that Brad was counting—it required to take care of the bill and get their meals to go were an exercise in torture. He would have been perfectly happy just to leave the gift card and some cash to cover their wine and tip and forget the meal—he was starving, but not for anything packed in a container. The only thing that kept him from grabbing Toni's hand and dragging her out of the restaurant immediately was the fact that he knew they'd soon be working up an appetite. And since his fridge was pretty bare, and he wasn't much of a cook under the best of circumstances, better they have some decent food available later.

Now, clutching the bag filled with to-go containers in one hand, and his other hand holding hers, he led the way through the crowded restaurant to the exit, trying to curb the edgy impatience clawing at him. Even though he'd barely touched her, hadn't even kissed her, he already felt like a powder keg with a lighted torch waving over it—one instant away from detonation. His house was only fifteen minutes away. He'd waited three months to kiss her. He could wait another fifteen minutes.

The instant they were outside, however, he realized he wasn't going to make it another fifteen seconds. Walking so fast he was almost jogging, he rounded the corner of the brick building and drew her into the deep shadows. Dropped the bag. Then pulled her into his arms.

"Can't wait," he said in a harsh whisper, barely realizing he said the words out loud.

"Thank God," she whispered back, winding her arms around his neck.

With his heart rapping against his ribs, he lowered his head. Her lips parted and she rose on her toes, meeting his mouth with an urgency that matched his. He'd meant this to be a soft, exploring kiss, but the instant their lips touched, the powder keg exploded. In a heartbeat, the kiss turned fierce. Demanding. Deeply intimate. Their tongues met, and with a groan, he stepped back several paces until his shoulders hit the brick wall. He spread his legs and, curved one splayed hand over the luscious swell of her ass, urging her tighter against him, while his other hand plunged into her soft mass of curls to hold her head.

She tasted…perfect. Felt…perfect. She squirmed against him, a full-body caress, all her feminine softness touching all his male hardness, and he swore he was going to lose his mind. His control teetered dangerously close to the edge and she wasn't doing a damn thing to keep it from plunging into oblivion. She fisted her hands in his hair, dragging his head lower and opened her mouth wider. With a growl he sank deeper into their kiss, dancing his tongue against hers with a rhythm that blatantly imitated the act his body was screaming to share with hers. Right here. Right now. He rolled his hips, pressing his erection against the juncture of her thighs, and she responded by rubbing herself against him.

A bit of sanity somehow managed to pierce the stranglehold of lust gripping him, warning him he needed to stop this madness—right now—while he still could. He wanted her naked. Hot. Wet. Under him. Over him. And this sure as hell wasn't the place.

With an effort that nearly killed him, he broke off their kiss and raised his head. Her lips remained parted and she was breathing as heavily as he.

Damn. He'd known sparks would fly between them, but this…this was unlike anything he'd ever experienced. His legs felt like rubber and his hands were unsteady. She looked up at him through glittering, half-closed eyes.

After licking her lips, a gesture that had him gritting his teeth, she whispered, "Whoa. That was…"

"Yeah. I know." He dropped a hard, quick kiss against her mouth. "We need to get out of here. Now."

She ran her tongue along his bottom lip and he groaned. "Agreed. And I think maybe you'd better not kiss me again until—"

"We're somewhere we can't get arrested?"

"Exactly. How far away do you live?"

He forced himself to set her away from him then pushed off the wall. Grabbing her hand, he scooped up the bag of food and started out at a rapid pace toward the parking lot. "Fifteen minutes." Fifteen interminable minutes.

"I'm only five. So I vote for my place."

"Done." He glanced at her and his jaw tightened at the sight of her beautifully messed curls and swollen lips. "But even five's going to be hard."

Her gaze flicked to his tented pants. "Very hard."

So damn hard, walking was uncomfortable. "If you keep looking at me like that, we won't make it out of the parking lot, possible arrest or not. Where are you parked?"

She pointed just ahead and he caught sight of the '64 Mustang. "You?"

"Next row." He waited while she unlocked her door. "It's an homage to your legs that I can't take my eyes off them long enough to admire your very excellent ride," he said, watching her slide into the front seat.

She shot him a sexy smile. "Thanks. Follow me."

Hell, yeah. Anywhere she wanted to go. He jogged to his pickup and tailed her through the dark, quiet streets of Santa Rey. He opened the windows in an attempt to allow the cool, ocean-scented air to relieve the feverish sensation coating his skin, but it did little to abate the heat consuming him.

Five minutes and eighteen seconds later—not that he was

counting—Toni pulled into the driveway of a small stucco ranch on a peaceful side street. After parking behind her, he grabbed the food, exited his truck, and cut across the neat postage stamp of a lawn. Just as he joined her, she opened the front door.

He followed her in, and with his gaze on hers, pushed the door closed behind him. She dropped her purse and walked toward him with a sinful sway of her hips that momentarily stupefied him. Before he could fully recover, she reached behind him and locked the door. Then she set her hands on his chest and pushed him back against the wood panel. Reaching up, she twined her arms around his neck.

"Now finish what you started," she whispered against his lips. The bag of food hit the floor, and with a groan he yanked her against him.

Toni moaned as Brad's mouth came down on hers, hot, hard and demanding. Never in her life could she recall wanting a man this much—feeling such sharp, raw hunger, such desperation.

"Normally I prefer slow," she said between panting breaths and frantic kisses, her fingers impatiently jerking his shirt from his waistband. "But not now. I want your hands and mouth on me. Mine on yours." His body buried in hers. Hers wrapped around him. And all these damn clothes simply had to go. Her hands plunged beneath his shirt and settled on the warm skin of his ridged abdomen. *"Now."*

"Now sounds good to me," he muttered against her neck. Clearly he felt the same urgency as she, and clearly he knew his way around women's clothing because no sooner had he spoken than the zipper on her dress was down, the material was bunched around her waist, her strapless bra was on the floor, and his hands were cupping her breasts.

A gasp of pleasure escaped her as he teased her nipples. His tongue blazed a trail down her neck, over her chest, then drew one tight, aching peak into the wet heat of his mouth. Toni arched her back, offering more of herself, an invitation he instantly took her up on. Each tug of his lips, each circle of his tongue shot fire straight to her womb. Moisture pooled between her thighs and she shamelessly gyrated against his hardness, desperately seeking relief.

He made a sound that resembled a growl, then turned them. With her shoulders pressed against the door, she watched him drop to his knees, dragging her dress and panties down with him. When the velvet and bit of lace hit her ankles, she stepped out of the pool of material and kicked it aside, leaving her wearing only her heels.

"Spread your legs," he said, the hoarse words blowing hot against her stomach as he pressed kisses to her quivering skin. Feeling as if she were about combust, she set her legs wide apart. And was rewarded with a long, slow swipe of his tongue over her swollen folds.

A moan escaped her, one that turned into a gasp of pleasure when he thrust two fingers deep inside her. "Beautiful," he murmured, then lazily circled his tongue around her clitoris. "Wet. Hot. Delicious."

The back of her head hit the door and her eyes slid shut. He lifted her right leg and settled it over his shoulder, opening her more fully for his fingers, mouth and tongue. Need knifed through her and she fisted her fingers in his hair, unable to hold off the orgasm screaming toward her like a bullet. He performed some sort of magic with his mouth and fingers and her climax roared through her, hot pulses of intense pleasure that dragged a cry from her throat.

The spasms had barely tapered off when she felt him scoop her up in his arms. And a damn good thing he did, too. Otherwise she would have slithered to the floor in a mass of trembling, sated flesh. Still, even as she reveled in his strength, the independent feminist in her felt compelled to say, "I can walk." A weak protest at best. An outright lie at worst.

He dropped a quick kiss on her lips. "This is completely selfish on my part. I can't keep my hands off you."

"Well, in that case, carry on." She wound her arms more firmly around his neck and leaned forward to lightly scrape her teeth over his earlobe. "Literally."

"Bedroom?"

She toed off her shoes, pointed down the hallway with her foot and he started walking. "Sorry I came so fast," she said, nibbling on his neck. God, he smelled good. Tasted good. Like warm, clean, freshly showered man.

"No apology necessary. I can't wait to see how fast you can come again."

She huffed out a laugh. "Given how long it's been since I've had sex and given your extreme sexiness, I think it's going to be an embarrassingly short period of time. I'm afraid I'm feeling somewhat…" she gave his neck a little bite "…insatiable."

"That's a shame. Really. God knows I have plenty of reasons to complain because of that, but I'll try to keep a stiff upper lip and take it like a man."

"Stiff will serve you well."

"Stiff is not a problem, believe me."

He strode into her bedroom and set her on her queen-size bed. She landed on the pale yellow comforter with a gentle bounce. When he started to unbutton his shirt, she immediately scooted to the edge of the mattress and stood.

"Oh, no," she said, shooing his fingers aside and applying herself to his shirt buttons. "You undressed me. You don't get to undress you, too."

"Okay." He raised his hands and filled his palms with her breasts.

Toni laughed and firmly set his hands back at his sides. "Nor do you get to distract the undresser. I didn't distract you when you were stripping me bare."

"Wanna bet?"

She cocked a brow and resumed flicking open buttons. "What did I do?"

"You stood there." He brushed the backs of his fingers up and down her abdomen. "That's all it took."

"Clearly you're easily distracted."

"Actually, I'm not. It's more that you're incredibly distracting."

She finished with the buttons and slowly pushed the shirt down his arms where it fell on the carpet with a quiet whoosh. Her avid gaze took in the fascinating display of toned muscle then zeroed in on his tattoo. "Very nice," she murmured, splaying her hands on his ridged abdomen then gliding her palms slowly upward. "Your calendar shot was lovely, but it doesn't do you justice, Mr. December."

"Glad you liked it…" His voice trailed off into a low growl of approval when she leaned forward and lightly traced his tattoo with her tongue. Her hands skimmed down to his belt which she quickly opened, along with the button on his pants. Then she gently pushed him until he sat on the edge of the bed. He leaned back and with his weight propped on his elbows, he watched her through glittering eyes as she slipped off his black dress shoes and tugged off his socks. Then her gaze slowly tracked up his long legs and muscular torso. With his pants unfastened at the waist and that huge bulge pressing behind his zipper, he looked positively sinful.

Stepping between his legs, she slowly lowered his zipper then curled her fingers around the waistband of both his pants and underwear. He lifted his hips and she slid the garments down his legs, dropping them on the floor where they landed next to his shirt. Her avid gaze fastened on his erection which rose thick and hard, curving upward nearly to his navel.

"Spread your legs." It was the same thing he'd said to her, and, like her, he obeyed the command. She ran a single fingertip up the length of his shaft, enjoying the sharp breath he sucked in. Enjoying even more the long breath he exhaled when she wrapped her fingers around him and squeezed.

"I'm not going to last if you keep doing that," he warned in a strained voice.

For an answer, she leaned down and in the name of payback gave his erection a long, slow lick. His drawn-out groan encouraged her to repeat the lick, ending with a lazy swirl of her tongue around the head before drawing him deep into her mouth.

His breath came in a sharp hiss. "Toni…" His fingers sifted through her hair. When she swirled her tongue around him again, he made an agonized sound and urged her head up.

"Can't take anymore," he said, between urgent kisses against her lips.

Female satisfaction filled her. Perfect. Right where she wanted him. She reached for one of the condoms she'd bought earlier that day and had stashed in the drawer of her bedside table—minus the one she'd tucked in her purse—and tore open the package. After sheathing him, she straddled his hips and slowly took him into her body until he was buried to the hilt.

Toni rocked her hips and her long sigh of pleasure mingled with his groan. She rode him, slowly at first, running her hands over his chest, exploring every muscle, loving how they tensed and jumped beneath her fingertips. He rolled his hips in perfect unison to her quickening movements while his hands molded her breasts and his long fingers teased her aching nipples. When her climax overtook her, he grasped her hips and thrust upward as she ground down, embedding him deeper. Their moans and ragged breaths filled the room. Deep spasms shook her, and when they faded into delicious aftershocks, she melted against his broad chest like warm honey.

Where he found the strength to move she couldn't imagine, but seconds later she found herself on her back looking up into his eyes. She stretched beneath him, reveling in the delicious sensation of his body on top of hers. Still inside hers.

He pushed back a tangled curl that clung to her damp cheek then brushed his lips over hers. "Sorry *I* came so fast that time."

"Your timing was perfect."

"Good. Next time will be better. I'll last longer—now that the edge is off."

A huff of laughter escaped her. "I don't know how much better it could possibly get. But, hey, I'm willing to find out."

"Glad to hear it." He touched his forehead to hers. "Toni...do you have any idea how much I've wanted you?"

Her heart performed a swooping dive at both the tender gesture and the quiet words that sounded way too serious. And serious was to be avoided at all costs. Her mind knew it, but for reasons she neither liked nor understood, her heart didn't seem to be falling in line. Which meant it was time to stop thinking.

Framing his face between her hands, she shot him a wicked half smile. "I think you demonstrated how much. But...what would you say if I told you I need some more data. Just to be sure."

He nuzzled the sensitive spot where her neck and shoulder joined. "I'd say let's take this to the shower and I'd be happy to provide further information." He lifted his head and looked into her eyes. "What would *you* say about *that?*"

"I'd say that's the perfect answer."

7

TONI WAS putting together a birthday bouquet of red and white roses, freesia and white hydrangea when Jayne arrived at Blooming Pails the next morning. Her pregnant friend studied her for several seconds, then said, "Three."

"Three?"

Jayne nodded. "I'm guessing that neon glow emanating from you is the result of three orgasms."

Toni shook her head. "Wrong."

Jayne's face fell. "You didn't have sex with him? Good God, you *are* made of titanium."

"Oh, we had sex. You're just wrong about three." Toni peeked at her over a white rose. "Try six."

Jayne's eyes goggled. "*Six?* You had six orgasms last night?"

"It actually might have been seven. I think I had an out-of-body experience at one point and may have missed one."

Jayne plopped onto the nearest stool. "I want details."

A wave of heat engulfed Toni. She couldn't possibly tell Jayne the finer points of what she and Brad had shared. And not just sexual intimacies. No, they'd also shared laughter and conversation during their reheated meal where they'd discovered many common interests. They both enjoyed action flicks. Sports. Classic cars. Butter-pecan ice cream. Had similar political views. She'd never met a man with whom she felt so at ease and who was so easy to be with.

And as for the sex, it had been…incredible. After those first two frantic encounters, time had seemed to stand still as they'd spent hours in leisurely sensual exploration. Touching, talking, laughing, learning. If she lived to be one hundred, she'd never forget the way Brad had plucked the petals from the rose she'd given him and strategically placed them on her naked body. Had then settled himself between her splayed thighs and with their hands entwined above her head and his gaze steady on hers, had made soft, slow love to her with the scent of roses rising between them.

Blinking away the image, Toni forced a laugh. "You want more details than six, possibly seven orgasms and one out-of-body experience? Suffice it to say, it was a pleasurable night."

"Obviously." Jayne chuckled. "Can you even walk?"

"I'm a bit tender," Toni admitted, looking down to hide the flush heating her face. "But in a good way."

"Did you get any sleep?"

"Not much, yet I'm feeling surprisingly exhilarated."

"Hardly surprising. The postcoital glow you're tossing off could light up a cave. So when are you seeing him again?"

Toni's fingers briefly faltered, then she shrugged. "What makes you think I am? The operative words in one-night stand are *one* and *night*."

Jayne's mouth dropped open. "Are you crazy? How could you even consider not seeing again a man who gave you six orgasms and an out-of-body experience? You need to lock yourself in a room with him and toss away the key."

"You seem to be forgetting that I'm not looking for a time-consuming, work-disrupting boyfriend. Most especially not a firefighter one."

"So just make him your love slave."

"I don't want a love slave."

Jayne reached out and touched her hand to Toni's forehead. "How is it you don't have a raging fever that's causing this delirium of yours? I think he'd make a great boyfriend. You could change his nickname from Elf to Mr. Orgasm."

Hmmm…Mr. Orgasm had a certain ring to it. Then reality returned with a thump. "So let him be *your* boyfriend."

"My husband would strongly object. And what I'll need in a few months is a babysitter, not a boyfriend."

"What I need *right now* is help picking out two dozen white roses for an anniversary bouquet. Not a boyfriend."

Jayne pursed her lips. "How did you leave things with him?"

"I thanked him for a lovely evening. Told him I'd enjoyed our 'one little dinner.'" She made air quotes around the description of their evening. More like their one big sex romp.

Jayne's brows shot up. "He didn't ask to see you again?"

"He asked, I refused. He left, I came to work, and that's all there is to it."

"He accepted your refusal? He didn't argue?"

"No." And Toni refused to acknowledge the unreasonable prick of hurt that had caused. She was *glad* he hadn't protested. His acceptance had simply surprised her. She'd been sorely tempted to say yes to his invitation, which was reason enough to refuse. She couldn't afford a man cluttering up her life right now. Didn't want another relationship. Didn't want anyone or anything that would divert her attention from making her business a success and impinge on her independence.

"Obviously he doesn't want a relationship any more than I do," Toni said lightly. "We had our night and now it's back to work. Back to reality." *Back to long, lonely nights,* her inner voice whispered. She ignored the pesky voice and wrapped her finished bouquet in green tissue paper. Fine. So the nights would be long and lonely, but she wouldn't have to answer to or please anyone other than herself. Her time was her own—to devote to herself and her business.

"So you wouldn't care if tonight he treated some other woman to six, maybe seven orgasms and an out-of-body experience?"

A blast of white-hot jealousy pierced Toni right through the heart. And scared the crap out of her. Damn. This wasn't good. She tossed back her hair and forced a smile. "Why would I?"

"For someone who wouldn't care, it looks like steam is about to shoot from your ears. I recently read an article that stated one of the differences between lust and love is with lust you don't feel possessive, but when love is involved, you're very possessive."

Toni looked toward the ceiling. "There is no love involved. I barely know him."

"It's not as if you just met him yesterday. He's been coming in here for the past three months. And those six, maybe seven orgasms tell me you know him pretty damn well."

"I don't know him well enough to confuse lust with anything that resembles love."

Jayne shook her head and made a *tsking* sound. "Honey, I knew Tim was the guy for me three minutes into our first conversation. We were engaged two months later and married three months after that. That was five years ago and I'm so deliriously happy I can barely stand it." She reached out and took Toni's hand. "I know you're not looking for a boyfriend, but the truth is there's no good timing when it comes to these things. I certainly wasn't looking when Tim came along. Do you want my opinion?"

"Is there any point in me saying no?"

"Nope," Jayne said with a grin. "Listen—the right guy won't take away your independence. He'll enhance it. Maybe Brad isn't the right guy, but I think that any guy who turns you on so much that you lose count of your orgasms and who makes you turn green at the thought of him touching another woman warrants another date."

"I didn't turn green," Toni lied. "And it wasn't a date."

"Honey, you were greener than our fake Christmas tree. And it *was* a date—obviously a damn good one, too."

"It doesn't matter anyway," Toni said, ignoring the sinking sensation in her stomach. "He seemed perfectly happy to accept my decision not to see him again." Right. And the feeling cramping her insides right now as she spoke those words was relief. Yeah. Relief. Whew. What a relief.

"Maybe he just didn't want to argue about it then." Jayne's gaze fixed on something beyond Toni's shoulder. "Seems we're about to find out."

Toni turned and her heart jumped at the sight of Brad walking across the street toward the shop. He carried a long rectangular white box, just like the ones she used to pack long-stemmed flowers.

"This should be interesting," Jayne said, and there was no missing the smirk in her voice. "I'll be in the back, starting on the anniversary bouquet."

"Don't you dare leave me—"

"Alone with that gorgeous, sexy, six—or was it seven?— orgasm man?" Jayne broke in. "Yeah, I'm a monster. You can thank me later. Just remember—there's nothing wrong with having a one-night stand *twice*."

No sooner had Jayne disappeared into the back of the shop than the door opened and Brad walked in. Their gazes met and although Toni tried her damnedest to appear nonchalant, she wasn't certain she succeeded. Looking into his eyes, a myriad of images from last night played through her mind. Their soapy hands caressing each other in the shower. Warm water cascading over them as she braced herself against the cool tiles and pushed back, arching her spine to take him deeper. His body on hers. Hers on his. Him thrusting deep inside her. Her crying out his name—

"Hi," he said.

She blinked away the sensual memories and pulled in a much-needed breath. "Hi."

He crossed the tiled floor and set the long white box on the counter separating them. "What's this?" she asked nodding toward the box.

"For you. I wanted to give you flowers, but…" he looked around the shop then back at her "…it seems you already have plenty of those. So I improvised."

Dammit, she didn't want to be charmed. Didn't want to feel this bubble of giddy pleasure gurgling inside her. "It looks like a flower box," she said, sliding off the bright red ribbon. "Did you visit the competition?"

He reached out and ran one fingertip down her cheek. "You don't have any competition, Toni."

Everything inside her did something that felt suspiciously like melting. She wanted to call a time-out. Give herself a few minutes to regroup. To steel herself against him. It simply wasn't right how he turned her to mush like this.

Not trusting her voice, Toni opted to remain silent. She removed the lid, separated the layers of white tissue paper and stared. At twelve long-stemmed roses made from—

"Chocolate," she murmured, looking at the glistening candy flowers mounted on extra long lollypop sticks.

"Somehow roses remind me of you."

Warmth rushed into her cheeks. Before she could think up a reply, he continued, "I figured since you deserved roses and like chocolate…" His words trailed off and she looked up to find him staring at her with a serious expression. "I know I agreed to just one dinner, to just one night, but after last night…I want more." He reached out and took her hand. "I think, at least I hope, you do, too."

God help her, part of her *did* want more. The lonely and he's-so-sexy-and-funny-and-charming-and-sexy part of her wanted another night like last night. Who wouldn't? But her cautious side, the part that needed to live for herself and concentrate on her fledgling business told her that she was playing with fire. And with a firefighter no less—the one profession she'd vowed to avoid at all costs.

"Toni…" He entwined their fingers. "I've gone on lots of dates but never one like last night. There's something between us, something I've never felt before. I felt it the first time I looked at you."

"That was lust, Brad. I'm sure you've felt that plenty of times."

"But not like *that*. It was lust but *more*. And I'm old enough and experienced enough to know the difference."

"I told you…I don't want a boyfriend."

"I didn't particularly want a girlfriend, but here we are."

Toni's heart was thudding so hard she wondered if he could hear it. In light of his honesty, she couldn't in good conscience give him any less. "The problem is…I'm scared. I really don't want…this. Not now. Please try to understand—I've spent the last few years fighting to reestablish myself, first after the end of my disastrous firefighting career and then after finally pulling away from my smothering family. I'm finally on my own. I don't want to give that up. And I have a business that needs all my attention. I can't ignore my responsibilities."

"I don't expect you to give up anything. Wouldn't want or ask you to ignore your responsibilities. One of the things I like about you is that you aren't a clinging vine. And if it makes you feel any better, I'm scared, too." He lifted her hand and touched his lips to the backs of her fingers. "How about we be scared together?"

Toni tried to summon her willpower, but couldn't seem to find it. Which was scary and frustrating and downright annoying. She finally heaved a resigned sigh. "You know, I don't want to like you."

"I don't want to like you, either." One corner of his lips quirked. "Especially if you aren't going to like me back. Problem is, I *do* like you. A lot." He reached out and tucked a wayward curl behind her ear, an intimate gesture that made her heart stutter. "Have dinner with me tonight."

"You already asked me that this morning."

"And you said no. Which is why I'm asking again."

"You didn't argue about it this morning."

"That's because cowboy wisdom taught me that there're two ways to argue with a woman—and neither one works." He shot her a devilish grin that dissolved whatever was left of her knees. "So instead of arguing, I figured I'd just ask again."

"Just one more little dinner?"

"You've got to admit, the first little dinner went pretty damn well."

Did it ever. She had to face facts—maybe there was a woman on the planet who could say no to another date with this guy and his chocolate roses, but she wasn't that woman. What harm could one more date do?

"Okay. One more little dinner. Do you like pasta?"

"Love it. You want to go to an Italian place? Francini's on Moore Street is very good."

"Actually, seeing as how we couldn't wait to leave the restaurant last night, what would you say if I asked you to eat at my place? I'll cook."

He treated her to another one of those slow, devastatingly sexy smiles. "I'd say I'll bring the wine."

8

BRAD PULLED the cork from the bottle of merlot and glanced at the clock on his kitchen stove—ten minutes to eight. Perfect.

Toni was due to arrive in ten minutes for what would be their third date. And based on how well the other two had gone, it was going to be a fantastic night.

Leaving the wine on the counter to breathe, he took a last quick look around his small ranch house. The place was freakishly neat and clean—hell, he'd even vacuumed. Not that he was normally a slob, but he'd made sure there were no dust bunnies or dirty socks littering the floor for Toni's first visit to his home. Candles lit? Check. Soft jazz playing? Check. Lights dimmed? Steaks marinating? Check, check. Condoms in the bedroom? Check. Condom in his jeans' pocket? Check. And God knows he needed one there. He'd learned very quickly to be very prepared when he and Toni were alone together.

He heard her car pull into the driveway and shook his head at the anticipation that rushed through him. He couldn't ever recall experiencing this acute sense of eagerness. He'd never wanted to see a woman more. Touch one more. Share a meal and conversation with one more. Make love to one more.

He hadn't seen her since she'd made him dinner at her place three nights ago, but she hadn't been out of his thoughts for an instant, and he suspected that that was going to be an ongoing affliction. Hell, she hadn't been out of his thoughts *before* he'd made love to her. Wasn't much chance she would be now that he knew what every inch of her skin felt like. Tasted like.

Their date at her place had been…incredible. In addition to being beautiful, smart, witty and sexy as hell, the woman could cook. She'd bewitched him in the kitchen with her delicious pasta, then blown his mind in the bedroom. Three times. He hadn't been able to see her the following night as he was scheduled for a shift at the station, or the night after that as she'd already had plans with her friend and coworker Jayne. Which brought them to tonight.

He was relieved she'd accepted his invitation without an argument, although he hadn't been thrilled when she'd referred to tonight as their third one-night stand. If she still thought this was just sex…well, she was dead wrong.

His common sense told him that he needed to take things slow—that he'd spook her if he came on too strong. And it was just a good idea in general not to rush into emotional entanglements. Of course, in the past that had never been a problem. How ironic that now, with Toni, he was more than ready and willing to zoom ahead, and she was the skittish one.

So he'd take his time, let her take hers, allow their relationship to bloom slowly, but in his heart, he knew time wasn't going to make any difference. In his heart—his heart that Toni had stolen the very first time he saw her—he didn't doubt for a minute where this was going to end up.

A knock sounded on the door and he drew a careful, calming breath. Right this minute, his goal was not to pounce on her the instant he saw her. In spite of the inferno raging in him, he'd be cool. Refined. Well-behaved. They had the whole night ahead of them. He was perfectly in control. No problem.

Then he answered the door. And in a heartbeat, *cool, refined, well-behaved* and *in control* took a direct hit. She was just so damn appealing and gorgeous, with those big brown eyes and full pink lips and dark curly hair. His gaze skimmed over her tan knee-length raincoat which was belted at her waist, then lingered on her bare legs and high heels. Clearly she was wearing a dress. Lucky him.

He took her hand and drew her forward, leaning down to give her a kiss—a kiss he forced himself to keep deliberately light. Because if he didn't, they wouldn't make it out of the foyer.

"C'mon in," he said, stepping back, proud of his restraint in not pouncing on her like a starved dog.

"Thanks."

She moved into the small entrance and he briefly closed his eyes, breathing in a lungful of the subtle flowery scent she left in her wake. Damn. How was it that she smelled better than any woman on the planet? He took a few extra seconds closing and locking the door so he could corral his badly dented willpower. Then, after drawing another calming breath, he turned around.

"I hope you like…" His voice trailed off as he watched her open her raincoat. The garment slithered down her arms to puddle at her feet. She stood before him, naked except for her heels and a pair of tiny red-and-white-striped panties. He froze in place—

although how that was possible when he felt as if he stood in an oven he didn't know.

"You hope I like what?" she asked in a smoky purr.

Damned if he could remember. His gaze zeroed in on her erect nipples. "Huh?"

"What's the matter, handsome? Cat got your tongue?"

He had to clear his throat—twice—to locate his voice. "Actually, I think I swallowed it."

"A pity, as I was hoping you'd be putting that talented tongue to good use." She turned, revealing that her barely-there panties were a thong. "I redeemed the gift card you gave me from Mimi's Intimate Apparel." After finishing a slow twirl that left him feeling more glazed than a doughnut, she stepped toward him with a sinful sway of her hips.

"I hope *you* like," she said in a sexy whisper.

Whatever miniscule amount of cool, refined and well-behaved he might have retained evaporated in a puff of steam. With a growl he yanked her against him. Kissed her with all the pent-up want and need and urgency that had been clawing at him since the last time he'd touched her.

"God, I missed you." The unstoppable words came out as a groan against her neck. One hand skimmed down her smooth back to curve around her lush bare bottom while he filled his other hand with her breast.

"Show me," she demanded, gyrating against him while she jerked his polo shirt upward. "Show me how much."

In the space of mere seconds he had her pressed against the door, his shirt was on the floor and his erection freed and sheathed with the condom he—thank God—had had in his pocket. Her thong was disposed of with one hard yank. With raw, desperate hunger scraping through him, he curved his hands around her ass and lifted her. And buried himself in her silky wet heat with a single hard thrust.

Her gasp turned into a throaty moan and she wrapped her legs around his hips. He would have told her to hold on tight, but words were beyond him. He pulled nearly all the way out of her tight warmth, then sank deep again. And again. Over and over, each thrust harder, deeper, faster. Sweat broke out on his brow, and he gritted his teeth against the intense pleasure, trying to hold off his climax as long as possible. The instant she cried out and pulsed around him, he let himself go.

When the shudders racking him finally faded, and with her still wrapped around him, he slowly sank to his knees, then settled his butt on his heels. Her head flopped limply against his damp shoulder, and he remained buried deep inside her. Still breathing heavily, he tunneled his fingers through her wildly mussed hair and drew her head back. She looked stunned and dazed. Sated and sexy as hell. And more beautiful than any woman he'd ever seen. The area around his heart seemed to go hollow, then filled so quickly he felt as if he were drowning. Which pretty much described the way he'd felt since the minute he'd seen her three months ago.

"Toni," he murmured against her lips. And then he gave her the slow, deep, intimate kiss he'd meant to give her when she arrived. Before she'd dropped her coat and fried him where he stood.

When he lifted his head, her eyelids fluttered open. She trailed her fingertips over his jaw, then her lips slowly curved upward. "Whoa, baby. My favorite dinner—Hard and Fast Against the Door. What's for dessert?"

"That wasn't dinner, that was just the appetizer."

"Even better. What's for dinner?"

"Damned if I can remember. My entire thought process jumped the track when you dropped your coat."

"Want some cheese with that whine?" she said with a teasing grin.

He leaned forward and nuzzled her soft, fragrant neck. "Wine…I have wine."

"That's a good start."

"Actually *this*…" he drew her body tighter against his "…was a *very* good start."

"I agree." She raised one brow. "Seems you *did* miss me."

He had. Much more than he was willing to admit for fear of scaring her off. "Maybe a little. Obviously I was happy to see you."

"Got that."

"Wearing so little."

Her lips twitched. "Got that, too."

His gaze flicked down to her breasts which were pressed against his chest. "Shame you don't have any clothes with you."

"I have some in my car."

He brushed his lips over hers. "Sweetheart, believe me, you won't need them."

Twenty minutes later, after a quick shower, Brad tossed on a pair of boxer briefs, loaned Toni a T-shirt, then led her into the kitchen. He noted her looking around while he poured their wine and he wondered if this might be a good time to broach the subject that had been on his mind for days—Christmas. And them spending the holiday—or at least part of it—together. He'd delayed mentioning it for fear she'd say no, but since Christmas Eve was tomorrow, he didn't have a huge window of time left to work with.

"I like your house," she said, leaning against the counter, her gaze tracking over the white kitchen cabinets, then into the den with its coffee-colored sectional sofa, oak entertainment center and flat screen TV. "Do you own it or rent it?"

"Own. My grandfather passed away a few years ago and left me a little money. I figured a house, even a small house, was a good investment."

Handing her a glass, his gaze wandered down her form. The soft white cotton clung to her every curve and barely covered the essentials. "I like the way you look in my T-shirt."

She smiled and accepted the glass. "I think you're just easy to please."

"Actually, I'm very particular. Especially about who wears my T-shirts."

She raised her glass. "Happy holidays."

"Happy holidays," he repeated, touching his rim to hers. After taking a sip, he said in a casual tone, "Speaking of the holidays, what are your plans?"

"I'll be heading to Santa Barbara tomorrow after work for Christmas Eve dinner—aka The Huge Italian Seafood Festival— at my mother's. Spending the night there, then Christmas Day at my sister's house. Much eating, opening of gifts and the inevitable arguments will ensue. How about you?"

"I'm on duty from seven tomorrow morning til seven Christmas morning. After that I'll catch some sleep then head over to my folks' house. My brother and his wife will be there, too." He moved to stand in front of her. Reached out and tucked a silky curl behind her ear. "I was thinking maybe you'd like to join us. Either for dinner, or dessert, or just a drink."

She went perfectly still. Even in the muted light he could see she paled a bit. "You mean like…*meet the family?*"

Uh-oh. Didn't sound like she liked the idea. Part of his brain warned him to back off, but the other part told him to push on. Hell, she'd have to meet them sooner or later. Besides, he'd already issued the invite—he couldn't take it back now. "They don't bite," he said lightly. "At least not much."

The loudest silence he'd ever heard seemed to echo through the room. Finally she set down her wineglass, then stepped away from him. "Look, Brad, I don't think—"

A faint musical ring tone interrupted her words. She frowned and cocked her head. "That's my cell phone. And it's Jayne's ring tone. I left her at the store to finish a centerpiece. I'm sorry—I don't think she'd call unless something was wrong." She hurried toward the foyer where her coat hung on the brass coatrack.

"No problem," he called after her, grasping on to any excuse to not have her finish the very unpromising sounding thing she'd been about to say. He felt, literally, saved by the bell. "I need to see to the steaks anyway. Take your time."

TONI ESCAPED to the foyer, feeling literally, saved by the bell. Brad's suggestion that she meet his family, share part of the Christmas holiday with him, with them, had stunned her. Meeting the family was…serious. Which was why most guys avoided it like the plague. God knows she had no intention of bringing home any man she didn't intend to marry. Unless, of course, she wanted to scare the guy off—one meeting with her evil-eye-giving family would surely send him screaming into the night.

No one brought their one-night stand to meet their parents. And no one invited their casual sex partner to a holiday meal. It simply

wasn't done. Clearly Brad believed that their one——okay *three-*
—night stand was something more than sex.

It is *something more than sex, you doofus,* her inner voice
testily informed her. *Just because you don't want it to be and keep
denying it, doesn't make it any less true.*

Drat. Her and her pain-in-the-ass inner voice were going to
have a serious talk right after she finished with her phone call. She
fished her cell from her coat pocket and flipped it open.

"Hi, Jayne. What's up?"

"Hey, Toni. I'm so sorry to interrupt your date—"

"No problem. Trouble with the centerpiece?"

"No. It's finished. But when I was putting the copy of the in-
voice on your desk, I found something odd and figured I'd better
ask you about it."

"What is it?"

"An order. It was underneath the book of bank-deposit slips.
It's in your handwriting, but it hasn't been entered in either the
appointment book or the order ledger."

Toni frowned. Impossible. As soon as an order was taken it was
entered into both logs. "What's it for?"

"Saint Mary's Cathedral. For five dozen poinsettias, six altar
arrangements, and three dozen smaller arrangements. You noted on
the order that the church van would arrive at 10:00 a.m. on the
twenty-fourth for pickup. Since the twenty-fourth is tomorrow—"

"Oh. My. God." Toni froze. Then the bottom seemed to fall out
of her stomach. For several seconds the room actually went dark
and dots swam before her eyes. Pressing her hand against her
churning midriff, she leaned against the wall and tried to catch
her stuttering breath.

The order for Saint Mary's Cathedral. The *huge* order. The sort
of high-profile order that could mean tons of business for her. The
sort of order that could result in enough revenues to insure a successful bank evaluation. She'd spoken to the church secretary on
the phone earlier in the week. Taken the order. She'd been very
excited about getting it, but at the same time distracted. In a rush.
Because by the time she hung up with the woman Toni had realized she was running late for her first "little dinner" at Sea

Shells with Brad. So instead of doing what she should have done—taking the time to enter the order in the proper books, she'd left it on her desk and hurried off to get ready for her evening with Brad, promising herself she'd take care of the paperwork first thing in the morning. Instead she'd clearly set the bank-deposit book on top of the order. And had completely forgotten all about it. Until just now. Oh, God.

How could she have forgotten? How could she not have re-membered it for *four whole days?*

But, of course, she knew the answer.

Brad.

Since that first night together, she'd been wandering around in a sensual, lust-glazed, emotionally confused haze. Instead of concentrating on her work and her business, she'd allowed her thoughts to wander to him constantly. She'd known getting in-volved right now was a mistake—that her business required all her focus. But had she listened to her better judgment? No. Instead she'd allowed her attention to be diverted. And now she was fac-ing a business disaster of biblical proportions. If she'd failed to fill the order… God, she couldn't even think of the consequences. The lost business of such a big client, and the other work that could have potentially come her way if she satisfied them. The black mark against her and her reputation. As it was, she wasn't certain she'd be able to pull it all together.

"Toni, are you okay?"

She moistened her dust-dry lips. "Actually, no. All I can say is thank goodness you found that order and called me."

"So it's legit?"

"I'm afraid so." She quickly explained her error.

"Oh, boy," Jayne said. "That's not good. We don't have enough on hand to fill this order."

"I know," Toni said, her mind racing. "I'm on my way to the shop. The flower market opens at 4:00 a.m. I'll put together as much as I can using what we have, then I'll be at the market when it opens."

"I'll start preparing what roses we have right now," Jayne said.

"No. You've been on your feet all day and even stayed late to-night to finish the centerpiece so I could leave." She pressed her lips together. Another example of how she'd allowed her personal life to interfere with her business. "Go home to your husband. This is my mess and I'll fix it. I'm eternally grateful you found that order." As she spoke she shrugged her arms into her coat and scanned the floor for her missing shoes and panties.

"Even pulling an all-nighter there's no way you'll get all those arrangements done by yourself. Even with the two of us, it's going to be tight. I'm staying to help."

Gratitude filled Toni. "That's more than I deserve for having made such a terrible mistake. Have I told you lately that I love you?"

"You just did. I love you, too. Hey, anybody's memory would get wiped clean after six or seven orgasms and an out-of-body experience."

Which is precisely what had happened. And precisely what she wasn't going to let happen again. For now, all she could do was pray she'd be able to get the flowers she needed when the market opened at 4:00 a.m., and finish the arrangements on time. Otherwise her name—and Blooming Pails's—would be mud.

After assuring Jayne she was on her way, she shut her phone, slipped it back in her coat pocket and was struggling into her stilettos when Brad came into the foyer. "I have to go," she said, the words running together as she impatiently rotated her foot to coax it into the high-heeled shoe. "Huge problem at the shop. A missed order. Client needs it in the morning. I'll be pulling an all-nighter."

Concern filled his eyes. "Is there anything I can do to help?"

Yes. Stop being so distracting. Stop making me want you. Go away so I can focus on what I need to concentrate on—which isn't you. Come back in a year or two. Then maybe I'll be ready for you.

Those were the words she actually needed to say to him, but didn't have the time or the courage to do so now. "Thanks, but no." She pulled her car keys from her pocket. "Sorry. I need to leave. Now." She gave him a quick peck on the cheek then sprinted to her car and drove away without looking back, determined to put her focus back where it belonged.

Which meant that this had been her last night with Brad.

All she needed to do now was tell him.

9

AT QUARTER PAST SIX the next morning, holding a cardboard caddy bearing two extra-large coffees, Brad crossed the street leading to Blooming Pails. Only a few streaks of dark mauve colored the pre-dawn sky, but the inside of the flower shop was brightly illuminated. He could see Toni behind the counter, her brow bunched as she moved methodically down a lengthy row of floral arrangements set up on her long counter, adding flowers to each one. His heart sped up at the mere sight of her and he shook his head. Damn, he had it bad.

He glanced down at the coffees. He figured Toni would need one to get through the day after her all-nighter, and he needed one, as well, since sleep had mostly eluded him the night before. And not because of his disappointment at her needing to leave— although there was no denying his regret at that turn of events. No, it wasn't the fact she'd left that concerned him—it was the *way* she'd left.

The cool, impersonal kiss. The cool, impersonal way she'd looked at him. There had been something in her quick exit that gave him the sinking feeling she wasn't simply running to fix her work problem. It was more like she was running away from him. And his invitation to spend some time together on Christmas Day. That invite had definitely been a mistake as it had clearly freaked her out. He'd practically seen the wall she'd immediately erected between them. Not that she hadn't had one there all along, but at least that barrier had contained a few weak spots, ones he'd held out hope of soon scaling.

She was upset about more than a work emergency. Something she hadn't told him. Something he strongly sensed he wasn't going to like. He'd wanted to ask her last night, but had forced himself to let her go, telling himself they'd have time to discuss it in the morning, after she fixed her work problem.

He'd spent the restless night trying to convince himself he was reading too much into her reaction to his invitation. To her lack of warmth when she left. That she'd been upset and distracted. But no matter how hard he tried to persuade himself, he couldn't untie the knot of apprehension squeezing his insides.

Well, in just a minute he'd find out one way or another whether his gut instincts were right. He just hoped to hell they were wrong.

Brad jogged the last few steps across the street, and holding the cardboard coffee caddy in one hand, tapped on Blooming Pails's glass door. Toni looked up and hesitated. And in that brief hesitation, a feeling of dread suffused him.

She came around the counter slowly, as if reluctant to do so, and approached the entrance. He tried to ignore the fact that she didn't look at him. Not until she'd unlocked the door. "Hi," she said.

He told himself the reason she didn't smile was because she was clearly exhausted. "Good morning," he said. "Merry Christmas Eve. I come bearing gifts." He handed her one of the coffees.

That brought a slight uplifting of one corner of her mouth. "Thanks."

Unable to keep from touching her, he brushed a fingertip over the violet shadows beneath her eyes. "How's it going?"

"If nothing disastrous happens, I'll finish about thirty seconds before the van arrives to pick up the order."

"And you thought you'd be crunched for time."

She gave a weak laugh. "Yeah. Silly me."

"Is Jayne here?"

"She stayed until I left for the flower mart a few hours ago. The poor girl was exhausted."

"You must be, too."

"I am. But I'm not five months pregnant."

A silence that felt distinctly uncomfortable to him swelled between them. Finally, unable to stand it any longer, he said, "Something's wrong."

The fact that she didn't immediately deny it confirmed his worst suspicions. She looked at the floor, then raised her gaze back to his. What he saw in her eyes—or rather what he didn't see there—tightened the knot in his gut. He knew damn well what was coming.

"Brad…I…" She blew out a long breath. "I think you're a great guy and I've enjoyed the time we've spent together, but I can't do it anymore."

His knotted stomach seemed to drop to the floor. "If this is because I asked you to spend Christmas with me—"

"No, it's not that. Not really, although that forcibly reminded me that we want different things. I told you from the start I wasn't looking for a boyfriend, yet that seems to be the direction we were heading."

"And would that really be so terrible?"

"I foolishly allowed myself to think maybe it wouldn't. But yes, it would. At least for now. This fiasco with the order…it was totally my fault because I was focused on *you* rather than on what was important."

Hurt—and dammit, anger—slapped him. "Gee, thanks."

She shook her head. "I'm sorry, that sounded bad."

"I don't think there'd be a way to make it sound good."

She pressed her lips together, then shook her head. "No, I suppose not. The bottom line is that I don't have the time or energy to devote to a relationship now. By doing so, I nearly caused irreparable harm to my business and at this point I can't afford that."

"Everyone makes mistakes, Toni."

"Yes. And my first one was allowing a one-night stand to continue for more than one night."

She couldn't have cut him more effectively if she'd plunged a knife into his chest. But that wound also pushed his anger closer to the surface. Anger at himself for not being able just to walk away. And at her, for not giving them, him, a fair chance.

"You're blaming me for this order screwup?"

"No. I'm blaming myself. For allowing myself to—"

"To what? Feel? Care? Get involved?"

She pressed her lips together then gave a tight nod. "Yes. I don't want…this. Whatever it is that's happened between us."

"Then what, exactly, *do* you want?"

"For my business to succeed. For the bank review to go well. Not to lose everything I've worked so hard for."

"What about other than your business? What do you want for *you?* Your life outside Blooming Pails?"

His question clearly brought her up short. She blinked, hesitated, then frowned, and he wished like hell he knew what she was thinking. Finally, she said, "For right now I don't *have* a life outside Blooming Pails. I failed at my last career and I'll be damned if I'll fail at this one."

"You didn't fail at being a firefighter, Toni. Firefighting failed you."

"Maybe. But I still feel as if I have something to prove. To myself. That I can be successful on my own. And to my family, who, as I told you, in spite of their love for me, on some level wants me to fail here so I'll come home to them and the family business. Which I refuse to do. Which means I can't afford any more mistakes. Or distractions. Which means there can't be any more me and you. It's too much. Too fast. Too soon."

He pulled in a slow breath, then said quietly, "You know, I wasn't looking for this, either. But I'm willing to play the hand I was dealt here. I'm willing to make the time to find a way to make this work."

"Which is where we differ, because for right now, I'm not willing. I just can't."

A muscle ticked in his clenched jaw. "You mean you won't."

"All right, I won't. I have too much at stake, too much riding on the success of my business. The bank review is only three months away. I need to keep my priorities straight. This mess…" she waved her hand to encompass the multitude of arrangements she was working on "…happened because I didn't."

"So you turn off your feelings, just like that," he said, his voice tight. "Or are you prepared to look me in the eyes and tell me you don't have any for me?"

Her already pale face went a shade whiter, and finally something flickered in her eyes. But instead of the warmth and caring he'd hoped to see, it was regret. "I… Of course I *like* you. You're…a great guy."

He stood frozen in place. "But…?"

"But the timing isn't right for me. I'm sorry, but I can't be with you, with anyone, right now."

"Not right now?" His anger and frustration came through in his clipped words. "Then when, Toni? When will it be convenient for you?"

"I—I don't know. I need time—"

"How much time? Two weeks? A month? Three months? After the bank review? Or will you tack on a few more months after that?

Resentment flashed in her eyes. "You're pressuring me."

"Maybe you need to be pressured."

"No, I don't. As for a time frame, I simply don't know. All I do know is that I'm not prepared to continue our…whatever you want to call it now. And naturally I don't expect you to wait around until I figure out when I might be ready."

Anger and hurt warred inside him. The determined look in her eyes made it clear there was no point in arguing further. "So that's it. You don't want us to see each other anymore."

"It's for the best."

A humorless sound escaped him. Best for her, obviously. At least he hadn't admitted the depth of his feelings to her. Hadn't made that big an ass out of himself.

"I…I'm sorry, Brad. I hope you understand."

"Don't worry. You've made yourself perfectly clear." Throat tight, he nodded toward the counter. "Guess you'd better get back to work, and I need to get to the station. Merry Christmas, Toni."

Yeah. Merry damn Christmas.

Without waiting for a reply, he pulled open the door and quickly strode toward his pickup, feeling…gutted. How was it possible to feel so angry and so numb at the same time? And how long would it take to repair a broken heart?

He already knew the answer. It was going to take a damn long time.

ON CHRISTMAS MORNING, Toni woke up in her old room at her parents' house and stared at the skeins of sunlight peeking through the curtains. The muted sounds of breakfast filtered up the stairs, the coffee grinder humming, her mother's and grandmother's voices. Probably they were arguing over whether to brew decaf or regular. Or whether the eggs should be scrambled or fried. She pictured her dad, sitting in his favorite chair, working a crossword puzzle, oblivious to the disagreement taking place no more than ten feet away from him.

With a sigh, she sat up on the edge of the mattress then pushed back the tangle of flattened curls clinging to her face. She didn't need a mirror to know she looked like roadkill. Which was really only fitting as she felt like roadkill. Actually, she felt like the potholed, weather-scarred, oil-stained street underneath the squashed, rotting roadkill.

Setting her elbows on her knees, she rested her dully aching head in her hands and closed her eyes. And found herself fighting to hold back the tears that had threatened to spill over ever since Brad had walked out of Blooming Pails and her life yesterday morning. For there was no doubt he was gone from her life for good. The look on his face when she'd told him she didn't expect him to wait around for her was branded on her brain. That combination of anger and hurt made it clear he had no intention of waiting around. Or of bothering with her again.

Toni tried to summon annoyance at herself for feeling so weepy—it was ridiculous. She was *glad* he was gone. She'd *wanted* him to go. She'd made the right decision. The last thing she needed right now was a distracting man. He'd pressured her with invitations to meet his family and to put an end date on how much time she needed. Her concerns about her business and the potentially damaging mistake she'd made were reasonable and dammit, he'd been unreasonable. And to top it all off, he was a firefighter. Although she honestly hadn't given much thought to his occupation over the last few days.

So, if she'd made the right decision, why did she feel so…wrong? So…numb?

So devastated.

Exhaustion, obviously. Yesterday, after fulfilling Saint Mary's order—with an entire four minutes to spare before the church van arrived—she'd endured a hectic day at the shop. Yet in spite of the busy whirlwind, Brad had never left her thoughts. *So that's it. You don't want us to see each other anymore.* She'd never forget the shattering sense of loss that had hit her when he'd walked away. There could be no doubt he'd cared for her. And had wanted to continue their…whatever it was. Friendship. Relationship. Sexual escapades.

She squeezed her eyes tighter shut. She'd gone to their first "little dinner" anticipating one night of no-strings sex. But somehow, some way, in spite of her not wanting it to, their time together had turned into more than just sex. *Are you prepared to look me in the eyes and tell me you don't have any feelings for me…*

She hadn't been able to. Had admitted she liked him—

A bitter sound that was half laugh, half sob escaped her. *Liked* him? God, she should be handed an Academy Award for delivering that line with a straight face. *Like* was an incredibly tepid word to describe the maelstrom of feelings Brad inspired in her. Feelings that she wanted, needed to forget. Feelings she despaired of being able to forget. If only she'd met him six months, a year from now. Once Blooming Pails was established and her stomach wasn't tied in knots over bank evaluations. Of course, she didn't doubt for an instant that in six months he'd have someone else. Some other extremely lucky woman. A woman Toni already hated. The thought of him touching someone else filled her with a despair she could only describe as agonizing. And the thought of another man touching her simply didn't compute.

The sound of dishes clanging and raised female voices intermixed with Italian words reached her ears and she groaned. How she was going to face another big family dinner today she didn't know. Last night's had just about done her in. In spite of her best efforts to act cheerfully, her mother, sister and Nana Rose all had zeroed in on her misery like wolves around a fresh kill. Her refusal to open her personal life for their examination had only increased their curiosity, which had led to the usual pattern of a bombardment of questions followed by the piling on of guilt— not only for not answering their nosy questions, but also for not getting married and having babies. All that fun was finished off by one of her mother's hysterical outbursts that all this upset— which Toni had naturally caused by not offering up her personal life for the family's consumption along with the Italian seafood feast—had cast a pall on the entire evening.

Yup, just another jolly holiday with the fam.

Normally she could handle it, but right now she just didn't feel capable of doing anything save pulling the covers over her head and praying for this aching sense of loss clawing at her to go away. For the question that kept reverberating through her mind to cease its echoing. The question she was sickly afraid to ask herself.

Had she made a mistake?

Yes, her inner voice instantly answered. *A big, fat whopper of a huge mistake. He's a great guy and you're an idiot for letting him go. So the timing's bad—so what? Deal with it. A guy like Brad comes around once. And you're an idiot.*

"Argh!" Hoping to dislodge that stupid voice, she fisted her hands in her rat's-nest hair and yanked. All she got was more dull throbbing in her head.

Not ready to go downstairs and face whatever drama was occurring there, she decided a shower was her best bet. She rose and was digging through her overnight bag for her shower gel when her cell phone rang, the ring tone indicating the caller was Jayne.

She briefly considered not answering it—Jayne had already given her hell yesterday for cutting Brad loose and she simply wasn't up to another episode of *Are You Crazy?*

But ignoring the call on Christmas was too bah, humbug, so she picked up the phone from the night table.

"Merry Christmas," she said, plopping back onto the edge of the bed. "Was Santa good to you?"

"Toni…have you seen the news?"

Something in Jayne's voice made her tighten her grip on the phone. "No. I just woke up. What's wrong?"

"I just saw it on TV. A fire. Late last night at a warehouse in Ocean Harbor Beach. Two firefighters were injured and taken by ambulance to the hospital."

Toni's heart lurched into her throat. "Brad?" she whispered, her entire body icy with sudden fear. Dear God, no. But she knew perfectly well how dangerous firefighting was. And how that danger could be increased if the mind and body weren't totally focused on the task at hand. Brad had looked tired and had been upset about what had happened between them…had he lost his focus because of that? Had his mind wandered, leaving him vulnerable to mistakes? One that could have led to injury?

"I don't know—their names haven't been released. I thought you'd want to know. Maybe call him."

"Y-yes, of course. I'll do that."

"Call me and let me know if you find out anything."

"I will. You, too."

She snapped the phone shut and pressed her hands against her churning stomach. Dear God. He had to be all right. *Had* to be. Every time a firefighter was called to duty they risked injury and even death. But the rewards…helping people, saving lives, tipped the scales. Made the risks worthwhile. She understood all too well what drove Brad to be a firefighter. But the thought of him injured—or worse—rendered her unable to catch her breath.

She glanced at the clock—10:00 a.m. Brad's shift had ended three hours ago. Murmuring fervent prayers that he was all right, she dialed his home phone which clicked immediately to voice mail. She listened to his recorded message and the sound of his voice brought tears to her eyes. Dear God, what if he *was* one of the injured firefighters? She couldn't bring herself to carry that question any further. After leaving a brief message to please call her right away, she dialed his cell phone. Once again his voice mail came on and again she left a message.

The instant she clicked her phone shut, Toni began tossing her things into her overnight bag. She needed answers. Now. And they weren't here in Santa Barbara.

10

INSISTENT POUNDING and buzzing sounds roused Brad from a deep sleep. With a groan he lifted one heavy eyelid. Bright sunshine filtered through the blinds, slipping over his bed where he sprawled facedown—in the exact position he'd fallen after he'd dragged his exhausted ass home after a long, tension-fraught shift.

He tried to ignore the noise, but it quickly became apparent whoever was banging on his door and leaning on the doorbell wasn't going to give up.

With a muttered curse and a herculean effort he pushed himself up, wincing at the stiffness in his neck. Since he'd only managed to toe off his sneakers before collapsing onto the bed, he was already fully dressed. Good thing, because he wasn't operating on enough cylinders to do anything as complicated as pulling on a pair of jeans.

"All right, all right," he grumbled, making his way to the foyer. "I'm coming." More than a little annoyed, he yanked open the door. "What do you…" His voice trailed off at the sight of Toni. Toni, who sported a wicked case of bedhead, no makeup and tear-streaked cheeks.

Damn, but she was gorgeous.

She stepped into the foyer, teasing his senses with the scent of flowers that always came with her. He closed the door and turned to face her. One look at her and all the anger he'd felt the day before faded away. He wasn't sure why she was here, but whatever the reason, he was damn glad for it. Her gaze zoomed over him, then her bottom lip trembled and two fat tears dripped from her huge eyes. "You're okay," she said in a shaky voice.

"I'm glad you think so. I think you're okay, too. Better than okay actually, but—"

"I mean, you're not hurt. You weren't injured in the fire last night."

Understanding dawned. "No. It was two other guys. But they're both fine—treated and released."

She briefly closed her eyes. "Thank God. I called the hospital but they wouldn't tell me anything, so I came here. I can't tell you how relieved I was to see your pickup in the driveway." She pulled in an unsteady breath. "When I heard about the injured firefighters I thought…" She swallowed and another pair of tears dribbled downward. "I had a terrible feeling it was you. I was so afraid."

"I'm fine. But I appreciate the concern." The fact that she was here, had been worried about him, ignited hope that only hours ago had been dead. Reaching out, he brushed his fingers over her wet cheeks, a gesture that only served to bring on a fresh onslaught of tears. "Hey," he said, feeling masculine panic edging in. "No crying. Seriously. House rules."

A sob escaped her, followed by another. "Ah, hell, Toni, don't do that." But clearly it was too late because in a heartbeat she was crying in earnest. An anguished sound escaped her and she erased the distance between them. Her arms went around his waist and she buried her head against his chest and cried as if her heart were breaking.

Feeling utterly helpless, but glad for any excuse to hold her, he drew her tighter into his embrace and gently rubbed her back.

"Shh," he murmured against her wildly messed hair. "I'm fine. Completely fine. All in one piece." Several minutes passed, then, unable to take it anymore, he cupped her face in his hands and leaned back. "Toni, sweetheart, *please* stop crying. You're killing me."

She looked up him with those big wet brown eyes, and whatever tiny piece of his heart she hadn't already owned was instantly deeded to her.

She gave a big sniffle then said, "I'm an idiot."

He couldn't stop the quick laugh that escaped him. "You are not."

"I am. I pushed you away and that makes me an idiot. A *miserable* idiot. I didn't know it was possible to hurt so much until you walked away yesterday morning. And then again this morning—when I thought you were hurt. That's when I realized it."

"Realized what?"

"That I'm an idiot." She framed his face between her palms. "I'm sorry. So sorry. I *do* care about you. So much it scares me. In the interest of full disclosure, I need to tell you I've never felt this way about anyone. Ever."

Brad closed his eyes for several seconds, letting the relief rushing through him wash away the pain and hurt that had been crushing his chest. "In the interest of full disclosure, I can only say I'm really glad and relieved that it's not just me."

She rested one hand on his chest, right over the spot where his heart thudded hard and fast. "When I made the mistake with the order…I felt everything I'd been fighting for and working so hard for slipping away and I panicked. I believed the only solution was to push you away. So I did. And nothing, ever, made me more unhappy."

He brushed his thumbs over her wet cheeks then leaned down and kissed her very gently. "I'm glad."

"That I was unhappy?"

"Yes. Because if you'd been happy, then you wouldn't be here right now."

She considered, then nodded. "True. In that case I'll forgive you for being glad I was sad."

His lips twitched. "Thank you." Then Brad sobered. "I owe you an apology, too. I know I was rushing things, pushing you, and I'm sorry. I tried not to, but Toni…everything with you just felt so…*right*. But I can back off. We'll take things as slowly as you want. And you can have as much time as you need. You're worth the wait."

She laid her hand against his cheek. "Thank you. But I've realized I don't want or need time. Yesterday, when you asked me what I wanted for my life outside Blooming Pails—the question startled me. Made me realize I hadn't allowed myself to think about anything other than my business. So I took some time and thought about it. And I realized I want companionship. With someone honest and kind. I want someone to share my life and hopes and dreams with. Someone to laugh with. Someone who makes me feel needed. Wanted. Who I need and want." She stroked her fingers over his stubbled jaw. "Turns out that except for the firefighter thing, *you* are exactly what I want. And it turns out, I can live with the firefighter thing."

Heat, and something else, something deeper, glowed in his eyes. "You have no idea how glad I am to hear that."

"And I want you to know that I would have come to my senses eventually—like by the end of the day. I was halfway there already. But when I heard about the injured firefighters, it made me realize right then and there that I'd been—"

"An idiot?"

"Yes." She narrowed her eyes. "Are you going to rub my nose in that?"

He smiled at her disgruntled expression. "Nah. I'm just glad you figured it out sooner rather than later." He leaned in for another kiss, one he meant to be light, but that quickly turned into a passionate, tongue-dancing exchange. When he lifted his head, they were both breathing hard.

"Brad…what would you say if I asked if it's possible to fall in love in a week?"

Happiness filled all the spaces inside him that only yesterday had been rendered numb. "I'd say that since you're asking a guy who fell in love three months ago in the span of about one minute, yeah, a week is definitely possible."

Her gaze searched his. "If the invitation is still open, I'd like to join you and your family for Christmas dinner."

His heart performed a somersault-like maneuver. "The invitation is still open," he assured her. "But they're going to think you're my girlfriend."

"Which is better than what you'd get from my family. You'd be interrogated by my mother, sister and Nana like a murder suspect, and be on the receiving end of multiple death stares from my brothers."

"No problem. I don't scare easily."

"So I've noticed. Just one of the things I love about you." She smiled. "One of the *many* things. And about your family thinking I'm your girlfriend…I'd like to be. If you'll have me, in spite of the crazy hours I'll need to put in at Blooming Pails until who-knows-when."

"If I'll have you? *If I'll have you?*" He picked her up and twirled her around until she squealed. After setting her back on her feet, he grabbed her hand and led her into the kitchen. "If I'll have you?" he repeated, shaking his head. "Crazy woman." He opened the drawer where he kept his receipts and sifted through several pieces of paper before finding what he wanted.

"Take a look at this, Miss If-You'll-Have-Me."

"What is it?"

"Something I wrote after our first 'one little dinner.' I'd mentioned my Christmas list, so the next day, I actually wrote one." He handed her the paper.

"'My Grown-up Christmas List,'" she read. Then her eyes widened. "The only thing on this list is my name."

"Twenty times," he agreed. "'Cause all I wanted for Christmas was you."

A smile bloomed across her face. "Be careful what you wish for, Mr. December. Looks like you're getting it."

"That's because I'm on Santa's nice list." He swung her up into his arms and headed toward his bedroom. "But what would you say if I told you I'm also on his naughty list?"

She smiled into his eyes. "I'd say I'm a very, very lucky girl."

* * * * *

UP ON THE HOUSETOP
Jamie Sobrato

To Mom

Prologue

A village near Mombasa, Kenya

THE FIRE glowed brightly in the darkness, crackling and filling the air with the scent of burning wood. Lorelei could have become mesmerized by it so easily, the same way she might have been entranced by a television screen back in the U.S. at night after a long day of work.

But tonight, it only warmed her. The storytellers had long since finished spinning their tales, the drummers had retired to their cots and the last vestiges of the evening's gathering had trickled away.

Next to her, a gnarled old man who had most unexpectedly become one of her closest friends in the past few years was looking at her as if he could see her soul. She squirmed uncomfortably, because, she feared, he really could.

"You must go home now," Kinsei said in his heavily accented English.

They had been trading her English language instruction for his knowledge of herbal medicine ever since Lorelei had first come to Kenya. It had started as her way of smoothing out the relationship between her, the local Peace Corps doctor, and him, the local medicine man.

"I'm not sure I'm ready to go back to the U.S."

"Not America. I mean, you must go to your *home*. Where your family is. The place of your coming into this world."

A wave of nausea nearly overcame Lorelei, not just at the thought of going back to her hometown, but because Kinsei was eerily, against all her scientific logic, always right. The few times she'd dared to contradict his advice, disaster had struck.

"You have been feeling restless, have you not?"

She nodded slowly.

"And you have unsettled business in the place where you be-came a woman."

Oh, dear. Her mouth went dry. She looked at the fire, and then quickly back at Kinsei again, because he knew that when she couldn't look at him, he'd struck the most tender of nerves.

"The place has made you so unhappy in the past, that you go all the way to the other side of Mother Earth to escape it, but you cannot escape what dwells in your heart."

"Is this your way of getting rid of the annoying white doctor?"

Kinsei laughed hard. He always said there was no other way to laugh.

"No, no, my dear. You are ready to go. This is why I say so."

"I'm afraid."

"You have so much pain in your heart, you need to conquer it."

"I don't know how."

"Think of someone who hurt you the most. Who is it?"

Without thinking, Lorelei blurted the name *Ryan Quinn*. God, she didn't even think of him very often anymore, but when she did, she still felt as if she wanted to vomit. All her teenage angst, summed up in one name….

Her first love, her first lover, her first heartbreak.

"You must go back to him and find a way to have power over your pain."

"I don't understand."

"If he killed your family's goat, then you take the goat of his family. You see? It is the way to achieve balance, and happiness comes after balance."

"So if he broke my heart, I have to break his?"

"I never thought you such a violent woman."

Lorelei laughed now, realizing how her meaning had gotten lost in translation. "No, in English, to break someone's heart means to hurt the person you love very badly."

"Ah, I see. You must not be vengeful. But this man who set fire to your heart, you must take back from him the power he took from you. He took your virginity, you take it back."

She had stopped wondering how he knew details of her life that she hadn't told anyone. He just did.

"How, exactly, might I do that?"

"You must have sexual passion with him, and then walk away. In this act, you will be taking back your sexual power."

Lorelei's insides rebelled at the idea.

"And don't let your silly Western ideas get in the way of this wisdom. It is the correct thing to do."

There wasn't a relationship therapist on earth who would have agreed with Kinsei, but he had never steered Lorelei wrong. She bit her lip and let the fire mesmerize her now.

Take back her sexual power? Go home again? Leave this place she'd come to love?

She'd have to sleep on it.

1

Ocean Harbor Beach, California
Six months later…

DR. LORELEI GIBSON didn't recognize the hot guy sitting on her examining table at first. She was preoccupied and exhausted. The pace of the Ocean Harbor Beach Hospital E.R. was still a drastic change from her last job, and she'd already been on her shift for eleven hours when she walked into room 8 and looked at the clipboard.

"Hello, Mr…Quincy. Let's see what's going on here."

"It's Quinn, not Quincy, and I just got hit in the head by some falling floorboards—that's all," he said in the usual manner of manly men who didn't like to admit they were hurt.

Quinn, not Quincy, she noted on the chart, scratching out the mistake someone in admitting had made. Quinn-not-Quincy wore a pair of firefighter's pants and boots and a white T-shirt. When her gaze lingered for a few moments on his face though, she choked back a little gasp of surprise.

Ryan Quinn.

She thought of Kenya, and Kinsei and his advice to her before she'd left Africa. She'd tried to dismiss his words, but she couldn't. Not completely. He was part of the reason she was here in Ocean Harbor Beach, trying to make peace with her past.

And now here he was, this piece of her past, sitting on her examining table, as if Kinsei himself had delivered him up for her.

He looked a little different than he had fifteen years ago, when they'd been in high school together—older, more mature, more weathered by life, but still gorgeous, even more so than in his younger years.

This was the problem with coming back to her hometown after so many years away—it was like walking through a graveyard, with ghosts hopping up to scare her at every turn. Although they were ghosts she'd come to face, their appearance didn't scare her any less.

She didn't have many—any?—pleasant memories from her adolescent years. She'd been an awkward, nerdy, socially inept, chronically weird kid, too brainy for her own good and too young, from having been moved ahead two grades, to grasp the intricacies of adolescent social life.

And she'd had a raging, painful, endless crush on Ryan Quinn.

In spite of the significant role he played in her memories, she knew it was entirely possible he wouldn't remember her at all. They'd slept together exactly once and while for her it had been a momentous event—her first time—for him, it had just been a meaningless teenage conquest, probably one among many.

She swallowed the bile rising up in her throat and forced herself to focus on the present.

"Looks like your CT scan came out with no abnormalities," she said as she finished reading over his chart.

Lorelei approached him, set aside the clipboard, and took out her light. She shone it in his eyes and watched his pupils contract normally, then instructed him to follow the light with his gaze as she moved it left, right, up and down.

"Have you felt dizzy at all? Nauseous?"

"Nope. I blacked out right after getting hit in the head, but only for a few minutes."

She noted her observations on the chart.

"You look familiar," he said, frowning at her name tag, and her throat constricted. "Lorelei Gibson… Did we go to school together maybe?"

She was sixteen again for a moment, wondering why the love of her young life was pretending she didn't exist the day after they'd made love. But she pushed aside the feelings of angst and inadequacy and reminded herself that she was now a grown woman who'd traveled around the world, served in the Peace Corps and finished medical school at the top of her class. Those old rules about who was cool and who wasn't didn't apply anymore, and those old rejections should not matter at all.

"Perhaps," she said, sounding more casual than she felt. "I did grow up here, but I left after high school."

Recognition dawned on his face, and she felt herself shrinking inwardly. "Rat Girl!"

Lorelei winced at the cruel nickname she'd been branded with in freshman year after volunteering to loan her two pet rats to their biology class to act as class pets for the year. Her intelligence, and her uncool interest in all things creepy and crawly, had made her stand out from her peers right away, and they'd awarded her a lovely moniker to match her pets.

When he caught her expression, he realized his mistake. "Oh, God, I'm sorry. You must have hated being called that…Lorelei. We were lab partners one year, right?"

If she hadn't been blushing before, she definitely was now. Because soon, he was going to remember the disastrous end of their senior-year lab partnership.

When she'd mistaken his kindness for attraction, she'd finally worked up the courage to blatantly flirt with him. And one day while they'd been gathering sulfur water at the local hot springs for their project, she'd kissed him right on the mouth in the middle of a discussion about the effects of sulfur on invertebrates.

And then, right there in the hot springs, the kiss had turned into an embrace, which had turned into heavy groping, which had turned into them taking off their clothes for a dip in the springs, which had turned into them making love in the pool of steaming water.

To Lorelei, that one evening had been complete bliss. And the next day at school—utter hell. He'd never looked at her, never talked to her, never offered any further help on their lab project. He'd simply pretended she didn't exist for the rest of their senior year.

Lorelei had been heartbroken.

She pushed away the horrible memories and tried to move on. They weren't here for a high-school reunion. "So," she said, pretending she'd been reading important things on his chart. "You blacked out after getting hit on the head?"

He nodded, but he was still looking at her as though he was trying to remember something. "That's what I just said."

"For a couple of minutes?"

But she could tell by his expression now that he was remembering the hot springs. "You and I, senior year, we…"

Oh, God.

But why was she so scared? She wasn't that inexperienced girl anymore.

"We what?" she said flatly.

"We, um, did that sulfur project together, didn't we?" he said, obviously uncomfortable with her intense stare.

She frowned as if she was having trouble recalling. "Did we? Wow, you've got a better memory than I do," she lied.

He looked at her a little oddly. "Yeah, we did."

"I'm sorry to hurry this along, but we're pretty backed up today. Do you happen to know exactly how long you were blacked out?"

"Oh, right, sorry. Maybe a couple of minutes?"

"Okay, good. It looks like you're fine. If you start feeling dizzy, nauseous, have any trouble with your vision, or generally just feel like something isn't quite right, please come back in right away."

He nodded. "Okay."

"Take it easy for a day—no running marathons for at least twenty-four hours."

"Am I cleared to go back to work?"

"Yes, so long as you're not doing any heavy lifting for a day. You can take over-the-counter pain medication if you're feeling any discomfort from the bump on your head."

She edged toward the door.

"Okay, thanks. Hey, it was good to see you again. Welcome back to Ocean Harbor Beach."

Lorelei smiled as best she could. "It's good to be back," she said as she hurried out the door, feeling as if she were fleeing the scene of a crime.

In the hallway, Maria Valdez, one of the day-shift nurses, was passing by. She stopped in her tracks. "Are you okay?" she asked.

Lorelei blinked dumbly at the question, not sure how to answer. "Not really," she said. "I'll be in the break room for a few minutes."

She headed down the hallway, her heart thudding wildly in her chest, feeling for all the world as though she was in high school again.

2

"REMEMBER that girl Lorelei Gibson from high school?"

Ryan's coworker, Kyle Witcomb, who'd been sitting in the E.R. waiting for him, blinked uncomprehending. "Um, no. Are you going to live, or what?"

"Sure, just got a bump on the head is all. I told you guys I didn't need to come to the E.R."

"Yeah, well, you were slurring your words and talking non-sense at the time."

"And, now I'm fine, so let's get out of here," Ryan said, then headed toward the E.R. entrance.

No matter how long he'd worked as a firefighter, he never got comfortable with the sight of people sick or in pain. It always made him feel that he should be doing something to help, and if he couldn't, it drove him crazy.

Once they were outside in the cool, sunny December day, free of the sights and smells of tragedy, he let out a sigh of relief. His thoughts went immediately back to Lorelei.

"That girl from school I mentioned—I know you'll remember her. She was in our biology class, and she had those pet rats—"

"Rat Girl?" Kyle said, frowning. "That weird science-geek chick who always wore hats to school?"

Ryan winced at the nickname. He still felt like a jerk for blurting it out to her in the examining room. But he had much bigger things to be ashamed of. After they'd had sex, he'd spent the rest of the year pretending she didn't exist, unwilling as he'd been to admit he was attracted to her.

"Yes," he said, his tone a little testy. "That's her. She was my doctor today."

"No kidding? I've never seen her around here."

"She said she just moved back into town. I gotta tell you, she doesn't look so weird anymore. She was pretty damn hot."

"No way. I remember one time, she came to school smelling horrible, like she hadn't bathed in weeks, with blood all over her clothes. When our homeroom teacher demanded to know what had happened, she said she'd found a dead dog on the side of the road and carried it around looking for its owners."

Ryan said nothing. His thoughts went back to adolescence, when he hadn't had the balls to publicly lust after a girl like Lorelei. All the kids in school had known she was brilliant, but that had only made her stand out even more as an oddball. It hadn't helped that she'd been so much younger than the other kids in their graduating class.

He hated that he'd been one of the jerks who'd made her feel like an outcast. Sure, he'd been thrilled when they were assigned as lab partners senior year, but only because he knew it guaranteed him an A. The fact that she'd apparently developed a crush on him and thought he'd be interested in being more than lab partners had been lost on his eighteen-year-old self—that is, until she'd thrown herself at him the last night they'd worked together and he'd callously accepted her offer of sex without considering at all what it might mean to her.

He'd only let himself consider later that her complete awkwardness as they'd fumbled with each other's bodies, and the pain he'd caused when he entered her, might have meant that she'd been a virgin. Which had only made him retreat even more from facing her, because it meant he was an even bigger jerk than he'd wanted to admit.

He'd been immature back then, and only officially interested in girls with shiny hair and hot bodies. He'd never even told any of his friends that he'd slept with Lorelei.

Ryan wished he could make it up to her for the following days and weeks after they'd had sex, when he wouldn't talk to her or even look her in the eye.

She must have absolutely hated him.

She had every right to.

"What's the matter with you?" Kyle said.

"Oh, nothing," Ryan lied. "I was just thinking about how being a doctor's a lot like being a firefighter—saving lives, working under pressure, making a difference for people—"

"Dude, you and your bleeding heart might want to go on home now and take a rest. Maybe curl up with your favorite teddy bear and watch a chick flick."

Ryan gave Kyle a friendly shove. "Screw you."

"The chief said you should go home for the day. I'll drive you back to your place if you want."

"I should go get my car from the station."

"You sure you're clear to drive?"

"She didn't say I couldn't."

They both climbed into Kyle's truck and started off toward the fire station.

"You going anywhere for the holidays?" Kyle asked.

"Nope. I'll be working. My parents are at my aunt's in Arizona, so there won't be a family get-together."

"Hey, I'd have you join me, but I've got vacation time and I'm heading south to visit family."

"That's all right," Ryan mumbled, distracted as he stared out the window.

His head still ached from getting bonked, and Christmas was the last thing on his mind right now. He couldn't stop thinking about Lorelei. Did it make him a shallow jerk that now that she was hot, he felt bad for having been an ass to her?

Yeah, it pretty much did. He cringed at himself. Except, well, she'd probably always been this hot. It had just taken him growing up and seeing her through mature eyes to understand it.

It wasn't just that she was pretty in a more conventional way now. He hadn't really thought much about her in all these years, but what he did remember about her was all good. She'd been so smart and quirky back then, he hadn't had the good taste to recognize what a cool person she was. But now he knew better…

And yeah, okay, she was hot.

That didn't hurt.

He had to do something to say he was sorry for his asshole behavior all those years ago. He owed her big-time. Maybe take her to lunch, or bring her some flowers or…

Or what? He didn't even know if she was married, or had a boyfriend or if she still even liked guys.

Well, hmm, he was almost positive he hadn't seen a ring on her finger. He had a second-nature habit of scanning women for one. But maybe what he owed her most was to leave her alone.

Still…

At the very least, he needed to apologize to her. But would that just remind her of something she'd rather not think about? Would she even remember now what a jerk he'd been? Was he just crediting himself with too much significance in her life?

No, he needed to just leave her alone. If their paths ever crossed again, he'd take that as a sign and find a proper way to apologize, but until then, there wasn't really anything to be done.

The moment he thought it though, he found himself wishing "until then" would happen right away. Like today, or tomorrow, or…no later than the day after that.

3

LORELEI could feel the heat from the fire, but she didn't smell smoke. The foot of her bed was on fire, flames licking the air and singeing the heirloom quilt her grandmother had made. She tried to pull the quilt away from the fire, but it was too late. Ruined.

Only when she saw that she couldn't save the quilt did she think of saving herself. Terror seized her as she scrambled off the side of the bed. The flames were spreading across the floor now, engulfing the entire bed and half the room—blocking her way to the door.

She tried to cry out, but no sound came from her throat. And then, as if she'd been heard anyway, someone burst in the door.

Across the flames, she saw Ryan Quinn. He aimed his hose at the bed and fired a blast of water that instantly put out all the flames.

With the fire extinguished, she could see that he wasn't wearing a shirt, only his fireman's pants and boots, and a red hat that looked oddly like the flimsy plastic kind she saw kids wearing when they played fireman. His chest was all sculpted muscle and smooth tanned skin. God, he was gorgeous.

Was that just a costume he was wearing?

"You got here fast," she said.

He tossed aside the fire hose and crossed the room, then took her into his arms Rhett Butler–style.

"I thought you'd never call," he said in a breathless voice.

Then they were both on the bed, naked, kissing and caressing in such a frenzy that Lorelei couldn't tell where she stopped and Ryan began. She was sixteen again, acting out her wildest adolescent fantasies. In fact, when she looked down at herself, she saw that she wasn't entirely naked. She was wearing nothing but a pair of pink striped knee socks she hadn't worn since high school.

Weird.

But then, the sensation of Ryan's mouth on her neck erased all thoughts, and she could feel a relentless need building within her, a sweet, delicious ache that demanded he be inside her.

She grasped his hips and pulled him hard against her, spreading her legs wide and as he found her wet, hot center with his erection. She moaned, arched her back, and begged him, "Please, I need you now."

And then he was there, right where she needed him. Inside her, filling her up, creating an even more delicious ache that was building fast, fast, so fast.

He moved inside her, and then her inner muscles were contracting around him, and she was gasping, crying out, as her body was overcome by climax.

But then he started moving inside her so fast and hard, it was making the house shake. The headboard banged against the wall so loudly, she was sure the neighbors a house away could hear.

Or maybe it was a hammer. Or a car driving into the side of the house…

Lorelei's eyes shot open. She stared into the darkness of her bedroom, her brain catching up with reality.

Her body was tingling, as if she'd just had an orgasm. Her heart was pounding.

She *had* just had an orgasm.

But…

She was here alone. She'd been dreaming. There'd been no fire. There'd been no Ryan Quinn bursting into her room with his fire hose to rescue her.

His *fire hose?*

Could her brain's pathetic symbolism get any more obvious?

She groaned and sat up in bed, bewildered by the banging sound on the roof that had invaded her dream. Her highly erotic dream…*that had just given her an orgasm.*

Jeez. She needed to get laid.

This wasn't the first time she'd woken up with the certainty that she'd just come in her sleep—it had happened a few times before, always after a long stretch during which she was getting zero action in bed.

She sighed and squinted at the ceiling, her brain trying to process what the noise was.

She wasn't in Kenya anymore. She was in her old family home, in bed, in Ocean Harbor Beach, California, and…

The roof of the house was about to fly off. Or at least, that's what it sounded like. Then she remembered that the weather forecast had called for rain with wind gusts of up to seventy-five miles per hour tonight, and, judging by the noise outside, the weatherman had been pretty accurate. Lorelei had a feeling she wasn't going to get much more sleep unless she did something about the loud banging sound coming from the roof.

After a twelve-hour shift at the hospital that had turned into a fourteen-hour one, she really, really could have used a good night's rest. But the noise was only getting louder. She flung her covers off and got up, grabbed her robe and went to check the fire in the wood-burning stove.

Her family beach cottage had seen better days. Her grandmother had passed it on to her mother, but now that her mom was living in a condo in a seniors' community, she had no interest in the upkeep that went into taking care of the cottage.

And her lack of interest showed in a big way. After sitting empty for the past three years, being battered by the constant wind from the Pacific and occasional arctic storms that blew in off the ocean, the cottage was in terrible disrepair. Lorelei had been thrilled when her mother offered to let her have the place—it had seemed like serendipity, after she'd made the decision to come home—but she'd had no idea how far in over her head she was getting.

With the house—and the emotions involved in coming back to Ocean Harbor Beach. She didn't have many friends here to come back to. Those few she'd kept from high school had scattered to other parts of the world thanks to careers and marriages. And those who remained—like Ryan Quinn—were ghosts she wasn't sure she wanted to confront.

Except, Kinsei insisted she had to.

Kinsei was a crazy old man who had three wives, a terrible pipe-smoking habit and wore a loincloth. Why, exactly, did she feel the need to take relationship advice from him?

Because she knew she really did want to move on from the pain of her past. She wanted to let go of her childhood angst and make a life for herself here in her hometown. She didn't want to run away from her dreams anymore. So here she was, attempting to live out the dream she'd always held dearest, of working happily as a doctor in her hometown, and she was having to confront her dreaded past in order to do it.

And what she needed to confront right now was that her house was falling down.

Now that the first big winter storm of the season was closing in on the coast, Lorelei had a feeling she was going to see just how bad the cottage's condition truly was.

She kept telling herself that after two years in the Peace Corps, she could accomplish anything, but so far, she'd proven to be pretty inept at home improvement. She'd thought that the resourcefulness she'd learned in Kenya would serve her well in tackling the renovation project, but, it turned out, she was better at adapting to life as a doctor in a third-world culture than she was at stripping floors or repairing leaky roofs.

And speaking of leaky roofs...

That banging sound coming from the ceiling in the living room was situated over a spot where she could see water dripping onto the floor. She walked across the room and peered up at the leak.

"Dammit," she muttered, her mind producing images of costly structural damage done by long-term exposure to rain.

She needed to do something. She'd hoped the storm would hold off until morning when she'd have more energy to get on the roof and nail down a protective tarp, but she'd been kidding herself. The rain was probably only going to get worse as the night wore on.

She found a bucket under the kitchen sink and placed it where the water was dripping. Then she slipped her feet into a pair of gardening clogs and went outside to look at the roof. Fat raindrops pelted her skin, and an icy wind penetrated her robe and chilled her to the bone instantly. She tugged the fabric tighter around herself and walked to the side of the house.

There she found the source of the noise. As she'd suspected an area of the roof had taken the brunt of the coastal winds for years, so that now some of the shingles were missing, while a piece of the roof itself flapped in the wind like a bad toupee, lifting up and slamming back down with each wind gust.

She had to do something about it. If she waited all night, that whole section of the roof might be gone in the morning.

Flush with a sense of self-reliance, she ran to the gardening shed in the backyard and tugged out the ladder, then dragged it across the yard and laid it on the ground next to the house. After that, she went back inside, took off the housecoat and found a hooded sweatshirt that would serve her better for climbing onto the roof. After two years in Africa, she no longer owned any rain gear, and she made a mental note to buy an all-weather kind of coat soon.

She tugged the sweatshirt on over her pj's—a pink flannel top and pants covered in big red polka dots—then put on her running shoes, which would be better than the clogs for climbing.

She had a large blue tarp next to the door, the very same one she'd been telling herself for the past week that she needed to nail over the problem spot in the roof until serious repairs could be done, and next to it, a nail gun she was a little bit afraid of but that had so far proven less injurious to her than the old hammer-and-nails method.

Okay, what else would she need up there?

A loud crashing sound came from the roof again, and she winced.

Her cell phone…in case she needed to call anyone for help.

Not that she'd need help. But there was a storm outside, and, well, she'd never been up on the roof of a house before. She wasn't quite sure what to expect. It was going to be a piece of cake, she told herself. No problem at all. She'd just get up there, nail down the tarp and get back down. It would take ten minutes max.

She could do it.

Yep, no problem at all.

She grabbed her cell phone off the table by the door and put it inside the pocket in the front of her sweatshirt, wrapped the nail gun up in the tarp, then tucked the bundle under one arm. Finally, she marched outside into the rain, feeling as resourceful and self-reliant as a pioneer woman.

Once she had fought the wind to get the ladder balanced against the side of the house, she was feeling slightly less confident, but when her weight was on the ladder, there'd be no problem at all…she hoped.

For once in her life she found herself wishing she had a nice strong man in her life to hold the ladder—or maybe even go up on the roof while she held the ladder—but she banished that thought before it could take root.

Men, even the biggest, strongest ones, were intimidated by her. They usually didn't want their women to be smarter and more successful than them. And those who weren't intimidated usually just couldn't understand her at all. She marched to the beat of her own drummer, and while as a kid that had been the source of most of her misery, as an adult, it gave her joy to be herself. Unlike in her adolescent years, now she didn't give a damn if men were turned off by her funky fashion sense, her outspokenness or her sometimes-odd interests.

Except, well…maybe she should give a damn, considering how hard up she was, to be having orgasm-inducing dreams all by herself in bed.

Not wanting to dwell on thoughts of the man who'd inspired the dreams, Lorelei stared up at the top of the ladder, rain pelting her face, and tested its footing by placing her weight on the first rung. She shivered at the icy wind that penetrated her pj bottoms. The bundled tarp tucked under one arm, she quickly climbed the ladder before she could lose her nerve.

At the top, she carefully placed the tarp on the roof, then eased herself up beside it.

Okay, now what? She'd never been on a rooftop before, let alone in a storm. By now she was half soaked by the driving rain, and the wind felt strong up here. She carefully started unrolling the tarp as best she could over the problem spot.

As soon as she had one corner of it free, she took out the nail gun and drove several nails into the corner. Then she rolled the tarp out farther, using her knees to keep it down in the wind, and crawled across it to nail the next corner down. This one needed to hang over the edge of the roof, and getting so close to the edge made her a little queasy. But she managed it.

Feeling more confident, she made quick work of the third corner, then crawled across toward the fourth corner. A wind gust blew the tarp up into her face before she made it there, a gust so hard she had to duck down and press herself to the roof to keep her balance. She muttered a string of curses and edged herself toward the corner of the tarp again, quickly nailing it down with three nails as she used her knees to hold the corner in place.

Finished, thank God. But when she tried to crawl back toward the ladder she couldn't move. Her leg was stuck. She looked down at the spot her leg refused to move from and saw that she'd managed to nail one leg of her pj bottoms to the roof along with the tarp.

Of all the stupid things she'd ever done…

She muttered a string of curses.

Think. What to do? She tugged at her pant leg again, figuring if nothing else she could rip them off, but the roof was slanted, and if she tugged hard she was likely to fall right off.

Okay, so, she'd just have to slip the pj bottoms off and leave them up here. The world wouldn't end if she crawled back down the ladder in her underwear. Shivering and soaked, and trapped in a kneeling position by her inept nail-gun work, she dropped the gun, untied her shoes and kicked them off, then shimmied out of the pj bottoms.

There, that wasn't so hard. In the morning her pj's would be stuck up here for all to see like a surrender flag made by Victoria's Secret, but that was better than her being stuck up here with them.

When she was done, she hurriedly put her shoes back on and crawled to the edge of the roof where the ladder was… No, make that, where the ladder had been. The same wind gust that had nearly blown her off the roof, had apparently blown the ladder over, and it now lay in the grass, utterly useless to her.

Another string of curses escaped her lips.

Now what?

She didn't know anyone well enough in town anymore to call them after midnight to come help her out of this ridiculous bind. Growing colder and wetter by the second, she began to see what she was going to have to do.

Call 9-1-1.

As soon as she thought it, she also realized that would mean the fire department would probably come. And, that meant there was a small but real chance it would be Ryan Quinn who'd have to come up here and rescue her in her underwear.

4

RYAN STEPPED off the truck and braced himself against the driving rain and wind that lashed him. As he strode across the lawn lit by the engine's flashing red lights, he turned on the flashlight in his hand and shone it ahead so that he could see where he stepped. Behind him, the removable ladder was being brought down from the truck by his buddy Kyle.

It had been a week since Ryan had seen Lorelei in the E.R., but he hadn't stopped thinking about her. She popped into his thoughts at odd times of day and night, like right now, as he strode across the yard of a house where it had been reported a woman was stuck on the roof.

Stuck on the roof? This stormy night, of all nights? Well, it wouldn't be the oddest thing he'd ever seen on duty.

This place, he recalled, was where Lorelei had lived when they were teenagers. He'd come here a handful of times to work on their science project, but he wondered who owned the place now. He didn't come to this neighborhood often. His own house was little more than a surf shack, a place down the coast he'd been renting for a few years near the best surf break in the area.

Whoever lived here hadn't taken very good care of it. Last time he'd seen a place in such bad shape, he'd found a meth lab inside. He braced himself for having to deal with some meth head on a rampage, stuck on the roof after trying to fix the TV antenna or something equally dumb.

On the other side of the house, he found a ladder lying across the grass, which probably explained the person trapped on the roof.

Kyle positioned the ladder for Ryan and braced it, then Ryan began to climb up. A minute later, he was peering over the edge of the slanted roof.

The first thing he saw was a pair of bare legs, bent in a squatting position. His gaze followed the legs upward to the rest of the woman, whose face was familiar to him.

Lorelei.

Sweet heaven.

Lorelei, looking wet and cold, but not hurt. He tried not to grin. She had an expression on her face somewhere between anger and self-deprecation, as if she knew how ridiculous she looked but couldn't quite bring herself to laugh about it.

"Lorelei," he said. "Hi. Are you hurt at all?"

"No, just wet."

"Let's get you down from here. Just take my hand," he said, reaching out.

She looked at his outstretched hand, then back up at him. "I don't have any pants," she said, her teeth chattering between the words.

"Dare I ask why?"

"I…nailed them to the roof by accident." She tried to say it with a straight face, but laughter bubbled up from her throat, and Ryan couldn't help laughing, too.

"That must be the polka-dot surrender flag over there flapping in the wind," he said, nodding to the bit of pink fabric ten feet away.

"Yeah."

"Take my raincoat," he said, unbuttoning it as he spoke. Before she could protest, he shrugged it off and handed it to her.

She put it on, and sure enough, it was long enough to cover her to midthigh. "Thanks," she said, still shivering as she eased herself across the roof and turned so that she could go down the ladder.

He placed a steadying hand on her back, but his gaze was fixed on her bare legs, thin and shapely. He got a flash of heat in his groin as he imagined her thighs spreading for him, imagined those legs wrapped around his hips.…

Whoa, there. Time to remember his purpose, which was to help her off the roof, and then maybe, if he dared, apologize to her for his asshole behavior in high school.

They made quick work of the ladder, and at the bottom, Ryan picked up a blanket that someone had brought and left on the ground, and wrapped it around Lorelei.

"All's well," he said to Kyle. "I'll help her back to the house while you get the ladder."

"Sure thing, man."

Ryan followed Lorelei around the side of the house to the back door. Once she was inside, she turned to face him, took off the blanket, and unceremoniously removed her jacket. He took them when she held the stuff out, and then his mouth went dry as he took in the sight of her stripping off her sweatshirt and grabbing a towel to dry off.

He watched as she toweled off, transfixed at the way her panties pressed against the flesh at the apex of her thighs and her nipples showed through the thin fabric of her wet pajama top. And before he lost all good sense, he shrugged on his raincoat again in the hope of hiding his growing erection.

She had a woman's body now, with heavy breasts and a narrow waist, smooth skin and a shapely ass. She looked glorious there in her tiny white panties and pajama top, wet hair clinging to her cheeks and shoulders—not like any teenage fantasy he'd ever had, but like a totally grown-up one.

He would have loved to reach out and touch any part of her—hell, every part of her—to confirm that she was not a figment of his imagination. Then he'd pull her close and warm her against his naked body—

"Thanks," she said. "You can go now."

Right. Of course he could.

"I hope you'll, um, wait until after the storm to do any further nailing of clothing to your roof."

She grinned sheepishly. "I've got a leak. I was trying to cover it with a tarp."

"Looks like you've got your hands full with this place, huh?"

"My mom let it fall into disrepair. She hasn't lived here for years. I thought I could move in and renovate it, but, yeah, it's turning into quite an ordeal."

"I used to work construction—maybe I could help," Ryan blurted before he could stop himself. What the hell was he thinking?

He wasn't thinking, at least not with the head he should have been using. His brain was too clouded by erect nipples and wet panties to think clearly now.

"Oh. Wow, um, thanks, but I couldn't ask that of you. I mean, maybe if you know any good contractors or carpenters or roofers, you could recommend someone?"

"Absolutely. But seriously, one of my hobbies is carpentry. It would be my pleasure to help—anytime."

It occurred to him then that maybe while she was standing there in her wet panties wasn't the best time to be having this conversation. There—a sensible thought.

She gave him an odd look.

Ryan felt his cheeks burning. God, all he was supposed to do was apologize, not try to insert himself into her life. Why was he being such an ass?

Because she was a beautiful, nearly naked woman, and he was a guy. It wasn't any more complicated than that. Besides, she looked even hotter soaked with rain than she did dry.

He forced his mind off the wet-naked-Lorelei fantasy that was threatening to overcome him and back to reality.

"Listen, I know it's late, and you're cold, and I have to get back to work. Maybe we could talk about this later. I'd be happy to give you some names of people to call, if nothing else."

"Sure, thanks. That would be great."

"How about tomorrow? Will you be around for me to stop by?"

"It's my day off."

"Great, I'll see you then," he said, then turned and walked away before he said anything else stupid in the face of her panties.

He needed to get a grip. But dammit, he wanted her. His whole body was so pent-up with frustrated desire, his dick pressing against the front of his pants, his mouth parched…it was a minor miracle he hadn't grabbed her and made love to her right then and there.

No, he wasn't going to behave like a Neanderthal. Not again.

Not when he had a chance to make things right. He'd help her with her house, if she'd let him, and when the time was right, he'd tell her how sorry he was for his behavior in high school. His self-respect depended on it—he couldn't walk around in the world knowing he'd been a jerk without making amends for his actions.

That was it. He'd apologize, and all would be right in the world again.

He absolutely wasn't going to sleep with her again. Well...not unless she really wanted to.

5

AS SHE WAITED for someone at Monroe Brothers Roofing to pick up the phone, Lorelei stared up at the growing water stain on the ceiling and muttered a curse. Living in a house should not be so hard. She was beginning to think the hut she'd lived in in Kenya had not been such a bad idea. At least when a thatched roof leaked, no one was surprised.

Finally the phone was picked up, but it was only a recorded voice explaining, "Monroe Brothers Roofing is currently unable to take on new roofing jobs for the immediate future, due to high demand for roof work. Please call us back in February if you need an estimate for new work. If you are a current customer—"

Lorelei hung up the phone and muttered a curse at the phone book. The other two roofing companies she'd already tried were not working during the winter months. She was beginning to feel as if she were starring in a bad movie version of her own life, in which the hapless, overeducated doctor meets her match in a house determined to fall down rather than be renovated.

Her brooding was interrupted by a knock at the door. As she went to answer it, she did a quick check in the mirror and saw that she hadn't yet brushed her hair, and her face, untouched by makeup, bore the puffy, dark-circled evidence that she hadn't slept much the night before.

Whatever. Anyone who dared to knock on her door at nine in the morning after an epic thunderstorm would get the frightful sight they deserved. It was probably a neighbor knocking to ask if she had electricity—the answer was no, she didn't—or to tell her that some of her belongings/tree branches/whatever had blown into their yard and needed to be removed.

But the moment she jerked the door open, she regretted having answered it at all. Ryan Quinn stood on her doorstep, still wearing his uniform.

Him again. Was fate trying to beat her over the head with him or what? She said a silent *Fine, you win* to Kinsei and gave in to the truth of the matter. He was right. She was going to have to sleep with Ryan to get rid of him from her life for good.

"Hi," he said, grinning sheepishly. "Sorry to bother you so early—"

"I've been up for a while," she said, cutting him off. She didn't want to stand here engaging in niceties right now, not when she looked like this.

How was she supposed to conquer the ghosts of her past with bad hair and raccoon eyes?

Her gaze dropped to his hand, and the bouquet of red and yellow daisies he held. He presented them to her.

"These are for you," he said.

"Oh," she said dumbly, taking the bouquet. "What for?"

"Can I come in for just a minute?"

"I'm…kind of busy right now," she said, torn between not wanting to be rude to her future conquest and not wanting him to get any more of a look at her poorly groomed self.

"Sorry, I just need a minute to talk to you. Please?"

He might have been the source of her worst teenage angst, but that was then, and right now, he looked so earnest, she couldn't manage to feel the least bit cold and hostile.

He flashed a weak grin, and she looked down at the flowers in her hands. Flowers? Really?

Curiosity nearly overcame her desire to send him away.

How could she refuse? Kinsei would probably curse her if she did. But the old man didn't understand a girl's need to prepare herself for seduction.

"Um, sure, I guess." She stepped aside and opened the door wider for him to enter. Upon doing so, she got a view of all the leaves, tree branches and debris from the storm that would now need to be cleaned up, adding to her ever-growing list of household tasks.

But the problem vanished from her head almost immediately, because when she turned to face Ryan again, she was struck by just how damn attractive he really was. Still. After all these years.

He filled up the space in her entryway, and the flowers—what was with the flowers? She smelled them. They were a lovely contrast to the dreary morning sky outside.

His expression turned to a mixture of serious and sheepish. "I wanted to check on you, first, and make sure you're okay after your ordeal last night. And bring you those references you asked about."

Lorelei blinked. This concern was in sharp contrast to her long-held belief that he was an insensitive jerk. "Other than being a wee bit sleep-deprived, I'm fine."

"Good." He handed her a list of names and numbers. "These are my recommendations of people to contact for work on the house."

"Oh, thanks," she said, and took the paper. She looked at it, and the roofers were ones she'd already tried. Her heart sank.

"What's wrong?"

"Any chance you know of a roofer who isn't booked solid with work right now?"

"Oh, you've already tried them, huh?"

Lorelei nodded.

"Well, that's perfect. So you don't have any choice but to let me help you repair the roof—and remove your pajama bottoms from their rooftop imprisonment."

"No, really, I can't ask you such a big favor. We don't even know each other."

"I'd really like to help. I feel like I owe you," he said, his gaze steady on her as if he was hoping she'd understand another level of his meaning.

"You don't owe me anything," she said too quickly. Was he thinking of what had happened in high school? Did he remember?

The flowers, the offer of help, the early arrival on her doorstep…it was all adding up to…what? Was she really going to get laid that easily?

Following Kinsei's advice usually involved much work and sacrifice. Success didn't crawl into her lap like a lovesick puppy.

"The other reason I'm here is a bit more awkward. I…" He hesitated. "I owe you an apology for what happened when we were teenagers."

Lorelei blinked again, her brain refusing to catch up to his words. "What?"

"I behaved like a total jerk when we were in high school together. I know that now, and I'm very sorry. I wish I could go back and change my actions, but I can't, so the best I can do is offer amends now. I was hoping you'd let me make it up to you by helping you with the house repairs."

An unexpected surge of anger rose up in her, and she blurted, "So it's like a trade? You take my virginity and fifteen years later you fix my house as repayment?"

He went pale, and she could tell by his pained expression that she'd hit him where it hurt.

Good.

She wasn't finished.

Screw Kinsei's advice. She was pretty sure telling Ryan Quinn to go to hell was exactly what her soul needed to heal from the past.

"That's right, asshole! I was a virgin. Did you even know that? Would you even have cared? I gave you my virginity, and you repaid me by treating me like I didn't exist for the rest of the school year."

"Lorelei, I'm really, really sorry. I deserve whatever you'd like to say to me."

She knew she was supposed to be gracious in the face of his heartfelt apology, but did he really think he could show up here

fifteen years later with a sad little bouquet of flowers and a cha-
grined look and make all her pain go away?

She'd never felt so angry in her life. It was as if all her teenage
angst was welling up again, only this time, she was strong enough
to do something about it.

She thought of Kinsei again. He'd never steered her wrong.
She was suddenly sure of what she wanted to do. She'd let him
make amends, if that's what he wanted to call it—he could amend
his way right into her bed and relieve all the sexual tension that
had been building up in the months since she'd last gotten laid,
and then she'd drop him like a hot potato, and this time let him
sit around wondering what the hell had gone wrong.

Some little adolescent voice that dwelled deep in her heart let
out a victorious battle cry at that thought.

"Wow," she said. "This is certainly an unexpected turn of events.
I never thought getting stuck on the roof would lead to this…"

"I know an apology and a bouquet of daisies can't begin to
make up for what I did to you, but—"

"I appreciate the gesture," she forced herself to say without
sarcasm. "And…what the hell. I'd be happy for you to help me with
the house repairs, if it would make you feel like we're, um, even."

"Thank you," he said, nodding solemnly. "I'd love to help."

"Why don't you stay and have some coffee with me, tell me
what you've been up to all these years, and I can tell you what
needs to be done to the house."

He smiled. "I'd like that a lot."

Lorelei led him into the kitchen, where a pot of coffee had just
finished brewing. At least the gas stove was still working, even if
the electricity wasn't. With its own fireplace that she'd gotten
going as soon as she'd woken up, the kitchen was the warmest
room in the house.

On the far side of the room, her pet rabbits, Thor and Lucia,
were huddled together, taking in the warmth of the stove from a
safe distance. They had free rein of the house, since they were
litter-box trained, but they tended to like staying in the kitchen
near their food.

"Have a seat," she said, nodding to the table. "Have you had any breakfast yet?"

"Actually, no. I came straight from the end of my night shift, to the flower shop, to here. I wasn't planning to, but…" He paused awkwardly, as if he wanted to say something but wasn't sure if he should. "But I really don't want to trouble you."

Lorelei ignored him as she put the daisies in water then started pulling out ingredients to make a breakfast frittata with mushrooms, peppers and cheese. She'd never been good at this small-talk stuff. She much preferred getting to the heart of matters. It made her bedside manner alternately loved and hated, depending on the patient.

"Hey, you have rabbits."

"Meet the new king and queen of the household. Thor is the brown one with the ever-disdainful expression, and Lucia is the white one."

"You just got them after you moved in?"

"Yep, from the local bunny rescue place."

He crossed the room, knelt down and attempted to pet the rabbits, who studiously ignored him until he came too close, and then they fled into the imaginary safety of their litter box.

"They don't like strangers. Ignore them and they'll come check you out in their own sweet time."

He smiled and sat down at the table again. "I always thought you'd become a veterinarian."

"I thought about it, but for as long as I can remember, I've wanted to be a doctor. I still love animals as much as I did as a kid, though."

"I always liked that about you. Didn't you have a python or something in high school?"

"Yep, and a couple of lizards, and the rats, of course, and a scorpion and…"

"You must have driven your parents crazy."

"They made me find new homes for most of the animals when I left for college. It was devastating."

"Yeah, I know how you feel. I had a dog until last year when she died of old age. It's like losing your best friend."

Lorelei went silent as she found all the ingredients she needed, thinking of the animals she still missed. The rabbits were a good fresh start though. She loved their bratty little personalities, and they kept her company in this drafty old house, their presence a constant fuzzy reminder to be Zen about all things.

"Want to hear something totally crazy?" Ryan said as she began shredding parmesan cheese with a grater.

"How could I not?"

"When I picked up those flowers for you at the flower shop in Santa Rey? There was this Christmas tree with little cards all over it, and a sign that said if you buy a card, the proceeds would go to charity."

"Oh, yeah, I think I heard about that on the radio the other day."

"So I bought one of the cards, and…this is going to sound really weird, but…I think you'll understand why I felt like I had to come here right now and apologize when you hear this. And I swear, I didn't know what was on the card before I bought it."

"What was it?"

"It's a gift certificate to Linden Rock Hot Springs."

Kinsei's face appeared in her mind. That sneaky little man… She might be a doctor with a scientifically trained mind, but the medicine man had taught her to believe in the inexplicable.

In a soap opera, this would be the part where Lorelei would halt the cheese grating and turn slowly to stare at Ryan. A weighty, emotional moment would pass between them as they contemplated the significance of his words, of the way fate—and one wily old Kenyan medicine man—had twisted and turned to make their lives intertwine again.

Linden Rock Hot Springs was where they'd had sex all those years ago. Back then, it hadn't been the luxury spa and retreat it was now. It had just been the hot springs located on undeveloped private property where teenagers and hippies loved to hang out naked. But its location overlooking the Pacific, among sheer cliffs down to the ocean and majestic cypress trees, had guaranteed that sooner or later it would be commercially developed.

But of all the cards for Ryan to have picked… Yeah, she could see why he'd come straight here, looking all earnest and sorry.

She felt the cheese grater slip from her hands as she looked back at him.

"Wow, weird coincidence, huh?" she said casually, as if she didn't already know it was the hand of fate telling her to get laid and overcome her past.

"Totally weird. I have to admit, it kind of freaked me out."

Lorelei turned her attention back to the cheese. She scooped the shreds up in her hands and dumped them into a bowl. Then she began washing and chopping vegetables.

"I guess, being a doctor, you probably don't believe in anything mystical," Ryan said to her back.

She shrugged, thinking again of Kinsei. "Back in medical school, I would have said no, but being a doctor, I've seen all kinds of things I can't explain. The only thing experience teaches me is that there's a lot I don't understand."

She mixed eggs with the frittata ingredients, then greased a pie pan, poured everything in, and put the dish in the oven to bake. It was her lazy-cook's method for making a frittata, since it didn't require her to stand over the stove and watch anything.

Once she'd poured them each a cup of coffee, she set the table with sugar and cream, then pulled up a chair across from Ryan.

"What about you?" she asked. "Do you believe in fate or ghosts or UFOs or anything?"

"I'm probably in the same camp as you. Experience has taught me to be open-minded."

"So," she finally dared to ask, seeing now how easy her resolution with the past might be. "Do you think fate is telling us we need to go back to the hot springs?"

"Yeah," he said, his voice sounding a little odd. "I feel silly saying it, but I do."

6

RYAN COULD hardly believe his luck. He'd never expected his apology to Lorelei to go so smoothly, and better yet, to end with her asking *him* to the hot springs. It would be the perfect way to make up for the past. He'd show her—and himself—that he wasn't the jerk kid he used to be.

As he sipped his coffee, he relaxed. With the heat from the kitchen stove and the morning light pouring in through the big picture window, the room felt cozy and intimate. If he closed his eyes, he'd have felt like he was home.

But with Lorelei sitting across from him, the last thing he wanted to do was close his eyes. He could hardly stop staring at her. She held such familiarity, this nearly forgotten piece of his past, like an old beloved toy that had slipped from his memory until he'd stumbled upon it by accident. Except, of course, she hadn't been sitting around in an attic waiting to be rediscovered. She'd been wandering the world, having what had no doubt been an interesting life, and he wanted to know what had filled the space between then and now.

Not that she owed him any such information. They'd had sex exactly once—he'd even been her first lover, which kind of blew his mind now that he'd had the fact confirmed—but everything he knew about her was based on his very limited perspective of who she had been fifteen years ago.

He wanted to know more, but she spoke up first.

"It must have been a busy night for you guys last night, with the storm and all."

"It was the most calls in one night that we've had all year. And that's saying something considering the fire season we had this year."

"Wow. I hope no one was hurt."

"Luckily, you were the most endangered soul I encountered," he said with a grin. "There was an oak tree branch that caved in a roof over on El Segundo Avenue, but no one was in the part of the house that was affected."

She smiled into her coffee. "I was horrified when you showed up to get me off the roof."

"I don't blame you. That was a pretty spectacular screwup, with the pj bottoms and all."

"I'm not as handy as I think I am sometimes."

"So you just moved in here a few weeks ago, huh?"

"Yes. For the past two years I was serving in the Peace Corps, in Kenya, and when my tour ended, I felt…drawn back home, I guess."

"That must have been an incredible experience."

"It was life-changing. I thought for a while that I'd never leave Africa. I had this dream of joining Doctors without Borders, but lots of different things…signs…whatever…just kept telling me I needed to come back here to Ocean Harbor Beach."

"I'm glad you did. It's great to see you again. I'm not really in touch with many people from high school anymore, but I always wondered what happened to you."

Which was true. He might have been a shallow, self-centered shithead as a teen, but Lorelei was unique enough that she had come to mind now and again, and he couldn't help wondering what had become of his most brilliant classmate.

"What have you been up to since high school?" she asked.

"Oh, the usual. Going to college, surfing, backpacking around Europe, getting married, getting divorced—perhaps not exactly in that order, but you get the idea."

"You've been married?"

"To a girl I met in college. Bad idea. It lasted two years, and then we realized we hated each other. Or, at least, I realized it when she told me she thought she was in love with my best friend."

"Ouch. I'm sorry," she said, wincing.

"It's okay. We already knew the marriage wasn't working when it happened. But it still hurt like hell. Definitely humbled me, made me realize I'm not God's gift to women or anything."

He grinned ruefully, and she smiled back.

"That's always a healthy realization. How long since you got divorced?"

"Five years."

"Dating anyone?" she asked, and if he had been his younger, cockier self, he'd have said her tone was kind of…provocative.

Could it be that after how horribly he'd behaved, she might still be attracted to him?

No, he was imagining things.

"Nope, how about you?"

"I'm afraid I've become one of those career-obsessed drones who has no social life," she joked. "Definitely not dating right now."

"I'll bet you left behind at least a few Peace Corps volunteers who were devastated to see you go."

She smiled ironically. "Perhaps, if only because I'm a hard worker and it meant they'd have to pick up the slack in my absence."

"That's not what I meant," he said, but she ignored him and went to the stove to check on breakfast, which was smelling pretty damn delicious right now.

She pulled the lightly browned egg dish from the oven, and Ryan's stomach growled. He'd been too busy to eat last night, except for a sandwich he'd grabbed around five in the morning on the way to a call.

A minute later she was getting toast out of the toaster. After preparing two plates, she placed one in front of him, along with utensils and a napkin. "It's a frittata," she said. "Would you like jam for your toast?"

"No thanks. This looks delicious."

"So." She took her place at the table again. "What do you do with yourself when you're not fighting fires?"

Ryan felt relieved that she really did seem to be genuinely interested in him as a person, because he was finding himself even more interested in her than he'd thought he'd be. Not only did she look dynamite in a tank top and panties, but she had an interesting career and past that he wanted to know more about. On top of the fact that she was brilliant, and, he thought, after taking his first bite of frittata—a great cook, too.

He found himself wanting to impress her. "I play the guitar, write songs, play in a funky little blues band sometimes…"

"Really? Is there anywhere I can see you play soon?"

"Hmm… Maybe."

He was struck with an idea. Maybe a brilliant idea. He'd write a song. For her. And play it at the hot springs, to say he was sorry.

It could be corny, or it could be the smartest thing he'd ever done to win a girl's heart.

Win a girl's heart? Was that what he really wanted to do?

Okay, so he didn't know Lorelei all that well yet, but he had a gut feeling about her that he couldn't shake. It had been settling in ever since he'd opened the gift certificate for the Linden Rock Hot Springs at the flower shop.

No, actually, ever since he'd seen her there in the clinic. He hadn't been able to stop thinking about her. She was everything he wanted in a woman. Ever since his divorce, he'd made note of what he truly loved in the women he dated, versus the things he thought he'd loved but ultimately realized were just the things society told him he was supposed to want.

He didn't want to make the same mistakes he'd made in marrying Heather. He wanted to find his real, true dream girl next time around. Someone smart and quirky and original and beautiful in the not-so-obvious ways—well, and okay, the obvious ways didn't hurt, either. Someone like Lorelei.

He wanted to prove to her that he liked her for who she was, and that he would never, ever take advantage of her again. If they were ever lovers a second time, he'd make sure she knew it meant something to him.

"You're looking awfully deep in thought. It's okay if you don't want me to see you play. But I do like blues guitar, if that makes a difference."

Perfect. Then she was going to get her own private show.

"It does," he said, smiling. "I'll let you know the next time I'm playing."

7

LORELEI checked herself out in the full-length mirror and was happy enough with what she saw. Her jeans were the rare, much-sought-after, perfect cut—the one pair she'd ever owned that made her ass look as if it belonged in a jeans ad. And her stretchy long-sleeved black T-shirt hugged her curves in all the right places. Her hair was sleek, and hung around her face in a stark contrast to how she usually wore it for work, pulled back in a haphazard bun.

She'd made plans with Ryan to take an evening soak in the hot springs first, then have dinner at the spa restaurant. She didn't suppose they were technically allowed to have sex right there in the springs anymore, not now that it was an official spa, but she'd been sure to wear her best bra and panties beneath her clothes, just in case the opportunity arose—and she had every intention of making sure it arose.

If nothing else, she'd be naked with him in the hot springs, and if that didn't put ideas in his head, she wasn't sure what would. Linden Rock was still, thank goodness, notoriously clothing-optional, and she planned to use that fact to her advantage. In spite of her discomfort with being found pants-less on the roof, Lorelei had always loved being naked in the great outdoors. It was one of the best feelings she knew.

Beside her, Thor the rabbit god stared at her rather disapprovingly.

"What? You think I'm being a slut? Well, if you weren't neutered, you'd be humping everything you could get your paws on, so I don't want to hear it."

Okay, so she talked to the rabbits. It was therapeutic for them, and for her.

A glance at the clock—thank God, the power was back on as of today—told her Ryan would be here at any moment to pick her up, so she slipped on a pair of boots, shrugged on a warm coat and headed to the living room. She caught sight of his headlights in the front window, flipped off the lights in her house, grabbed her purse, and headed out the door, feeling as if she was about to conquer the world.

Or at least the ghosts of her past.

She had never blatantly, intentionally seduced anyone before. She was a little surprised she even knew how. Not that she was the same awkward dork sexually that she'd been in high school. No, she'd never gotten any bad reviews on her skills as a lover, but she didn't believe in using her feminine wiles for nefarious purposes, either.

Flirting with Ryan the way she had over breakfast the day before—it was amazing how easy it had been. It felt natural, even. Probably because she really did want to sleep with him. He was as gorgeous as ever, and he wasn't eighteen anymore. He was a real man now. He had to be more emotionally mature than he was back then.

Even in high school, he'd had a sensitive air about him. He hadn't jockeyed for attention and status, but had moved with the self-assuredness that showed he knew he didn't need to. And he'd stood apart a bit from the crowd, always watchful, always noticing things. Well, noticing everything except Lorelei, apparently.

But now, he'd finally admitted what a jerk he'd been and apologized. Perhaps that should have been enough for her.

Yet she'd been so miserable during her high-school years, and Ryan had represented the culmination of her misery. After graduation, she'd fled Ocean Harbor Beach as fast as she could and never looked back. She'd gone so far as to attend a summer program at college just to get away as soon as she could.

Moving here was the most time she'd spent back home since high school, and she still wasn't quite used to it.

Outside, Ryan was getting out of his pickup truck, a dilapidated old thing he probably owned solely to haul his surfboard around. When he saw her, he smiled and said hi.

"Looks like we'll have clear weather, at least," Lorelei said, looking up at the star-studded night sky.

She'd had the day off, and she'd spent it cleaning up after the powerful storm. Now her yard looked normal again—well, normal for a long-neglected rat's haven of a front yard.

The forecast was calling for clear weather through Christmas. Not that it mattered. She'd be spending the holiday alone, far as she could tell. Her mother had already planned a seniors' cruise to Hawaii before she'd known Lorelei would be home for the holidays.

Well, at least she might give herself a little pre-Christmas revenge sex tonight. That would help make up for work being her only other thing to look forward to.

Ryan opened the passenger door, smiling down at Lorelei in a way that made her toes feel all tingly. "You look beautiful, as always."

"Thanks," she said as she slid into his truck, kicking aside a can of surf wax in the process.

The truck bore a bobbly dancing Hawaiian girl on the dash, and cracked vinyl seats that had seen better days. It felt familiar to her somehow.

When Ryan got in and started pulling out of the driveway, she asked, "Is this the same truck you drove in high school?"

"One and the same." He grinned proudly and gave the dashboard an affectionate pat.

"Wow, I can't believe it still runs."

"Neither can I. I've made a hobby out of fixing the old girl—it's become a labor of love."

So this was the same truck Lorelei had ridden in to the hot springs with Ryan all those years ago… Weird. And oddly appropriate, too, she supposed.

"Most people would, you know, just buy a new car."

"Believe me, I've been tempted, especially when I find myself broken down on the side of the road. But I like the things in my life to have some character, some history—you know?"

"Yeah. I guess it's the same reason I'm fixing up my broken-down family house rather than living somewhere else. Well, that, and I can't afford a mortgage anywhere in Ocean Harbor Beach."

She liked that he still had his same old truck after all these years. It suggested things about his character that were all good.

Except, of course, genuinely liking him would make the whole revenge thing a bit more difficult.

Lorelei bit her lip and pushed that thought out of her head as they turned off of her street and drove along the coast, with the ocean outside her window.

They traveled along the coastal road toward the hot springs, chatting about mutual acquaintances and who had done what or gone where or married whom since high school. Ryan, having stayed here in town, knew a lot more about such matters than Lorelei did.

When they reached the Linden Rock resort, he parked and turned to her. "I hope you don't mind taking a little detour before we go for a soak."

"Sure, what's the detour?"

"It's a secret."

Lorelei was intrigued. And when she saw him get out of the truck, reach into the rear and pull out a guitar case, she was even more intrigued.

"There's a little spot down this path I was hoping we could check out," he said, nodding in the direction of the gardens.

Lorelei followed him, and a moment later, they were standing in a gazebo draped with bougainvillea.

"Have a seat," Ryan said, as he removed the guitar from its case.

Her throat went dry. He wasn't really going to play music, was he? Right here? Right now? The thought made her nauseous, because it was just too romantic to be real. Where was the callous jerk she'd known fifteen years ago?

He began strumming a slow, bluesy tune on the guitar, as Lorelei settled on the bench seat across from him and watched. She'd never had a guy play music for her personally before. Then he began humming along with the tune, his voice deliciously sexy and low, and the breath whooshed out of her lungs. By the time he was singing the first bar of the song, Lorelei could feel sweat trickling down her chest between her breasts in spite of the cold, damp night air.

She watched, mesmerized as he sang about lost chances and

lonely nights, about broken hearts and longing for redemption. It took her well over a minute to realize what he was singing about and she could hardly believe her ears.

She strained to hear every word and make sense of it. Maybe she was mistaken. No way could he have composed this beautiful, soulful, melody in only one day.

But when he reached the lines about her virgin skin in hot water, heat rising around them, and being sorry for the silence, she knew.

This song…he had written it.

For her.

8

RYAN HELD the guitar until the final sound vibration had settled in it, and there was silence. Then he placed the instrument back in its case and looked up to see Lorelei staring at him, dumbstruck.

She tried to compose herself, perhaps arrange her features to suggest she wasn't moved by the song, but he knew that look. She'd felt what he'd intended her to feel.

And he could not help being satisfied knowing it.

"Wow," she said quietly. "You wrote that."

"It's a work in progress. That was my first time playing it through without any major screwups."

"You *wrote* that," she repeated, as if awestruck.

"Yesterday after I left your place."

"I'm…stunned. And flattered. Thank you."

He closed the distance between them and took her hand, pulling her up to a standing position in front of him. When he could see clearly into her eyes, he said, "I wanted you to understand how truly sorry I am for what happened the last time we were here together."

She nodded, averting her gaze for a moment, then looking back at him with an expression that seemed like determination.

"I accept," she said. "Now how about we go for a dip?"

"You don't have to twist my arm."

After he'd put the guitar back in its case and taken it to the truck, they went to the spa registration desk and checked in. They were given a map of the grounds and facilities, and they followed a path outside toward the ocean, to the hot springs, which were now dimly lit for the evening and equipped with chairs and meditation platforms nearby.

The place was, miraculously, deserted. Ryan said a silent thank-you to the universe. He had no preconceived notions of how he wanted the night to go—okay, maybe he had a few, and he'd reserved a room at the spa hotel just in case—but he did at least want them to be alone the way they had been fifteen years ago. It wouldn't have been the same with other people there to spoil the mood.

"Looks like we have the springs all to ourselves," Lorelei said, echoing his thoughts. "Nice, huh?"

"I don't suppose a cold Wednesday night five days before Christmas is all that popular a time to go spa-hopping."

"Have you been here…since, um…?"

"No," Ryan said quickly, which was true. "I think I'd lose some of my cred as a firefighter if I was caught contemplating my navel at a place as frou-frou as this."

She laughed. "I forgot you have to consider such things."

Ryan tried not to stare as she casually began taking off her clothes without even turning away. This he remembered from their first time here together, as well. He'd been awestruck by her lack of inhibition, especially when his experience with teenage girls had been dominated by awkwardness and self-conciousness.

Her ability to strip naked without a care in the world, both then and now, gave her an air of raw sexuality that was incredibly arousing to him. It was all he could do not to walk right over to her and take her in his arms.

And it presented him with another problem. He had a raging erection that was going to announce what he wanted to do whether he spoke a word or not, so as he undressed himself, he turned his back to Lorelei, then had to chuckle at himself over the ridiculousness of the situation.

Where was *his* lack of inhibition? What was wrong with her

knowing that she turned him on? Wasn't that what he wanted anyway?

With a deep breath, he tossed his pants aside and turned to get in the water, consequences be damned. Lorelei's gaze landed immediately on his stiff cock, but instead of looking away, she simply stared up at him, her eyes half-lidded, as if in a sexy challenge.

Damn, she was bold.

And he loved it. He'd never met a woman so at ease with herself as Lorelei was.

He lowered himself into the water and sighed at its heat, a heavenly contrast to the cold air around them. They could hear waves crashing against the beach down below.

"Here we are," he said dumbly. "Can you believe it?"

She eased herself into the water one leg at a time, and his gaze took her in, relishing the sight of her bare skin, the curly dark hair that covered her sex and the dark, erect nipples he so badly wanted in his mouth.

"Barely," she said. "Mmmmm, this feels amazing."

He tried to think what else to say, but at the sound of her little moan of pleasure, his mind went blank.

He could only sit there, dumbstruck, wanting so desperately to have her that he couldn't imagine not reaching for her right then and there.

"What is it?" she asked when she caught the odd expression on his face.

"I…this…um…"

What? What could he say? He'd lost all his words.

She eased herself across the rocks, coming closer to him. Closer, closer, closer still…

Then she was next to him, and before he could say a word…she unexpectedly straddled his lap.

His cock, so suddenly pressed against her, ached like crazy to thrust inside. He could hardly believe his luck.

"I have a condom," she said. "Don't worry."

She. Had. A. Condom.

Hallelujah.

She leaned in and kissed him then, a long, slow, deep kiss that stated her intentions as clearly as any words could have. Ryan's toes curled into the sediment at the bottom of the spring, and he grasped her hips, rocking against her and savoring the feel of her soft, delicious ass in his palms.

"We should get a room," he murmured when she broke the kiss.

"No," she said. "I want you right here, like before."

Yes, this was exactly like before. Her on his lap, straddling him, kissing him into stunned submission.

She'd been awkward then, unlike now, but clearly into him. And he'd been carried away in the passion of the moment, unsure, in his lame adolescent mind, why he was so turned on by his nerdy, odd lab partner, but unable to stop the forward momentum of passion unhindered by thought.

Now though... Now, he knew why he wanted her, and he knew he'd be lucky to have her. And there wouldn't be any stopping them this time, either.

When her hand slipped down his chest, between their bodies, and grasped his cock, he let out a ragged moan of pleasure. She began stroking him slowly, her lips slightly parted as she watched his reaction.

"Dammit, woman," he said. "You sure know how to make a guy feel good."

She kissed him again, and he shut up. But if she kept stroking him like she was, this was going to be over before it had gotten started, so he reached for her and pulled her hard against him, lifting her as he did so to bring her gorgeous tits to his mouth.

He sucked each one in turn, teasing a nipple with one hand as his mouth took care of the other. Then he slid his free hand down, between her legs, right across her clit, to gently stroke her opening. She was already slippery, ready for him to enter, and he groaned at the feel of her there.

Damn, but he wanted her badly.

Right here in the open, where anyone could see. He didn't care now. And apparently, neither did she, which made it all the more exciting.

Was this how he intended to show his contrition for past bad behavior? By repeating the same act? No, this time, he'd be the best damn lover she'd ever had, and he wouldn't ignore her the next day, or the next week—or ever. He'd give her the attention and appreciation and respect she deserved, because the feel of her body against him was all the convincing he needed that she was just as perfect for him as he'd suspected.

And this time, he intended to be remembered, at the very least, as a good lover.

Grasping her hips and lifting her slightly, he held his breath and plunged under the water, sliding down, and down still, until his face was between her legs. He found her sex with his mouth, flicked his tongue gently against her, held tightly to her hips as she writhed against his coaxing tongue. Then he plunged his tongue inside her and tasted her delicious, musky flavor, lingering there pleasuring her until his lungs could stand it no more and he had to come up for air.

When he'd broken the surface, his body between her legs again, he took a deep breath and gazed up at her surprised but aroused expression.

"Where's that condom?" he said in a ragged voice, and she held out her hand, revealing it on her palm where it must have been since she'd disrobed. So she'd come here knowing they'd get it on. One more thing he found to like about her style.

He took the packet from her and opened it with his teeth, then slid the rubber on and grasped her hips again. He couldn't wait anymore. He needed to be inside her before he went insane.

Looking into her dark brown eyes, he positioned his cock against her and held her hips tightly and thrust gently, back and forth, back and forth, not quite entering her. The satiny texture of her pussy drove him wild with aching, and he wanted to be in her more than anything he could ever remember, but he also wanted to know she ached for him just as badly.

Her back arched, she grasped his shoulders tightly and shifted her hips so that he could tease her no more, nearly forcing him inside her. The naked arousal in her gaze, in her half-parted lips as her breath quickened, told him what he needed to know, and he slid inside her in one smooth thrust. At the sensation of it, he expelled a ragged gasp of pleasure, and she sighed, letting her eyes fall shut.

Ryan felt himself melting into her as he thrust his hips, again and again, the water buoying them, making their movements effortless. To shield her from the cold air, where her body wasn't in the water, he wrapped his arms around her and held her chest against him, his short deep thrusts reaching as far into her as he could go. Each movement reverberated through his body like a little earthquake.

He could not remember the last time he'd felt so good, so right, and as his body coiled tighter and tighter, straining for release, he wished this night would never end.

9

IT WAS just like the first time, and it wasn't anything like it. The place was the same, and the people and the act, but the feelings and sensations were brand-new. Lorelei was not an awkward, love-struck teenager giving up her virginity to someone who didn't deserve it. She was a sexually confident woman who was well aware of what this act did and didn't mean, and she was taking back the power she'd lost all those years ago.

And, damn, it felt good.

She grasped Ryan's shoulders tightly as he lifted her and carried her to the middle of the spring, where they could both be immersed in the water and out of the cold night air. Her legs wrapped around his hips, he continued moving inside her in a standing position, and she could feel herself rushing quickly toward climax, just like in her dream, except not.

She closed her eyes to focus on the sensation of him moving inside her, stretching her and touching the most sensitive spots in her body, and she felt herself being transported back in time. The years vanished, and she was the same girl who'd been so hopelessly in love with Ryan, the same girl who'd offered her body to him in the hope of getting love back.

Here they were, joined together again, and finally it felt exactly as she'd once hoped it would. If she just kept her eyes closed, she could forget reality.

He was kissing her as if he wanted to devour her, making love to her as if somewhere inside of her was what he needed to survive. Lorelei held on to him, heard herself whimpering at the pleasure that threatened to overcome her…

When he stopped kissing her, his gaze locked on her and he stared into her eyes. He saw her, or maybe he saw through her, and she could not remember how they'd ever been at odds, or separate or even two different people with their own bodies and desires.

She had never had such uninhibited, animal sex right out in the open before, and she didn't want it to end. She savored each moment as if it might be the last…felt herself building toward something…her body tensing further and further still… Then her inner muscles began to quake, and she was surprised by the intense orgasm that overtook her suddenly.

Not caring who might hear, she cried out, gasping with the intense pleasure coursing through her. And a moment later, she could hear Ryan doing the same. He muffled his release by kissing her again, his tongue coaxing her to feel the moans that escaped his throat and entered her mouth.

When he'd finished spilling into her, he hugged her tightly and sighed raggedly. Then he eased out of her and set her down on her feet in front of him.

He held her against him as he caught his breath, and Lorelei became aware again that they were separate. Their bodies were two, not one. The deep hunger that had filled her had now been replaced by a delicious hum…and yet still, deep within, an ache remained, as if their one act of lovemaking had not begun to satisfy the desire that had burned within her for so many years.

"That was…incredible," he whispered into her ear. "I forgot how amazing you feel."

"I'm pretty sure we've both improved a bit over the years," she said, smiling, but the mention of their first time together caused something inside her to harden.

She recalled why she was really here, to do as Kinsei had said and conquer this painful ghost of her past. She couldn't get swept away in feelings that would only defeat her purpose.

"Come over here and sit," he said, taking her hand and guiding her back to the rocks where they could sit and still be chest-deep in the hot water.

They sat half facing each other, her legs draped over his, and stared up at the sky.

"You wanted that to happen, didn't you?" Ryan asked.

Lorelei found herself caught off guard by his frankness. "Of course I did," she said. "Didn't you?"

He chuckled. "Sure, but I didn't want to presume…"

"Why else would we come here?"

"To enjoy a soak?" he offered.

"Don't act coy."

"I don't mean to. I was just curious."

Lorelei found herself wanting to tell him here and now, why they'd just done what they'd done. It felt like the right time. And so she did.

"I needed to do this," she said. "To make peace with the past."

He gave her a curious look. "How so?"

She slid her legs out of his lap and sat up straight, not caring that her breasts were now exposed to the cold night air and all the world, too.

"I really appreciated your apology, but I felt like I needed more than that. I needed to reverse the wrong that was done here before. I've spent fifteen years hating what you did to me."

She stood up and started to climb out of the hot spring, but he grasped her wrist to keep her from going.

"Don't leave," he said. "Let's talk."

"I have to leave. It's the only way I can feel any resolution."

He let go of her, and she climbed out, grabbed her clothes and started getting dressed, still wet.

"So this meant nothing to you then?" he said. "You were just here for…*closure?*"

He spoke the last word as if it were something vile.

And maybe it was in this context, but she wasn't going to feel guilty.

"That's right," she said, then swallowed hard. "It means nothing."

WHY, LORELEI wondered for the next three days, did closure feel so damned awful? Wasn't having sex with Ryan again supposed to bring her balance and a sense of peace with her past and all that?

It hadn't given her anything but a sense of emptiness as she lay in bed alone every night. She buried herself in her work, but it didn't help.

Ryan had tried to call her a couple of times, but she'd screened her calls and hadn't answered, and he'd given up.

And then she'd felt bereft of him all over again.

She was sitting in the hospital cafeteria alone when her friend and colleague Maria Valdez sat down next to her, bearing a tray with two chocolate brownies on it.

"You look like you need one of these," she said, offering one to Lorelei.

"Thanks." Lorelei took it and broke off one corner, then put it in her mouth and chewed slowly. She could barely taste it.

"What's going on with you? You've been moping around here like your dog died."

She glanced over at Maria, at her warm brown eyes and half smile, and she shrugged.

"Hmm. Man trouble, huh?"

"Yep."

"It's the holidays. Seems to either make or break relationships."

"I didn't really even have a relationship. Just a…"

"A booty call?"

"No." Lorelei laughed in spite of herself.

"Whoever it is, you're sure looking like you want a relationship.Did he cheat on you? Lie to you? Steal your checkbook?"

"No, no and no," Lorelei said. "He's a good guy, I think. But I've been holding a grudge against him for something he did a long time ago, and I thought I'd finally evened the playing field—I thought I'd feel all empowered and victorious—but it just made me feel like shit instead."

"Of course it did. You're a woman. We can't do anything blatantly mean without feeling bad about it."

"I guess."

"Men get revenge—women just get hurt."

Lorelei swallowed another piece of brownie. She wasn't sure she bought Maria's sweeping generalization, but she thought of Kinsei. He was a man. He was the one who'd told her she'd feel better once she'd taken back her power from Ryan.

He'd never steered her wrong before, so what was going on now? Was it just that he'd given her advice meant for a man? She didn't think so. Maybe she just needed to stop taking other people's advice and make her own decisions.

"So now you're all alone for the holidays?" Maria said. "You're welcome to come join my family for Christmas Eve tomorrow. There's a ton of us—it'll be easy to get lost in the crowd."

"I'm scheduled to work, but thank you anyway."

"Whatever he did wrong, he's not worth feeling bad about, you know?"

Lorelei took another bite of her brownie as her gaze landed on the necklace Maria wore, a thin gold chain with a silver and gold angel charm dangling from it.

The angel's face, small as it was, managed to look so peaceful, so free of petty emotions.

"Maybe you should just forgive him," Maria said. "You know, the spirit of the season and all…"

Right. Forgiveness. Harmony. Wasn't that what Christmas was all about?

Lorelei frowned at the mist of fog outside the window, rolling in from the ocean. Did she have enough forgiveness in her heart? Did Ryan, now, after what she'd done?

She knew she couldn't sit here forever wondering. She had to go find out.

10

RYAN LAY on the couch in the darkened room across from the crackling fire, watching the colored Christmas lights on his ficus tree twinkle. The string of bulbs was his one nod to holiday cheer. But at nearly midnight on Christmas Eve, he was feeling a lot more wistful than cheerful. He'd turned down the various offers he'd received from friends to join them for holiday festivities, because after work today, he'd just felt like being alone.

Lorelei was still on his mind. But he understood she didn't care to hear from him, and he supposed he understood why. Not everyone could forgive. And maybe he didn't deserve to be forgiven.

But he wasn't all that thrilled with the way she'd treated him, either. He'd allowed her into his heart…the same way she'd allowed him into hers when they were teenagers.

So, yeah, okay, perhaps she was right, he deserved to be alone and miserable tonight. But he couldn't stop thinking of the way it had felt to be with Lorelei again, and the memories, so fresh in his mind, haunted him day and night.

Maybe he was just meant to be alone. He'd failed ever to find a woman who felt like his soul mate, and now, when he finally had found someone who seemed to fit his wildest fantasies, she hated him for the ass he used to be.

Such was life, he supposed.

His gaze landed on his guitar, and he sat up and grabbed it from the foot of the sofa. If nothing else, he could pour his wistful feelings into a new song. That was how he usually dealt with heartbreak, anyway.

He started a slow strumming, closed his eyes and let the words come to him.

He sang about *sorry* being such a sorry word, and forgiveness being so hard to reach, and…he just about made himself sick with how bad the impromptu song was, but he kept going, making up words as he went along, stopping, starting again, trying out the lines one way, and then another.

He was just about to give up his brooding musical efforts and go to bed, when he heard a knock at the door.

Ryan set aside the guitar and prepared to tell the neighbors that he was sorry the walls of his house were so thin, but when he opened the door, he found Lorelei, still wearing her hospital scrubs.

"Hi," she said quietly.

"Hi." His heart swelled in his chest, as if it was straining to get closer to her.

"I…I just wanted to stop by and say I'm sorry," she said quietly.

"No, it's okay. No more apologies."

"I heard your song."

"Oh. Well, then I do have to apologize for how bad it was."

"You wrote that?"

"Just now. I mean, no, I didn't really write it, I was just making it up as I went along."

"What was it about?"

"You."

She blinked, and he could see tears form in her eyes. One spilled out onto her cheek, and he wiped it away with his thumb.

"Want to hear a live performance?"

"Um…I just did. I heard everything. Sorry. I was eavesdropping, I guess."

"It's okay. All stuff I'd say aloud to you, if you'd listen."

"You don't need to."

"I don't?"

"It's Christmas Eve. Aren't we supposed to forgive on this of all holidays?"

Ryan tried not to feel too hopeful, but he failed. "I suppose so. Please come inside."

She stepped into the living room, with its unintentionally shabby chic decor, surfboards hanging from the ceiling, fireplace glowing brightly, and the pathetic little tree with one sad string of lights.

"Welcome to my humble shack," he said. "Can I get you something hot to drink?"

"Let's skip the pleasantries, okay?" she said, staring at him in that intent, hyperintelligent way she had.

She looked tired, as if she'd been working a long shift, but she was still beautiful. Her hair was pulled back, and her face was free of makeup, making her look younger than she was.

Ryan got a lump in his throat, seeing her standing right there in his living room, that had only moments ago felt so cold and empty.

"I shouldn't have done what I did," she said, "and if you have time, I'll explain why I did it. It has to do with an African medicine man, and fate, and teenage angst, and first love and other things I don't quite understand."

"I've got all night."

She smiled then, and all the tension vanished. She was, at once, the beautiful, odd girl he'd always known. The one he wanted to know inside and out. The one he was pretty damn sure he was falling in love with.

"So do I," she said, smiling still. "And I've got tomorrow, too, if you're free."

"I am," he said, then he bent to kiss her softly on the lips.

"Can I tell you a secret?" she said against his mouth a moment later.

"Yes."

"You were the first guy I ever loved."

"I was?"

"Yep."

"Wow…I'm honored."

"Do you know what they say about first loves?"

"I've heard different stories," Ryan said, slipping his arm around her and pulling her against him.

She felt warm and perfect.

"The only one I know to be true is that first love never really dies."

He let her words sink in, and he smiled. He glanced up at the clock. It was 12:01 a.m. now. Christmas day.

"Merry Christmas," he said, then kissed her again, holding her tightly, as he promised himself that this time, they'd get it right.

Epilogue

A village near Mombasa, Kenya,
Christmas Eve, One Year Later…

"WHY HAVE you not made her your bride yet?" Kinsei asked Ryan. "A woman like her will not wait around forever for a man."

"You should tell *her* that," Ryan said to the medicine man. "She doesn't want to get married. Says it's not a fair deal for women."

The man threw back his head and laughed hard. Ryan had seen him do this several times since they'd arrived in the village the day before, and it never failed to make him smile. Really, everything about this village that had been Lorelei's home made him smile. In spite of the relative poverty of this place populated by scrawny, beautiful children, elegant women, fat goats and squat little huts, the people he'd met seemed to possess something most Westerners lacked—true, unabashed, non-neurotic joy.

He wasn't sure he'd ever been so happy in his life as he had been since he'd arrived.

"What?" Lorelei said as she walked up, her long hair shining in the sun. "I can tell you two were talking about me."

"You American women know nothing of marriage," Kinsei said to her. "Ask my wives—they will all tell you they are happy being married to me."

Lorelei looked as if she didn't doubt it. On the flight over, she'd said that in spite of Western ideas about marriage, Kinsei's family was at least as functional and happy as any she'd ever seen.

"Kinsei, tell me you weren't just pressuring him to make me his bride or some nonsense like that."

"Nonsense? This is the most important thing you will ever do, getting married. It will bring your heart what it desires."

Ryan would have expected Lorelei to roll her eyes at the triteness of the sentiment, but he knew she was faced with Kinsei's track record. He was, against all reason, inexplicably always right, or so she claimed. And he could tell now how much weight she really did give the medicine man's words.

His heart did a little joyous flip-flop.

He'd told himself it didn't bother him at all that Lorelei wasn't really keen on marrying. He'd been happy enough that they were together, now cohabitating in her family house. They'd just finished renovations in the fall.

But Ryan understood in that moment that he really did want to marry her, not just live with her. He wanted to declare to the world that they were together for life.

Lorelei looked from Kinsei to him. "What do you think? Want to get married?"

"Of course he does," Kinsei answered for him. "Look at the man! He's hopelessly in love with you."

Ryan couldn't help laughing. This was not how he'd ever have envisioned his proposal of marriage going, but, with Lorelei, it was completely perfect.

He looked at the medicine man. "Could we, um…?"

"Okay, okay, I will give you privacy, so you can talk about your marriage. And when you are ready, I will marry you. Tonight, yes? Before the feast."

Without waiting for their approval, he turned and hobbled away on impossibly thin legs.

Ryan turned to Lorelei and smiled. "Are you sure you want this?"

"You heard the man—it's what my heart most desires. Don't make me get all mushy now."

She pulled him close and stood on tiptoe to place a kiss on his lips. When they finally pulled away, she said, "I can't think of a place I'd rather get married."

"Really? Right here, in the village?"

She nodded, smiling. "The wedding garb involves a sarong and no top. Are you convinced yet?"

"You mean, you'll be topless, or I will?"

"Both of us."

"Then what are we waiting for? Let's do it."

He picked her up and kissed her again, this time with the soul-deep satisfaction of his heart finally finding its greatest desire.

* * * * *

Silhouette Desire kicks off 2009 with
MAN OF THE MONTH, *a yearlong program
featuring incredible heroes by stellar authors.*

When navy SEAL Hunter Cabot returns home for some
much-needed R & R, he discovers he's a married man.
There's just one problem: he's never met his "bride."

*Enjoy this sneak peek at Maureen Child's
AN OFFICER AND A MILLIONAIRE.
Available January 2009 from Silhouette Desire.*

One

Hunter Cabot, navy SEAL, had a healing bullet wound in his side, thirty days' leave and, apparently, a wife he'd never met.

On the drive into his hometown of Springville, California, he stopped for gas at Charlie Evans's service station. That's where the trouble started.

"Hunter! Man, it's good to see you! Margie didn't tell us you were coming home."

"Margie?" Hunter leaned back against the front fender of his black pickup truck and winced as his side gave a small twinge of pain. Silently then, he watched as the man he'd known since high school filled his tank.

Charlie grinned, shook his head and pumped gas. "Guess your wife was lookin' for a little 'alone' time with you, huh?"

"My—" Hunter couldn't even say the word. *Wife?* He didn't have a wife. "Look, Charlie…"

"Don't blame her, of course," his friend said with a wink as he finished up and put the gas cap back on. "You being gone all the time with the SEALs must be hard on the ol' love life."

He'd never had any complaints, Hunter thought, frowning at the man still talking a mile a minute. "What're you—"

"Bet Margie's anxious to see you. She told us all about that R & R trip you two took to Bali." Charlie's dark brown eyebrows lifted and wiggled.

"Charlie…"

"Hey, it's okay, you don't have to say a thing, man."

What the hell could he say? Hunter shook his head, paid for his gas and as he left, told himself Charlie was just losing it. Maybe the guy had been smelling gas fumes too long.

But as it turned out, it wasn't just Charlie. Stopped at a red light on Main Street, Hunter glanced out his window to smile at Mrs.

Harker, his second-grade teacher who was now at least a hundred years old. In the middle of the crosswalk, the old lady stopped and shouted, "Hunter Cabot, you've got yourself a wonderful wife. I hope you appreciate her."

Scowling now, he only nodded at the old woman—the only teacher who'd ever scared the crap out of him. What the hell was going on here? Was everyone but him nuts?

His temper beginning to boil, he put up with a few more comments about his "wife" on the drive through town before finally pulling into the wide, circular drive leading to the Cabot mansion. Hunter didn't have a clue what was going on, but he planned to get to the bottom of it. Fast.

He grabbed his duffel bag, stalked into the house and paid no attention to the housekeeper, who ran at him, fluttering both hands. "Mr. Hunter!"

"Sorry, Sophie," he called out over his shoulder as he took the stairs two at a time. "Need a shower, then we'll talk."

He marched down the long, carpeted hallway to the rooms that were always kept ready for him. In his suite, Hunter tossed the duffel down and stopped dead. The shower in his bathroom was running. His *wife?*

Anger and curiosity boiled in his gut, creating a churning mass that had him moving forward without even thinking about it. He opened the bathroom door to a wall of steam and the sound of a woman singing—off-key. Margie, no doubt.

Well, if she was his wife… Hunter walked across the room, yanked the shower door open and stared in at a curvy, naked, temptingly wet woman.

She whirled to face him, slapping her arms across her naked body while she gave a short, terrified scream.

Hunter smiled. "Hi, honey. I'm home."

* * * * *

Be sure to look for
AN OFFICER AND A MILLIONAIRE
by USA TODAY *bestselling author Maureen Child.*
Available January 2009 from Silhouette Desire.

CELEBRATE
60 YEARS
OF PURE READING PLEASURE
WITH HARLEQUIN®!

We'll be spotlighting a different series
every month throughout 2009
to celebrate our 60th anniversary.
Look for Silhouette Desire® in January!

Collect all 12 books in the Silhouette Desire®
Man of the Month continuity, starting in
January 2009 with *An Officer and a Millionaire*
by *USA TODAY* bestselling author
Maureen Child.

*Look for one new Man of the Month title
every month in 2009!*

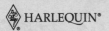

INTRIGUE

Sabrina Hunter works hard as a police detective
and a single mom. She's confronted with her
past when a murder scene draws in both her
and her son's father, Patrick Martinez. But when
a creepy sensation of being watched turns into
deadly threats, she must learn to trust the man
she once loved.

SECRETS IN
FOUR CORNERS

BY

DEBRA WEBB

**Available January 2009
wherever you buy books.**

REQUEST YOUR FREE BOOKS!

2 FREE NOVELS PLUS 2 FREE GIFTS!

HARLEQUIN®

Blaze™

Red-hot reads!

Inside ROMANCE

Stay up-to-date on all your romance reading news!

The Inside Romance newsletter is a FREE quarterly newsletter highlighting our upcoming series releases and promotions!

Click on the <u>Inside Romance</u> link on the front page of **www.eHarlequin.com** or e-mail us at insideromance@harlequin.ca to sign up to receive your FREE newsletter today!

You can also subscribe by writing us at: HARLEQUIN BOOKS Attention: Customer Service Department P.O. Box 9057, Buffalo, NY 14269-9057

Please allow 4-6 weeks for delivery of the first issue by mail.

IRNBPA208

HARLEQUIN®
Blaze™

COMING NEXT MONTH

#441 EVERY BREATH YOU TAKE... Hope Tarr
Undercover FBI agent Cole Whittaker never has trouble putting his life on the line…but his heart? He almost lost it once, five years ago, and he's not chancing it again. Until he takes on a security job—to guard the one woman he's never been able to forget…

#442 LONE STAR SURRENDER Lisa Renee Jones
Rebellious undercover agent Constantine Vega takes D.A. Nicole Ward on the sexiest ride of her life as he protects her from a vengeful enemy—but who will protect her from him?

#443 NAKED AMBITION Jule McBride
J. D. Johnson's ambition is twofold: reclaim the life that once fed his soul as a successful country musician, and win back his small-town Southern belle. Only, Susannah's been kicking up her heels in NYC. Good thing J.D. knows all the right moves….

#444 NO HOLDING BACK Isabel Sharpe
24 Hours: Lost, Bk. 2
Reporter Hannah O'Reilly will do most anything for a story—including gate-crashing reclusive millionaire Jack Battle's estate on a stormy New Year's Eve. But as the snow piles up and sexy Jack starts making his moves, Hannah is achingly aware there's no holding back….

#445 A FEW GOOD MEN Tori Carrington
Uniformly Hot!/Encounters
Four soldiers, four destinies, four complete short stories! While on a tour of duty, Eric, Matt, Eddie and Brian have become a family. Only now, on their way home from Iraq, they have no idea what—or *who*—awaits them….

#446 AFTER DARK Wendy Etherington
"Irresistible" is how Sloan Caldwell describes Aidan Kendrick. The reclusive millionaire mogul may seem a lone wolf, but Sloan's sirenlike sensuality will soon change his ways….